YOU MUST BE SISTERS

Deborah Moggach is the author of fifteen novels, including the bestseller *Tulip Fever*, and two collections of short stories. Her TV screenplays include the prize-winning *Goggle-Eyes*, *Close Relations*, *Final Demand* and the acclaimed *Love in a Cold Climate*. Her highly praised movie adaptation of *Pride and Prejudice* was released in 2005. She has two more or less grown-up children and lives in North London.

ALSO BY DEBORAH MOGGACH

DEBORAH MOGGACH

You Must
Be Sisters

VINTAGE BOOKS
London

Published by Vintage 2006

2 4 6 8 10 9 7 5 3 1

First published in Great Britain in 1982 by
Jonathan Cape

Vintage
Random House, 20 Vauxhall Bridge Road,
London SW1V 2SA

Random House Australia (Pty) Limited
20 Alfred Street, Milsons Point, Sydney,
New South Wales 2061, Australia

Random House New Zealand Limited
18 Poland Road, Glenfield, Auckland 10, New Zealand

Random House (Pty) Limited
Isle of Houghton, Corner of Boundary Road & Carse O'Gowrie,
Houghton, 2198, South Africa

The Random House Group Limited Reg. No. 954009
www.randomhouse.co.uk/vintage

A CIP catalogue record for this book
is available from the British Library

ISBN 9780099479727 (from Jan 2007)
ISBN 0099479729

Papers used by Random House are natural,
recyclable products made from wood grown in
sustainable forests. The manufacturing processes
conform to the environmental regulations of the
country of origin

Printed and bound in Great Britain by
Bookmarque Ltd, Croydon, Surrey

To my real sisters

one

'Well, that's the last of our birds flown,' said Rosemary, who was inclined to say things like this.

Her husband nodded, every muscle tensed to reach, across two roundabouts and a flyover, that large blue motorway sign. He could acknowledge her with a nod but he could hardly listen, what with an avalanche of cars, a thundering landslide of the things, bearing down on his left.

'Don't you think it's, well, rather final, darling?' she went on. 'Do you have that feeling too, Dan? Will you miss her?'

Amongst the many things Rosemary had never learnt was a good sense of timing. At times this could be charming, a bright flurry of inconsequence for which Dan, never much of a talker, was grateful. But now he was trying to concentrate. Could this be the wrong blasted flyover?

'I say, darling.' A finger pointed. 'Surely we go down there.'

She was right, of course. EASTBOUND: M4 LONDON. They'd have to double back, else they'd be swept out of Bristol towards some unearthly place like Wales. Rosemary was often right about this sort of thing. Also she beat him rather too often at golf.

At last. EASTBOUND: M4 LONDON. Dan put his foot down and the Rover shot forward.

'Laura's so silly,' Rosemary went on. 'I do hope she'll behave herself.'

'A great one for trying to shock, old Laura was – ' Dan corrected himself ' – is.' Suddenly he felt the loss of her. He had a sense of occasion and he knew that this was one. From today she was a university girl.

'Remember that dreadful young man from the butcher's?' sighed Rosemary. She gazed out at the flashing verge. 'I think she only brought him home to shock us, really. She knew we'd disapprove.'

Dan said nothing, so Rosemary adjusted herself more comfortably and switched on Radio 2. The young man's voice reassured her that nothing too terrible was happening to the world. Equally cheerful music followed. Radio 2 always made her feel better, and one advantage of Laura's departure was that it could be listened to without a pained silence from the back seat. Laura disapproved of Radio 2. *Ghastly pulp, Mummy. How can you bear it?*

Easily, thank you! thought Rosemary.

Laura was practising her expressions. Just now it was the slow meaningful one; she was good at that. She raised her eyes; she looked at herself with a steady stare, challenging, sensual.

What made it so fascinating was seeing herself doing it from the sides. She'd never had one of these triptych-type mirrors before. By adjusting the three panels, she had a most intriguing view of her profile giving itself its meaningful look. She took a drag of her cigarette and watched the plumes of smoke curling from her nostrils. That looked sophisticated.

She listened. Outside in the corridor she could hear the rustle of coats and the bumping of suitcases. Other girls were arriving. She took another drag of her cigarette; she watched the plumes. No, she wouldn't talk to them quite yet. They sounded so confident, banging their trunks around, calling out in loud voices. She would practise smiling; see what she looked like from the side. When her lips parted, did her teeth stick out?

She felt safe in here. Already she liked her room: its curtains matching the bedspread; its desk; its enquiring, bending lamp. *How charming!* her mother had said, rings glittering. *Look, darling, its own little cupboard and its own little bed. Aren't you lucky!*

For once Laura had actually agreed. She hadn't said so, of course; she'd just waited for her parents to go, her mother embarrassing her in front of all those other girls – first by the way she'd insisted on kissing her, second by that awful turquoise hat.

No, she wouldn't venture out yet. She'd just sit here and pile her hair on top of her head and see what that looked like from the side. Inspect these two new girls on either side of the known, frontal Laura. Interesting to see these two tilted profiles, each so thoroughly examining itself.

On the bed sat her trunk. The last ray of sun slanted through the window; it danced with dust and lit up the folds of her coat which lay draped over the luggage. She knew she ought to unpack but – a deeply satisfying feeling, this – who was there to tell her to?

'Nobody,' she whispered, her three selves smiling. The whisper hung in the air.

How much nicer just to sit here listening to the thumps against the ceiling and the slamming of doors, and do nothing at all but watch the smoke curl up into her own captured ray of sunshine! She never dared smoke at home – at least, only in her bedroom. It wasn't actually forbidden; that would have been easy to deal with. It was just tolerated rather painfully. But now she was at Bristol University she could do anything she liked. Right?

Strictly speaking, she did have a room of her own back in Harrow now that Claire had moved out to that flat in Clapham. But how can something be your own when the wallpaper has been chosen by your mother, and whenever she comes through the door her eyes flicker over the bed that you just happen to have left unmade? Stupid how irked that makes one feel. Not guilty, of course, just irked. Her father was even better at the old flickering-eyes routine: for instance, when she ought to be doing her homework and instead he caught her curled up with an Agatha Christie. He'd just flicker, and hesitate, and she would notice; then he'd close the door and go away, and bother, the book would be spoilt.

Laura turned her head slowly, keeping her hair up; she gazed at her profile. Ah! but here there was nothing to stop her doing what she liked, nothing at all.

'Such wild things,' Rosemary went on. 'Silly things, she does. Don't you think so, Dan?'

Dan gazed ahead at the darkening motorway. Red tail lights, strings of them, led towards London and his daughterless house. 'Not like Claire,' he said.

'Claire's so sensible, isn't she. Except teaching at that unspeakable school.'

Dan said nothing, so Rosemary went on: 'But Laura . . . she always has to be the rebel, doesn't she. The one who stands out.'

By now it was dusk; shadows in the room were deepening. Laura still hadn't quite dared venture out. It was so much easier sitting here at her mirror. But it was chillier now; her arms were gravelly with goose-pimples. And she was becoming uneasily aware that all the noises had stopped. Intent, she listened. What could the time be? She didn't know; she despised watches.

They must have gone down to dinner. Nobody had told her. Despite herself, she felt a homesick lurch in the stomach. First-day-at-school feeling.

She left her room and made her way down to where the dining-block must be. She stood outside the windows and watched them, rows and rows of them, rows and rows of silently chattering students, every one of them a stranger, every one of them eating his dinner and not one of them knowing she was missing. And why should they know? Silly of her to feel hurt that they didn't. She stepped closer and inspected the tables. They hadn't reached the pudding course yet; that was a relief. She took a deep breath and went in.

The sudden clatter stunned her and the lights glared in her eyes, so it wasn't until she had turned around from the serving-hatch with her full plate that she saw, with dreadful clarity, that everyone was wearing black.

She nearly dropped her plate. She'd forgotten about gowns. Hers was still in her trunk.

She stared at them, not daring to move forwards or back. But nobody returned her stare. Nobody seemed to have noticed either her or her gownlessness at all. They were all far too busy talking, all three hundred of them, heads nodding, forks waving, all making her feel so utterly left out. For a moment she actually wanted someone to notice she wasn't wearing a gown. Most unsettling, the whole thing. Oh to be back in the kitchen at home! Even quarrelling.

She sat down at a table. The person opposite had a commanding nose and shiny black hair. He held a chicken bone in his hand and was in the process of gnawing it. In his black gown he looked sleek and hostile, like a carrion crow. He looked up, shot her a beady glance and bent down again to peck.

Wherever she looked there were faces. She would like to give somebody a meaningful stare, challenging and sensual, but some-how it was easier in her mirror. The best refuge she could find was her plate, so she inspected it thoroughly – chicken, scoops of cemented potato, over-green peas. They disappeared as she ate, so then with the same thoroughness she inspected the scrapings – the tattered chicken bone, the sensible white china of her plate. All the others were new, of course, but why didn't they look it?

'Pudding,' said the crow. She jumped. People were getting up, fetching bowls. She got up and fetched one; it quivered with custard. A hammer rapped and voices hushed. With her spoon she stirred her custard skin into its own sunny depths; she listened to the speech of welcome. And now they couldn't speak, people relaxed and looked around with a general expansion of interest. Laura, too, relaxed a little, felt more included, raised her face and inspected a girl with bold eyes who had pushed her pudding to the side of her plate; someone who was casually scratching under his gown; a square-jawed hearty type who was gazing at the girl with the bold eyes . . . how assured they all looked! Someone already had his arm around a girl. Good grief, thought Laura, and I haven't even *talked* to anyone yet. Cosy home rose like a wave. She pushed it down.

It was better back in her own block. Girls tore off their gowns and, thank goodness, looked more approachable; along the corridor they wandered and into her room, inspecting her colour scheme compared with that of their own, introducing themselves. She explored too. The room on one side already looked fragrant and settled, with lace-covered Kleenex box by the bed. On the other side the room was more robust, with a corduroy troll sitting bossily on the bookshelf.

The Kleenex girl had efficiently remembered coffee things and mugs. Her face was white, unused-looking and floury with powder. Already in her bedroom slippers, she padded into Laura's room and invited her to have a cup.

They were joined by the troll girl who had an easy, sensible face and big jean-cramped thighs.

The Kleenex girl turned to the troll one. 'Glad I went down to dinner with you. I felt quite nervous.' She poured out the coffee. 'I'm funny that way.'

'I went by myself,' said Laura, 'and I felt awful. All those faces. They're all new like us, aren't they?'

'Except for a few post-grads and mature students.'

'Isn't that a deadly name,' said Laura. '*Mature students*. So terribly kind. It makes them sound about eighty years old . . .'

And so they chatted – about nothing much, it was true, but the unstrenuousness of the repartee made it all the more comforting. Out of the mass had emerged these two faces, the Kleenex and the troll one. They might not be soul mates but they were reassuring, as this mug of Nescafé was reassuring.

Later she unpacked and dragged her trunk into the corridor.

She stacked it beside the others. Each had initials on its lid; she felt less frightened of A.H., M.F.A., K.L. now. Were they even, perhaps, feeling the same as she was? She wandered outside where the windows of the other blocks shone brightly; identical windows, rows and rows of them. In some, shadows moved; in one a figure leant out, dark against the lamplight. She could see the glowing point of his cigarette. She gazed at that shape; compressed into its blackness seemed to be all the people she soon would get to know. She gazed at the glowing point; *meet me*, it said.

Ah yes, she was glad to be here. Boring at home, wasn't it? And her parents were so extremely annoying. Back in her room she stamped it as hers by peeling some colour plates from her 'German Masters of Painting' book and pinning them on the wall. And then she undressed and slid into her own bed, the skin over her face tight from washing and her body chilled by the strange, starchy sheets.

two

Laura was sure she got less letters than anybody else at Hall. The J pigeonhole always seemed to be stuffed with Joneses and Johnsons but never with Jenkinses, and the whole scene at breakfast seemed to be bent heads, rustling paper and secret smiles. Was she being over-selfconscious? Probably. Sometimes she got an overdue note from the library which, at a pinch, could last her through the cornflakes, but nothing could stretch it out through the bacon and eggs.

Of course she'd got a long, prodding sort of letter from her mother, but she hardly counted that. It was two weeks before she found a letter from Claire.

Claire's handwriting was poised and regular, the sort one sees on blackboards at school. Claire's writing had always been the same. When they were younger, hers, unlike Laura's, had never gone through the various distortions – Greek 'e's when they had been fashionable at their school, funny flat writing with square, instead of loopy, tails and then, later on, that beautiful, careful italic that comes with one's first Osmoroid. Claire's writing had always been settled as hers, Claire's. A strong-minded girl, that was why.

It was a nice fat letter. You got your money's worth with Claire.

Dear Laura,

How I long to hear all your news! I have a thousand questions – about your room, your friends – have you got a lot yet and are they all dreadfully clever? About your work – difficult? Stimulating? In fact, about everything. You have a slaveringly eager reader here.

I'm writing this in the Staff Room. The new headmaster has stunned the whole school by having a CLUB FOOT. Imagine that first assembly. Every word of his invigorating and stern address floated harmlessly away, unheard, as a thousand eyes were fixed, fascinated, on it. Did it hurt? How was he going to get down the stairs when his speech was over? Above all, what did it look like when his boot was off? Not a rustle, not a sniff, no one even picked his nose. Never has there been such total absorption. He must have been awfully pleased.

New tenants have arrived in the flat upstairs – an unmarried couple. Because they're unmarried, every sound I hear through the ceiling – thuds, rhythmic taps – I presume to be them On The Job, as my boys sentimentally call it or, as my West Indian ones say, Doing a Rudeness. I bet they're just clearing out the kitchen cupboard.

I've been home once or twice but little to report. They miss you a lot, of course, and Holly too. All their daughters gone. I've been down to see Holly at school and she seems to love it, though what she feels in those dark hours when the dorm lights are off, only she knows. I looked into the youngest girls' dorm and all the battered, one-eyed teddies on their pillows would make the strongest man weep. I wonder if you and I would have been different if we'd gone to boarding school.

Longing to see you. I think I'll be able to get down towards the end of term. The car is going well – it'll be your turn for it next term. Won't it be posh! Having a car your first year at university. But Mummy says your Hall is right away in the suburbs so I bet it'll be useful. You can make lots of friends by giving them lifts down to their lectures.

> *Lots of love,*
> *Claire*

Claire shared a flat on the ground floor of a red-brick Clapham terrace. It was a week later. She had just woken up from one of those devastating dreams where you fall in love – agonizingly, poignantly – with someone who in daylight hours would strike you as quite alarmingly unsuitable. Last night's lover had been the Assistant Maths Master, a balding man with pudgy hands. Claire lay in bed, glowing with misdirected love, and gazed through the crack in the curtains at the grey glimmer of dawn. Why couldn't her dreams show better taste? All that stuff about dreams showing one's deepest desires was nonsense. Yesterday, the thought of being clasped in the plump arms of the Assistant Maths Master would have made her laugh. Today, still drenched in her dream, she would feel quite peculiar when she saw him sitting in the Staff Room, puffing his pipe and complaining how no member of staff seemed able to keep his locker tidy. It would all wear off in a few hours, of course, but it would be interesting to see her oblivious object, the glamour of her dream strewn incongruous as tinsel over the shoulders of his serge suit.

Really, she thought briskly, kicking back the bedcovers, this is ridiculous. Why can't I find someone real, by daylight?

She went into the bathroom and looked at her shiny early-morning face, its eyebrows raised at itself in scrutiny. She started brushing her teeth. But where, in this huge city, can I find him? Just at this moment there must be hundreds of young men in their prime, lathering their faces, the same grey light coming through the same frosted window; they must be thinking just the same thing; but when can we meet? Lucky old Laura, she must be meeting hundreds.

Her eyes travelled over the faded wallpaper; she saw the millions of other faces at their early-morning mirrors, men's faces and women's, sprightly ones and tired ones, handsome and plain, and each person wondering what to wear today and whether to brush his hair to the side or perhaps forward? A cityful of souls all around her. If she let it, London could render her helpless.

'I say, Claire!' Yvonne's voice hissing through the door. 'I say, Clary, you've got a letter!'

It was from Laura. Claire took it into the kitchen.

'Gosh,' said Yvonne, padding up behind her in her quilted dressing-gown, 'do read it! I'm longing to know all about University Life, the lucky thing. I bet she's got loads of boyfriends!' She opened the bread bin, peered in it and sighed. 'You know, my diet starts today and it says I must have grapefruit, but grapefruits are so dear I decided I'd just have a *teeny* slice of toast instead. Do you think that's all right, Claire?'

'If it's really small.'

Claire took the letter into the sitting-room. Nikki, her other flatmate, had entertained last night and it was full of overflowing ashtrays. Claire drew back the curtains; the houses opposite, solid Clapham redbrick, stared back at her.

Thanks for your letter. I loved your description of The Foot. How's life at the flat with Nikki and the terrible Yvonne?

Talking about terrible things, I girded my loins and went to a Freshers' Ball last week. Truly a cattle market with all the males lined up one side and all us females, giggling and drinking halves of cider, up the other. At some mysterious signal half-way through the evening we converged, and I was glued to a succession of manly chests, some belonging to biologists, some to medics, once to a person who called me Norma and once to a person who called me Gloria. I kept up a bright stream of chatter that at moments of stress, especially with the Gloria one, became even brighter. 'Er, what exactly is an isotope?' I would say, furtively trying to push down a creeping hand. You'll be relieved to know I got back to Hall unravaged.

Work is harder than I expected. It's a shock to change from being top of one's class at school to being just any old average student. We have a fine yellow stone building for psychology and a lab full of rats that I'm getting very attached to. Boys in my class look rather moist and young, but in the second and third years there are dishier ones who wear old leather coats, things like that. Mummy and Daddy would disapprove of them –

'Grub's up.' Yvonne padded in with a tray. She gazed down at her piece of toast. 'Gosh, Clary, you're so lucky being *slim*. I wish I was like you. Oh dear, and I forgot to buy some saccharine, so I'll just *have* to have a spoonful of sugar. I can't bear tea without sugar. Do you think that's all right, Claire, just this once?'

'Just a small one.'

'But even if I have a teensy-weensy one that'll make a difference, won't it?' Yvonne looked plaintive. 'I mean, every little bit counts, doesn't it? But don't mind me; go on with your letter.'

Bristol is rather romantic, and Clifton is the oldest and most beautiful bit, just near the university. It's all elegant but tatty terraces, most of them Georgian. But Addison Hall is right away on the other side of the Downs in suburbia. It's glassy and modern, 4 men's blocks, 4 women's, a dining block where we work our way through mounds of chips, and a common room. The Hall stalwarts, like pub regulars, are making themselves clearer now, what with committees being set up and jolly functions to get us all to know each other. After this first year nearly everyone will move out into flats or digs.

My early days were spent – still are – in an agony of not letting myself be seen alone and wistful-looking. I mean, I like being alone, but it's difficult to show that one's liking it and not just being left out. I met a frightfully boring girl from school and we fell into each other's arms with wild relieved cries of recognition, and neither of us had the slightest thing to say to each other when we were in the same classroom all those years –

'I say, Claire!' cried Yvonne. 'Look at this.' She held out a printed form. 'It came through the post this morning and it says they'll send us this super series called "The Miracle of Your Body". And if we send off now, we can have the first book free! Look, all we have to do is send off this stamp they've given us – '

'The big red one,' said Claire, 'with the YES PLEASE on it.'

'That's right. It's very simple.'

'And if you don't want it you send the narrow grey one that just says NO.'

'That's right. Oh Clary, it's got such lovely-sounding things in it. *Some of the Most Moving Photographs ever Taken of the Miracle of Childhood* . . .'

'No, Yvonne.'

Anyway, enough for now. Please come down as soon as you can so I can show you everything. I'm making my room so special. But wait until I know more than about two people so I can introduce you to a nice lot. I'm buried in Freud who becomes more and more fascinating.

Love,
Laura

'Finished?' asked Yvonne. 'Tell me all about it. I bet she's got all the Men hanging on her little finger already. She's so nice-looking and so brainy too! That's what they like – not just a pretty face. Oh, I do envy her.'

'So do I. I'll show it to you tonight. Must dash now.'

Claire got into the Morris Minor that she shared with Laura and drove through the streets towards her school where 1,300 tough and restless pupils waited for her.

Those first weeks of autumn, Laura did the same things as everybody else. She walked across the Downs and into town for her lectures, none of which she had started skipping. She took painstaking notes. She rewrote her notes when she got back to her room. She sat long hours in the library working or, when the hot-pipe against her back seeped too deliciously through her skin, slumped asleep over her scattered textbooks, a real student.

She bought mugs for her room and, to be extra-special, real coffee instead of Nescafé. At first it was just the troll girl and the others who dropped in to gossip and speculate about everyone else. But soon they drifted their separate ways, and Laura found herself drawn into a group of English Literature students who did boisterous studenty things, like taking her out to a scrumpy pub where she drank two pints, cloudy and with lemon slices floating on the top. They sat in a swaying row, making up limericks. At closing time they linked their arms and linked their Bristol University scarves to become a knotted chain, and they staggered over the Downs to a late-night chipper.

Sitting on the grass with them, swallowing her fried cod, wiping her hands on the dewy grass and gazing at the figures munching in the moonlight, Laura felt a pang of nostalgia, already, for what she was doing. Memories in advance. These were the jolly things she'd tell her children about one day.

Then it irked her to be such a typical student. She could just imagine what her mother would say – *Oh, Laura's having a simply marvellous time, up to all sorts of fun and such nice young men. Rushing about, off to funny little pubs, up all hours; you know what students are like* . . .

That annoyed her. Definitely, now she thought of it. It washed the spice out of the incident. For, by some mysterious process, the minute her parents approved of something it became devitalized. Now she thought of it, that Len who worked at the butcher's – hadn't his fascination sprung from the simple fact that her parents were appalled? Their horrified politeness had made him look so *virile*.

She gazed up at the 300 identical windows of Hall. No, she

wasn't going to be like everybody else, was she? Hadn't she always been the sort to break out? No more of this cosy studenty life. The fact that she could write about it all, uncensored, in a letter home, made it suddenly tame.

three

The morning after the moonlit cod Laura ventured into the Berkeley Café. Up till now she hadn't dared; on peering inside, all she had ever seen was a blur of faces, and she was sure she'd know none of them. It always seemed full of older students, the ones who lived not in safe little Halls but in independent flats. She would like to be like them.

The Berkeley stood opposite the library. With its mock Tudor panelling it had a genteel tea-rooms atmosphere, but only at first glance. No Barbara Cartland hair-dos here. Laura got herself a coffee and peered through the smoke.

She could just make out a tableful of second year psychologists, the sort she admired, the sort who lived mysterious lives in flats and roared round Bristol on motorbikes. Leather coats, dark glasses, wild hair . . . they looked intriguing and existential and unsuitable. She took a breath and casually approached their table. Her excuse was that she slightly knew one of them, the one with the pale ropes of hair; he was called Andy.

Laura sat down and spoke to the nearest one: 'Would you like a cigarette?'

'Not for me,' he answered. He had a stubbly chin. He reached out for a packet of French ones. 'Not those; can't taste them any more.'

He sat back in a cloud of strong, acrid smoke. They went on with their conversation.

'It was shit,' said the third one, who had dark glasses. 'Christ, once that guy could direct.'

'Remember those shots,' said Stubbly Chin, 'outside the hut?'

'"The Red Desert". How could anyone forget. The way he handled her indecision. Those grainy close-ups.'

There didn't seem a lot Laura could contribute here. What was this desert business? She longed to know, to be one of them. She gazed into her coffee cup, occasionally sliding her eyes to the faded Levi'd thigh of Stubbly Chin, who was next to her.

Then Stubbly Chin said: 'I'm getting into alchemy. Might write my thesis on it – you know, the alchemist's power over the brain, the way, like, he altered concepts of time.'

'Far out,' said Andy.

'Bosch's the guy to study. Anyone got any Bosch books? His pictures just radiate alchemy.'

'I've got a Bosch book,' said Laura. They all turned.

'You have?'

She nodded, blushing.

'Hey,' said Stubbly Chin. His name turned out to be John. 'If you happen, like, to pass Wellington Crescent one day – number 6 – that'd be really nice. You could drop it in.'

'Oh yes, I will.' She felt the blush deepen with pleasure. She'd contributed at last.

They talked of other things. She watched them. Funny how what they said was different from what their eyes were doing. While they spoke, their eyes were flickering round the café, restlessly.

'I'm thinking,' said Dark Glasses, 'after I get out of this place, of getting it together in the country. You know, a few friends, growing all our own stuff.'

'Sounds nice,' said John. 'Really nice. Imagine most of this lot,' he gestured round the room, his voice assured, his eyes – could they be almost anxious? 'I can just see them, you know, nice safe house, mortgage, telly – you know, like the whole *family* scene.'

'Ghastly,' agreed Laura. How well he put it! Why then did she feel uncomfortable, shifting about in her seat?

'Ah, my girl, just you wait. Wait till you – what d'they call him – your Mister Right comes along. You'll be up to your ears in life insurance and dinner parties once a month.'

'No I won't,' said Laura. 'I'm just going to have lovers.' Now that sounded good.

'We'll see, we'll see. Anyway, catch me living a tiny life amongst all those other tiny lives way out in – well, Harrow or somewhere.'

Laura looked down at her hands. Shame that he'd actually said Harrow; as if he knew. Never, ever must she let it slip out.

Walking up the street later, she shook away her unease. No,

she decided they impressed her terribly. Such a change, they were, from the good-natured young lot at Hall, and such a change from those chinless wonders she was sometimes unfortunate enough to meet in Harrow, who actually asked her father 'What time would you like her back, sir?' and dreadfully uncool things like that.

That Sunday afternoon Laura went for a walk. She walked across the Downs and into Clifton. She was beginning to know her way around the alleys, terraces and curving streets, and easily found Wellington Crescent. It was a beautiful day in early November, and the golden sun lit the façades of the houses, façades whose shadows deepened as the crescent curved round in a large arc.

Actually, she was a bit chilly in her T-shirt but she hadn't brought a coat, partly because it had been warmer when she'd started out, and partly because she'd decided not to wear a bra, and with her nipples obvious as anything through the material she looked liberated. Outside number 6 she hesitated and took a breath.

John answered the bell. He looked at her blankly.

'Hello,' she said. 'I'm Laura. Er, remember?'

'Oh yeah. We met in the Berkeley.'

'Right. I've brought that book.'

'What book?'

'The Bosch.'

'Ah. I remember. Come in.'

His room was painted white. It had a rumpled mattress on the floor with an Indian bedspread over it, a lot of books, and on the wall a blown-up photo of what she couldn't swear wasn't a huge breast, very close up. Could it be?

'Lovely room,' she said.

'Yeah. Like some tea or something?'

'Yes please.' Yes, on closer inspection it couldn't be anything else.

He disappeared and she sat down on the bed, wondering whether she was welcome or not. But he didn't have anyone with him, and he was so glamorous and a second year and all. Surely she could stay for some tea?

He sat down beside her and poured it out. Then he reached for one of his yellow cigarettes and lit it.

'Can I try one?' she asked, looking at his hand as he gave

it to her. What exactly had she come for? Could she admit it, even to herself?

It was very strong. She gulped down some tea.

'You dig Bosch, then,' he said.

'Oh yes. He's so, well, strange.'

'Quite a guy, Bosch. His obsession with the anus, for instance.' Haze hung in layers round the room. He blew smoke out; the layers split, flimsily. 'As the erogenous zone. I prefer the good old front-entry myself, don't you?'

'Oh yes!' she laughed.

'I've yet to meet a chick who liked it, really liked it, from the rear.'

She laughed again, knowingly, but felt uncomfortable: having had it neither from the front nor the rear, ever. And aged nineteen too.

He went on: 'Anyway, perhaps one day I'll meet one and realize what I've been missing. But most English girls are so hung-up.'

'Oh no,' she replied with spirit. 'Not all of us.'

'Most of you. Not like French chicks. Now, *they* know how to turn a guy on. Wow, can they use their bodies. Sex is important to them.'

'It is for us too.'

'But just how important? You're – what's your name – Laura, right? A guy screws you; it's cool, right?' He leant back across the bed and stretched out his legs. He blew some more smoke into the haze. 'But which matters most to you, the guy or the fuck?'

'Well . . . it depends.' She was getting into deep water here, but she didn't know how to change the subject. She took another drag and another gulp of tea. She couldn't think what else to do so she drained her cup, taking a nice long time about it.

'For those chicks it's the fuck,' said John. 'Pure and simple. It's really, like, beautiful. No pretence.'

'Yes.' She thought for a moment. What could she say? 'Yes, I agree. There's something depressing about sincerity unless it's very intense and real.' She wasn't quite sure about that but it was better than nothing.

'It's amazing,' he went on, 'the fantasies, the compromises people swathe round themselves when all they want is a good screw.'

'Yes. People kid themselves. It's all their silly upbringings.'

'Right. You know, you're a girl after my own heart.'

Laura felt herself glowing.

'Come here,' he said, and pulled her back beside him. He started stroking her hair.

She tried to relax against him. After all, wasn't this really what she had come for? To start being liberated and adult?

'Hey,' he said, 'talking of that, why're we sitting here like a pair of idiots? I'm stacked like a fucking chimney.'

Before she knew it he'd unzipped his trousers, taken her hand and – heavens! plonked it on something stiff and stout.

Frozen with terror, she stared at the wall, at the books, at the goose-pimply photo, at anything.

'See what you've done to me?' he murmured. He took his hand away and hers was left there, ludicrously clasping it like a handle. She didn't look at her hand. She disowned it.

'Feels good, doesn't it,' he said. 'See? You've turned me on.'

Quickly she snatched her hand away and struggled up. 'Er, I think I ought to be getting back,' she gasped, still not looking at him. 'I really must.'

'Hey, relax. What's the matter with you?'

'Nothing,' she replied, primly smoothing down her hair and addressing the wall. 'Really, I, er, have so many things to do. Heavens, look at the time, too!'

'Look at me, for Christssake!' She heard the zip being pulled up. 'Why this coy virgin crap?'

Because I *am* a coy virgin, she thought wildly. 'I'm sorry,' she said. 'I just, well, don't feel like it.' Why can't I be honest?

'Look at me. Is this the way to leave a guy?' She turned round. He was dark in the face and furious.

She protested: 'But I didn't expect all this to happen.'

'Honey, do you mean me to believe that? You come here with your tits hanging out, throwing your libido all over the place . . .' He shrugged, and sat down on the bed again. 'Hell, will I ever learn. You're just like most of them; running around barefoot and thinking, like, you're really wild. But you always have a pair of shoes ready in case your feet get wet.' He sighed. 'Well, run along back to your nice Hall or wherever. Come back when you've grown up.'

She slammed out of the room, out of the front door, and walked quickly up the street. She wasn't going to run, not for anybody.

He might be looking out of the window. She felt unreal, as if the whole brief scene had happened to somebody else – and furious, and humiliated, and upset by those last things he'd said. Silly, theatrical words; he'd probably copied them from one of his beastly films. She wasn't going to think of it.

If only Claire were here, she thought, aching with homesickness. We could laugh about it together. But she isn't, and I don't feel like laughing. Oh, if only he'd *kissed* me first!

But as she walked across the Downs, her body shivering because it was dusk now, she couldn't stop herself thinking about those last things he'd said and she knew, though she hated him for saying them, that he hadn't been absolutely wrong.

four

. . . and then a big hook came down and puled Roggo up it puled and puled until he was dangeling up abuv the trees and the roofs the hook was not in his cloths it was stikking rite into his skin and the blud was cuming out and falling down the sky onto the tops of the houses it made big red pudels . . .

Claire raised her eyes. Her washing had stopped. She put down the exercise book and hauled her clothes out of the machine. But all the dryers were occupied, so she sat down again and took up the book.

. . . and then the hook droped him and he fell down and he was all rite.

How well she knew those hasty endings. They meant the telly had been switched on. 'Wasn't he hurt at *all*?' she wrote briskly in Biro, and opened the next book.

Its cover was greasy with wild explosions of crayon. She settled down with relish. Hector's homeworks were always the same; one had a nice secure sense of expectation as one opened the cover. Each homework was the next instalment of a blood-curdling serial of interminable length (six months so far) called simply *Jap Doom*. Despite its curiously dated feel it held Claire spellbound because the hero (called, needless to say, Hector) was left each time so close to death she could never see how he could possibly survive. But he always did. Hector gave good value.

Episode 24. The green ooze, all slimey with tentakles, came closer and closer. Hector struggled in his tite ropes – No, she'd leave this treat till last.

She opened the next book.

My Hamster. My hamster is brown and of medium size. He is very clean and tidy. All hamsters originally come from Syria and are imported . . .

Claire's heart sank. She yawned. This was goody-goody Jonathan, with his painfully neat writing. He'd taken a lot of trouble. Why did his always getting things right annoy her? She ought to be pleased, but somehow Hector was more fun.

She looked up. The dryer in front of her was being emptied by a portly old woman. Large satin knickers with legs came out, one by one, some pink and some greyish. The woman bundled them into a bag. Claire blushed for her and for the indignity of being poor and portly and having to use a launderette where you can conceal nothing.

She got up, pretending not to notice the other woman, and pushed her washing into the dryer. Then she sat back and watched it curve and fall, curve and fall inside.

The woman went out. Despite the churning machines, the launderette was now empty. At 10 p.m. on a Saturday night, the Lavender Hill Swiftkleen was a bleak place, its garish strip-lighting and shadowless corners creating a solitude made greater by the noises outside where cars hooted and women shouted. From time to time people came in to take out their clothes, but always in a hurry.

She felt reluctant to go back to her flat because upstairs there was a party going on, and she neither wanted to sit in her room with all those jolly noises coming down through the ceiling, nor to be taken pity on and invited upstairs where she'd know no one.

There was always Harrow, of course. She could go back there for the evening. The dog would welcome her with a lick, her parents with a Martini. And the house would welcome her with its delicious central heating – her flat was freezing just now. But that would be feeble.

Well, what about her sister then? She could always go and visit Laura. That was a thought.

When Claire was entering the launderette, Laura was lighting a candle. Then she lit a joss stick. She put her Bach Violin Concertos on the record-player. Then she lay on the bed and tried to feel spiritual. Or, to be absolutely honest, to forget that it was Saturday night and nobody had asked her out.

After all, what was so special about Saturday night? She decided that the charm of lying here gazing at the wreathing, curling smoke was actually increased by Hall being empty and everybody being out. She was unique, wasn't she? Yes, of course she was.

Her room helped to make her feel special. She liked doing things alone in it. Yesterday, realizing she'd be too late for Hall lunch, she'd bought brussels sprouts, spinach, salt and a saucepan. Alone at the gas-ring she'd cooked her first meal – amazingly enough, it was the first meal she'd ever made without witnesses or help. Its vegetarian quirkiness only made it more fascinatingly *hers*. She was beholden to no one, free to scrape it from the saucepan because there was nobody there to look pained. It was overcooked but lovely; a soggy green sacrament.

Half an hour passed . . . three-quarters . . . Bach finished and Segovia began. When he finished it would have to be Bach again; the only other records she possessed were Beatles and Rolling Stones, definitely unsuitable for this soulful sort of evening. She got down her book of Dürer etchings and thumbed through the pages. Peace settled upon her. She could even, for quite long spells, forget that business with John.

A knock on the door.

'Hi!' It was Mike, one of the jolly English gang. 'I saw your light and I thought hey, poor Laura, she shouldn't be in on a Saturday night. It's immoral.'

'Actually it's rather nice.'

'Well, nice or not, it's not right and you're coming to a party. I've heard of one and you've *got* to come. I insist.'

'You needn't feel sorry for me,' she said with spirit. 'I chose to stay in.' She was enjoying her solitary evening so much that this was, she decided, only a half-lie.

They crammed into a crowded car; they drove down into Bristol.

Sights, sounds and smells were pretty standard. She was getting used to these sorts of festivities. There was a hallway blocked with bodies who pressed and shoved past her as she entered. She immediately lost sight of Mike.

'You have *scrumptious* breasts,' came a voice from the shadows; a cupped palm was stretched out. She lifted it off and pushed past to the kitchen where, behind the regiment of bottles, she could see the touching evidence of everyday masculine occupation – a greasy Formica shelf upon which stood a bottle of tomato sauce, a bottle of brown sauce and a packet of Alka-Seltzer. Nothing else.

In glimpses she could see the floor, puddled with crimson wine. The lavatory, with Jane Fonda peeling off the wall, smelt unmistakably of vomit. Up the stairs she squeezed, up past entwined bodies, female stares over male shoulders. There was no one she recognized. At the topmost stair a shape stood up shakily and asked: 'Do you come here often?' then leant against the wall and giggled.

Yet another figure confronted her. 'Light of my life!' it cried, and tried to disentangle itself from the other bodies. She ignored it and had a sudden vision of her charmed, candle-lit room, within which she felt so special. She didn't feel at all special here. What a herd!

The next room was equally crammed. Seeking a familiar face, she caught sight of a bottle on the mantelpiece containing a sprig of holly. Christmas, unbelievably, was in a month's time. Christmas and home. It would be quite different at home after all this.

She stepped over more bodies and looked out of the window. A dark tree faced her, its arms outstretched into the wild night sky. It was shockingly real, in contrast to what was going on behind her. The herd, the mass, roomfuls of students snogging like fifteen-year-olds . . . But oh dear, she would so like to know just one or two! Wasn't it silly, to try so much to be separate and yet want so much to be part of it all, too. Silly and adolescent, to sneer at something just because one was left out!

Might as well go on looking at the tree. If she turned round someone might lurch towards her or, worse still, think she looked all wistful. Which she was, of course.

She looked at the branches; she felt expanded, soothed; just herself, alone with the tree. Much better than all those lurchers and gropers behind her. Since John, she was off that sort of business.

But she couldn't look at it for ever. She turned round, avoiding eyes yet perversely wishing she'd be intercepted in her avoiding, that somebody would want her. She saw the holly again and felt a lurch of homesickness. Actually, it swamped her; that ache when one is in a strange room, perhaps trying to sleep, with alien voices along the corridor and shadows in the corners, hunched shadows with long noses. Nineteen, and she hadn't grown out of it yet!

'Do you want to leave too?'

It was Mike, lanky homely Mike; she could have hugged him. They left, and together they walked up the street. After the party the air was silent, pressing in on their ears like the stillness after the telephone has been ringing and ringing and then has suddenly stopped.

'Dreadful party,' he said.

That solved that, then. How nice that it had been the party's fault; she felt much better. Nice, too, to have the familiar, known old Mike. She could tell him things, bony, public-schooly Mike who came – wait for it – from Norbiton. He didn't seem to mind that.

What happened next she could only blame, later, on the wine. Or perhaps on the need, at this particular homesick moment, for someone to lean against.

That was just what she was doing now, actually – leaning against him. They were back in his room at Hall and he'd just made some tea. Side by side they were sitting on his bed; he was rummaging through a book.

'I'll find it in a minute. It's so gorgeous, you must hear it.'

As usual, books lay scattered all over the floor. Mike was often seized with the urge to read out poems that he liked; the books lay where he'd discarded them. In his messiness he was as bad as she was.

'Don't be bored. It's here somewhere.'

She wasn't bored, she was reassured. An hour ago she'd felt so vulnerable, so newly-peeled amongst all those loud unnoticing people. But now she was safe. She relaxed against his tweedy jacket. Warming to him, she felt quite bold. She took the sleeve of his jacket between her fingers.

'You have hideous clothes,' she said cheerfully. 'Why can't you get anything trendy?' If only he weren't so nice and Norbitonish he could really be quite fanciable.

'Ah!' he cried. 'Got it. It's Wyatt.' His voice grew resonant; his poetry boom.

They flee from me, that sometime did me seek

With naked foot, stalking in my chamber . . .

Leaning against that shabby tweed, she listened to his voice and felt more and more soothed. It was nice to have somebody to sit beside, to lean against. A body. In this mass of people, someone to cling to. I've been needing one, she thought. Not an original observation, but a true one.

   . . . When her loose gown from her shoulders did fall,
   And she me caught in her arms long and small,
   Therewith all sweetly did me kiss
   And softly said, Dear heart, how like you this?

The boom changed to his ordinary voice. 'What an image, isn't it! *Her loose gown did from her shoulders fall.* So, well, erotic somehow. And yet so restrained.'

She stayed leaning against him. Feverishly, he thumbed through the pages. 'There's another lovely one I want to read to you . . .' His hair fell over his eyes as he bent down close to the book, scrabbling through the pages. She kept herself against him.

'It's somewhere here,' he muttered. 'A super lyric, sort of sensual yet religious . . .' He kept his head down. 'Must find it.'

Then, abruptly, his hand took hers, but still he kept his head down, thumbing through the pages with his remaining hand. His hand kneaded hers. 'You'll like this one . . . find it in a moment. Must be in the "Songs" section . . .'

The book fell to the floor and he turned to her. She glimpsed his face blindly seeking hers, and then it was against her skin and he was kissing her ear, again and again. And then his face moved over and his mouth came down on hers and luxuriously, deliciously, she opened her lips and boldly but oh so slowly she slid her tongue into his mouth. She could feel his body starting to tremble. So bold, so suddenly oblivious, she felt.

Over on to the bed they keeled, locked together, his arms tremblingly round her. Her eyes closed, she lay pressed against him, arching her body into his and boldly, caressingly, drawing up her leg and wrapping it round his thigh. How he trembled!

Just for one moment she opened her eyes, stared into the brightly lit room, stared at the red, intent rim of ear that was all she could see of him – he was buried in her hair again – and wildly she thought What *am* I doing? Or rather, these legs and these arms, what are *they* doing? Then she closed her eyes and felt only his limbs against hers. His breath was hot in her ear but he said nothing, just intensely, tremblingly, gripped her. His jacket slipped off;

she felt it; then suddenly his hand was under her skirt and struggling up her leg.

She stiffened. Oh no! With a jerk she unwrapped her leg and clenched it against her other one, trapping his hand mid-thigh. She opened her eyes and stared at that red rim of ear. No!

A silent struggle; heavy breathing. She stared fixedly at the bright, bookish room. But he was too strong, and suddenly his hand shot up to – she felt herself blushing – the hole at the top of her tights. Damn my tights! she thought.

'No!' she whispered.

'Oh Laura, for God's sake let me!' His urgent voice was muffled by her hair. His other hand – thrilled and appalled, she felt it – started to unbutton his trousers. It was insane, it was dreadful, it was almost comic . . . but she couldn't stop, not after that thing with John.

'Turn off the light then,' she whispered. 'And lock the door.'

He took his hand out. She sat up and smoothed down her skirt. He struggled to the door, his trousers held up round his hips by one hand. With the other he switched off the light. In the darkness she heard the key turning in the lock. His footsteps returned.

She heard a rustling of his trousers falling to the floor and then a small, almost undistinguishable sound that must be his underpants following them. Then, workmanlike, he tugged off her tights and knickers. Silently she screamed Oh no! This isn't what I wanted at all! I didn't mean it, not really – well, not quite really, not like this, anyway. I came to you for something else.

I'm nineteen, though. High time, isn't it?

The bed creaked as he got down beside her and pressed his hot legs against her bare ones. She clamped hers shut.

'Er, you on the Pill?' he hissed.

'What?'

'You on the Pill? You know . . .'

A silence.

'I'd better use something then, hadn't I.' He disentangled himself and she could hear him rummaging about amongst his clothes.

Oh, it's all wrong! she thought wildly. An hour ago he was my friend. It would have been easy then to have told him I was, well, virginal. Can't now. Hope he doesn't turn on the light; I feel so dreadfully silly dressed up on top and all bald on the bottom. It'd be better if we were at least naked. Hell!

She was more alone, terribly alone, than ever. Here she was, losing her best friend just when she needed him most. Hateful, hateful bodies!

Click. The light went on and she caught, transfixed, the sight of Mike, his hair sticking up, his socks on, his legs white as an old man's, the other part she daren't think about hidden under his awful nylon shirt . . . all lit up in a flash before she closed her eyes.

'Ah!' he mumbled. 'Got it.' Off went the light. He sat down on the bed with his back to her and she listened, appalled, to stealthy crackling sounds. She could hardly hear them.

'God, bloody thing,' he muttered. She gnawed her nails, her legs stiff as pokers in front of her. She felt she was laid out on an operating-table. 'Can't get the wretched thing on,' he muttered, an abyss away.

Then it must have been fixed because he turned round and heaved himself on top of her. She froze, her poker-legs rigid. He lay on top of her, knee to knee, foot to foot. It was horribly uncomfortable, all bones digging into her; she could hardly breathe.

For a moment they lay there paralysed. Then, horrors, he took her hand and pushed it down.

'Come on,' he muttered. 'Help me, can't you?'

She snatched her hand away. 'What have I got to do?' It was a nightmare.

'Help me get started again.'

There was a silence. Then she drew a deep breath.

'But I've never done it before.'

Silence. He rolled off her and sat up. 'What?'

'I've never done it before.'

'You mean you're a *virgin?*'

'Yes.'

A longer silence, a very long one. Then he said: 'So am I.'

A dazed moment, and then she burst into an explosion of laughter. After a moment he did too. Then, when they'd wiped their eyes, faces wet and bodies limp from laughing, he got up and switched on the light. He sat down beside her again, his thighs hairy, hers not, in a most companionable silence. After a while they picked up their underclothes.

Mike said brightly: 'You know, we could have a bash now if you feel like it.'

'No! No!'

He buttoned his shirt thoughtfully. 'I've always fancied you. You looked so experienced, too.'

'Honestly? But I thought you were. It was you who showed me all those poems about love's quick breaths and stuff like that.'

'That's different,' he said simply. 'That's poetry.'

Outside their window all the other lights in all the other windows were off. It must be very late. Mike got up and made some tea. Laura watched him; his bare legs seemed more attractive now they weren't threatening her.

'To innocence,' he boomed. 'To friendship.'

'Cheers,' she said, and added: 'My ears are sore.'

'Oh dear, sorry about that. I was carried away by passion, you see.'

Laura leant against the comfortable nylon-shirted shoulder. Good old Mike, she thought. She sipped her tea, nasty peaty stuff as all the milk was finished. They didn't bother to talk. Really, Laura thought, this debacle of arms and legs has made us much better friends, for what worse event could we go through together?

Platonic friends, of course. More than ever she realized: sex couldn't possibly work with someone so nice, so suitable. Goodness, her parents would actually *like* him!

Later, walking back past the dark buildings, every light but Mike's extinguished, she really felt quite refreshed and adult, for wasn't honestly admitting her virginal state the most adult thing she'd ever done? A hurdle had been jumped, a hurdle from which, in John's case, she had so pathetically shied away. What an exhilarating feeling!

She breathed the icy night air into her lungs, deeply, and strode up the steps to her block, a strong, adult girl, no longer feeble and no longer – she realized with pleasant surprise – so shamefully homesick.

'Laura!'

A blinding glare in her face. 'Laura!'

She stood still. By the voice it must be the warden, though she could see nothing but brilliance. The warden must be waving a torch.

'Step inside please, Laura.'

She must be leaning out of her special warden's room on the ground floor. Waiting, like a spider.

Inside, the warden switched off her torch and stood, weary

but unruffled, in her beige dressing-gown. She wore beige slippers too, Laura noticed with dislike – for she did not quite like to meet her eyes and kept her own lowered – dreary middle-aged beige slippers.

'I wonder if you've seen the time, Laura.'

'Er, no, actually.'

'Half past two. Half past *two*, Laura. Quite honestly, I don't really care for sitting up until half past two.' Don't then, thought Laura, but kept her eye on the slippers. 'Where have you been?'

'Er, with a friend.'

'Now, I won't ask you who that friend was. I will just ask you to tell me at what time, according to the rules, you are required to be back in your block. Could you tell me, Laura?'

'Midnight, except special permission.' How soppy and obedient she sounded! And she couldn't stop talking to those beastly slippers.

'That's right. Well, we won't say any more about it this time, Laura, but I do expect my girls to have the courtesy to abide by the rules. They're for your own good, you know. Goodnight.'

Now I'll let her have it, thought Laura. Now I'll tell her what I think of her!

'Er, sorry,' she said.

Blushing furiously, she found her way to her room. For some reason she felt quite trembly as she fumbled with the key. Stupid place; she really had outgrown it. The key shook in the lock. Just like school. Stupid rules, tonight of all nights, just when such important things had happened. When she felt so adult.

She got the door open. There was a note on the floor.

10 *p.m. Your sister telephoned to say that she is coming to visit you tomorrow. Expect her late in the morning.*
Warden.

Laura brightened.

five

Laura found it easy to work the next morning because she knew that in a couple of hours she would be interrupted by Claire. It gave a tighter feel to the Sunday; drawing in the gathers, so to speak, on a limp piece of cloth. As a rule, Sundays in Hall *did* feel a bit floppy. Much easier with a day structured with lectures, even if she decided not to go to any.

But with no lectures, she found herself sitting about and dreaming. Surprisingly often, these dreams were about home. Sundays at home were an awful bore, of course, but in her daydreams they became distanced into something past and sunlit. Sundays in the garden, her mother weeding round the plants in her own fastidious way, as if the soil was not quite nice; Daddy wearing the gardening-trousers he'd worn every Sunday since the War and doing something useful they'd all forget to comment on when it was done; Holly with a friend, either a blasé or a giggly one, she only seemed to have two kinds; Badger lying on the lawn snapping at flies and occasionally moving to another patch of shade, leaving a map, resembling the USA, of grey hairs behind him on the grass; Claire indoors reading . . . She could be quite nostalgic for home when she wasn't there.

She opened 'A Child's Conception of the World'. With Claire coming she could concentrate, couldn't she?

She couldn't. Last night, detail by blush-making detail, kept creeping up on her. How she was longing to tell Claire! She'd tell her about the John thing, too. Claire would laugh. Things were more fun when they were gone over again with a sister; giggled over and analysed from the safety of one's room.

Claire! She thought of her driving down in the Morris they shared with its hesitant windscreen-wipers. Down to the tiniest detail she could picture it, because she knew it so well – Claire crouched forward, knuckles mauve from the draughts, eyes narrowed against the blurred windscreen, dogged in her rattling Morris, buffeted and splashed by the passing Jags and Jensens. She must give her a good day. After all, it was seldom that she got

33

away. Usually at the weekends she was struggling with some under-rehearsed play or collapsing adventure playground. Old Claire was such a dedicated teacher.

She arrived. Laura asked about her parents first.

'Last time I saw them,' said Claire, 'Daddy was starting evening classes in painting. Isn't that touching? He says that with Holly at school and us two gone, he ought to branch out.'

'Good for him. But it's Mummy who needs the old horizon-enlarging.'

'I can't understand what she does all day now.'

'I know,' said Laura. 'She spends the whole morning in Harrods deciding whether she wants a pink or a blue fluffy bog-seat cover, and then she spends all afternoon taking it back because it doesn't match the plastic toothbrush-holder.'

'Honestly!' Laura was such an exaggerator. But there was truth there, too.

'You must be freezing. I'm going to make us some coffee.' Laura went outside to the gas-ring.

Claire gazed at the prints crammed all over the walls and the clothes thrown all over the floor. Laura always did things in extremes. When they were younger it had always been Laura who dared shout back at the boys in the Rec – to grown-ups, the Recreation Ground – boys who, with runny noses and peaky faces, had stalked them with jeers and bad words. Even in Harrow there were boys like that. And it was Laura who had led the expeditions to the block of flats at the bottom of the road, up the lift to the top floor and then out on to the roof. There they had played daring games, Laura always a little too near the edge, while underneath them they could see the sliding glitter of the arterial road – it was always night when they played there – and on the horizon the orange glow that meant London. 'We're looking for Mrs Fotheringay-Phipps,' Laura would answer, haughtily, any enquirer they might meet in the corridors. She looked so bossy that they always believed her. In those days her admirers had called her spirited, her detractors pert, and by the time she was adolescent they had joined together in calling her rebellious.

But to Claire she had just been the leader – Roy Rogers while she was Tonto (in the Rec), the eminent surgeon while she was the body (in the bedroom), the messy baby while she was the mother (when they were having tea in the kitchen and everyone was out). Laura had all the star parts.

But Claire didn't mind, even though she was the older and by rights ought to have been the boss. Her moment came with the recriminations when, Laura fidgeting behind her, she faced up to their irate mother and – far worse – disappointed father. She became an expert at extrication. This tidying-up she found curiously satisfying.

Laura returned. Claire asked: 'Remember that time you dug up all the potatoes on that man's allotment and put all the tops back in the soil – '

'And he thought they'd got blight because they got so withered, and sprayed and sprayed them – '

'And we put the potatoes in our room and forgot all about them, and Mummy found them all mouldy – '

'And you,' said Laura smugly, 'had to explain.'

They smiled into their steaming coffee cups. It was funny to talk about their youth in this ultra-modern room, devoid of any childhood memories except those assessed by the scientific books that stood on Laura's shelves.

'What's the first thing in your life you remember?' asked Laura.

'Ants in my pram,' said Claire promptly.

'That wasn't you, it was me.'

'Are you sure?'

'Of course. I remember them biting me. I can feel it now.'

'But then someone put cream on my arm and it felt better. It was yellow stuff and smelt of the dentist's.'

They looked helplessly at each other. 'Which of us was it?' asked Claire. 'We just merged for years. We did everything together.' She gazed at their similar hands curled round their coffee mugs – similar except for Laura's bitten nails and copper rings. They had parted ways a little – not much, just a little – since those days.

Claire drained her cup. 'Enough nostalgia,' she said. 'Tell me about your room. Is this where you work?'

'That's right. When I'm sitting here I can see who's in whose room in the block opposite.'

'And your own snug armchair! It's like a play set. Someone's figured it all out; every need catered for.'

'That's right. Sometimes I feel each one of us in his little room is going through the identical sequence. It's odd.'

They went up the corridor and wandered through the drizzle

to inspect the other blocks with their rows of identical windows. In the Common Room they could see a couple playing darts, another playing ping-pong, and in each armchair sat a figure rustling through the Sunday papers.

'How obedient they look!' exclaimed Claire. 'Using the facilities, doing what the building tells them to do.'

'That's what I mean. We're like ants in an anthill.'

Claire looked at Laura. 'That annoys you?'

Just then a newspaper was lowered. Mike's face appeared over the top, smiling. Laura, blush rising, said: 'Hello. This is my sister Claire.'

Mike looked at Claire with interest. What was he comparing? Claire's calmer face and brushed hair?

'Are there any more of you?' he asked.

'Only Holly. She's our little sister but she's only twelve.'

'Sit down,' said Mike, 'and listen to this.' He was still addressing his remarks to Claire. Could he possibly be selfconscious too? He must be, for he was avoiding Laura's eye. She was avoiding his, too, of course. They'd both feel better when he'd read something out of the newspaper. Then they'd be able to talk about it and this blushful moment would be over.

'Hang on,' he said, shuffling through the pages. 'Aha! Got it.' He looked up – at Claire, of course. 'Lend an ear.' He started reading, boomingly.

In one of Australia's most remote areas, mining executives have discovered the richest uranium deposit in the world. Assuming that mining rights would be easily obtained from the aboriginal owners, the company quickly signed contracts to sell millions of dollars' worth of ore. But what they failed to take into account was the aborigines' refusal to disturb the Green Ants which live near the site. The place is called the Dreaming Place of the Green Ants, and is deeply holy.

Mike looked up, addressing Claire. 'Listening?'

'Yes'

He was obviously moved by what he was reading. The grey ash lengthened on his forgotten cigarette. *'The executives have been offering them higher and higher sums for the mining rights. They started at $7,000: they have grown to $13,000,000. But,'* he looked up at them; he even looked at Laura, so swept along was he, *'the aborigines refuse to sell at any price. Confronted by the wrath of the ants and poverty . . .* well, they've chosen the poverty.' He put the paper down. The ash dropped to the floor.

His audience sighed, for it had moved them too.

Any further conversation was interrupted by the bell. Lunch-time.

'We all troop down,' Laura told Claire.

'Sounds fun.'

'Awfully regimented. I loathe doing things in the mass.'

Claire smiled. 'Do you?' she asked, looking at Laura's denim skirt, identical to countless denim skirts now passing them as they walked down the path.

They sat down with Mike. Claire ate with relish.

'A proper Sunday lunch!' she said between mouthfuls. 'With roast potatoes and all. I do envy you. I wish I could come to university. All the intriguing people, and everyone having their own lovely rooms . . .' She broke off because she sounded too wistful and instead gazed around. Serious boys, laughing boys, round-shouldered, T-shirted ones – could the 1970's be called the Decade of the Hollow Chest? – sombre, bespectacled boys who were probably doing Maths. When they went into digs their landladies would love them because they'd be tidy and roll their washing into a neat bundle. Plain girls, pretty ones, girls with certain make-up and uncertain eyes – clever, that – girls nobody would notice but who someone some day would want to marry more than anyone else in the world . . . Claire wanted to speak to all of them.

'Don't they look young and callow,' said Laura.

'You're very dismissive about everything,' said Claire. Appreciate it! she wanted to shout.

She didn't shout it, but as they left the hall she said: 'You're jolly lucky, you know.'

'Am I? You mean, it's all more fun than your flat? What would Yvonne be doing now?'

'Creeping into the kitchen and rustling through the Shortcake Fingers.'

'And Nikki?'

'Sticking on her eyelashes and dreaming about the strong brown thighs of her lover, and how he said her scent was as fresh as a meadow in spring.'

'Oh yes, they're all copywriters, aren't they.'

Nikki was a receptionist with J. Walter Thompson and bedded down with a succession of young executives known to Claire only by name and (in a whisper, because Yvonne disapproved) performance.

'Yes, I must say, it's nice to be here,' said Claire.

'Despite the rain.' They had decided to explore Bristol by car and were now driving across the Downs. They were alone, as Mike had left to do some work. 'I can see, looking at Mike, that you do lots of discussing and arguing. Things of the spirit.'

'Hmm. Sometimes bodies do seem to get in the way.'

At last Laura told her the episodes, John first, then Mike. When Claire had finished laughing she said: 'Yes, I could see that Mike fancied you.'

'What gave you that idea?'

'By the way he kept avoiding your eye, yet couldn't help himself looking whenever you shifted in your seat or scratched your leg. Everything you did, he noticed.'

'The thing is, I don't fancy him. He's too nice.' Too suitable, she thought.

'Idiot!' Claire laughed. She looked through the windscreen at the tall terraces, smudgy in the rain. People were always fancying Laura. She, Claire, had got used to it now. Laura's hair, streaked with yellow, could easily be described as tumbling round her face. Her own hair, brown throughout, just hung. And there was an aliveness about Laura, a quickness in her movements, a grace, that arrested the eye. Often when she left a room there would be a pause, almost a sigh, amongst those that remained. Anyway, she had a straight nose and freckles, two things that Claire had always lacked and would always lack. Laura had simply been the prettiest, though when they were children, of course, they'd never known it. The turning point had come when she had been thirteen and some parental friend, forgotten but for this one dreadful remark, had said to their mother: 'Claire's got such a *nice* face, but of course Laura's the beauty.' Both Claire and Laura, needless to say, had pretended they hadn't heard, but looking back Claire could identify that moment as a jolt into adulthood; one of those small shocks that take the facts you've always known, like prettiness, and suddenly shove them at you in a queasy, uncomfortably close way. Thud. Things won't ever be quite the same again.

The water was falling in steady drips through the roof, but from long practice they both knew how to tilt to one side so that it landed harmlessly between them. With all its leaks, they knew this car well. After nine weeks of *trying*, with everyone and everything, how nice it is, thought Laura, to settle down into the comfy, soggy car seat. How nice not to try to be clever or liberated or to know about films, but just to sit and chat to Claire. Claire's mind and body, inner and outer workings, were as familiar to her as the dials on the dashboard and the petrol gauge, stuck since time inmemorial at well below 'E'. Known and loved.

With a creak and a rattle the Morris climbed, painfully, the hill into Clifton and turned into the street with the shops.

'Everything's so beautiful,' said Claire. 'Even in the rain.'

The shops, being closed, faded into insignificance and allowed their lovely upper façades, tall windows and simple balconies, to state their presence down the street. Round a corner they turned and into a square.

'Never mind the rain,' cried Claire. 'Let's get out and walk.'

It was a pure pleasure to walk down the street. Up above them four storeys of golden stone faced each other across the trees whose trunks were glistening in the rain. The street was deserted. It was nice to be alone and talk about sisterly things without boring anyone else; nice, too, just to wander at will and not have to point out places of interest, as one would with anyone but a sister.

Just then they stopped. They had turned a corner and there in front of them stood a figure tugging at a cigarette machine. He was hunched over it, in his long flapping overcoat from the Army Surplus shop.

'Wow,' he said. 'This thing sticks.' The drawer shot back and he staggered, then he looked at them, pleased. He had very, very gentle eyes and a droopy moustache. Droopy hair, too. Everything drooped.

'Goodness, this is Andy,' Laura told Claire. 'He does psychology like me, but he's second year.' He'd been at that table in the Berkeley Café; she prayed that John had told him nothing about the episode that had followed that meeting. Andy's vague, benign look told her he hadn't; no little spark there.

Andy looked through Laura vaguely. 'You and your friend want to come inside or something? It's pissing down.'

'Well . . .' Laura hesitated. He'd think they were mad, but actually they'd been enjoying their damp wander through the streets. And yet . . . curiosity triumphed. So did his unsuitability, with his long and matted knots of hair.

They followed the stooping figure down the street and arrived at some basement steps. Andy went down and disappeared through a door. Laura halted, struck by another thought.

'Do you really want to?' she whispered.

'Yes. Why not?'

Laura had never been to Andy's place before, but as all his conversations seemed to revolve around the subject of cannabis, she presumed that his Sundays would revolve around its consumption. The fact was, to her terrible and secret shame she'd never actually had any of the stuff. And what about Claire?

They went inside. Andy seemed to have forgotten about them and was sitting down in the middle of the room. Claire and Laura hovered. The curtains were half drawn and a light bulb was lit, as if the room couldn't quite choose between day and night. Five or six people were sitting about on mattresses, and in the air was a damp bedsit smell mingled with a faint farmyard scent that must be It. Pot. Laura found a space and sat down.

'Come on,' she whispered to Claire, who suddenly looked foolish standing up there, clutching her handbag. 'Sit down next to me.'

A girl with lots of tiny plaits came in carrying a tray of tea. 'Oh,' she said when she saw Laura and Claire.

'They've come,' said Andy, 'to join us for the Sunday joint.'

'But we've already eaten, thank you,' said Claire.

Laura blushed. Someone laughed. The girl rolled large black-rimmed eyes at Claire, took in the woollen suit and proper hand-bag, and wordlessly squatted on the floor. She started pouring the tea. Andy had taken off his coat and was emptying the cigarettes out of their packet.

'Well, Laura and Laura's Friend,' he said, 'so you'd like to have a smoke, would you? Join the merry band.'

'When I was fourteen,' said Claire, 'my father gave me twenty-five pounds not to start and I was so miserly I never did.'

Laura hid her burning face. How could anyone, even *Claire*?

'Hey, hey.' Andy smiled at Claire, eyebrows raised. 'Not smoke – Smoke. Grass. Dope. The good weed.'

'Oh.' A pause. 'Oh, I see. Well, I don't think I could. I can't inhale, you see.'

Andy looked round at the others. 'Hey, hear that? Well, Laura's Friend,' he said, turning to her, 'just watch Uncle Andy. He'll show you how.'

By now he'd taken some papers from his pocket and filled them with tobacco from the cigarettes, and something else he tapped out from a little brass box. Everyone watched. He was the priest. Now he stuck the papers together into one loose sausage. 'A light,' he said, and the plaits girl leant over with the holy flame.

He put the sausage to his lips; it flared; through the smoke Claire saw his eyes bulge. For a horrified moment she thought he was asphyxiating. He drew the thing away from his mouth and then, with a sudden hiss and shudder as if he'd been stabbed, his lips drew back from his teeth. It was a long hiss, exquisitely painful, his lips stretched, his eyes glazed, the veins in his neck bulging. Then suddenly he subsided; his breath was let out in a shuddering groan. He slumped down, head lolling, and proffered her the smouldering sausage.

'Oh no,' she cried. 'I couldn't, really.'

'Hey, just try,' he said. 'Take it right down, deep.'

Those eyes were watching, waiting for it. Eyes all round the room. Claire quickly passed it to Laura.

'Are you sure?' Laura asked. She took it between her thumb and forefinger, her other fingers arched as she'd seen Andy arch his. She put it to her lips.

It burned down to her lungs; it tore, red-hot, down, and she was transfixed. Everything went black. She couldn't breathe.

After a moment she could open her eyes, just. But still she couldn't breathe. There was no hope of her ever breathing again. How could she, with her lungs full, her throat full, her mouth and head full?

The next hand hovered, waiting. Suddenly she could gasp. A fit of choking strangled her.

'Good grass, right?' said Andy. 'Not too strong; just a gentle high.'

'Is it?' Claire asked Laura with interest. 'What's it like? Do you often smoke it?'

Andy was listening, so Laura tried to seem blasé. Difficult when she was dying, but she tried. 'Er, sometimes.' Why, oh why couldn't she be as honest as Claire and admit she'd never done it? Why? Why couldn't she be as nice as Claire? The question reeled round her head. Why? In fact, the whole room was reeling. The Eric Clapton poster on the wall buzzed and wobbled. Hell! It was just like that awful thing with John all over again, but worse this time because she had, in some way she couldn't make out with her dizzy head, been disloyal to Claire.

The hissing next to her stopped. She turned to her neighbour; he was pressing his neck. Claire leant forward to look at him too. 'Why are you doing that?' she asked brightly.

There was a pause, then his eyes slowly opened. 'It gets me stoneder than stoned,' he said, then he closed his eyes again.

Enveloped in themselves, people didn't speak. The room was heavy with smoke and concentration. Then a voice came from the opposite mattress. 'I need jam,' it said.

'And why not,' said Andy. He heaved himself up and went into the kitchen, reappearing with a loaf and some jam. 'Let's get into the con – , the con – , how's it go?'

'Conserves,' said Claire helpfully.

'The conserves. Yeah, who wants a jam trip?' He cleared a space on the floor which was covered with things – ashtrays, teacups, 'Rupert Bear Annual' and a Sunday paper. It was open at the page about the aborigines.

'Have you read that article?' Claire asked Andy, pointing to it. He shook his head. 'It's very good.'

'Read it, then.' He turned round to the others. 'Listen to a story, children.'

Claire read it. When she had finished she looked up.

'Wow,' came an impressed voice.

'Yes,' she replied, pleased. 'It's extraordinary, isn't it.'

'Wow, those ants . . . big green ants, really big . . .'

'. . . with huge staring eyes . . .' came another voice.

'. . . and big shiny bodies, leaping through the woods . . .'

'. . . their eyes all red and their bodies all – all green . . .'

'. . . and pow! You're face to face with one,' said Andy. He started giggling. They all started giggling. 'A mighty monster ant. And you say, hey, don't touch me, mister monster ant, don't woggle your long green tentacles at me . . .' Giggling, Andy put a spoon into the jam and heaped it on to a piece of bread. He lifted it; the lump of jam slid off on to his jeans. 'Whoops.' He was shaking with giggles.

'But don't you see?' Claire cried. 'About the aborigines – ?' She stopped. They didn't understand what it was about at all; they didn't care.

The thing was back in her hand now; it was shorter and damper. She passed it to Laura.

'Er, no thanks,' said Laura, who was still fighting for breath.

She'd just noticed that the dropped ash had left round white holes in the knees of her black tights, holes the size of sixpences, widening and shrinking ones. The room still swayed to and fro, most oddly. 'We must go,' she said.

'Splitting?' Andy raised his head from the inspection of his jeans.

'Yes,' said Laura, longing for air. 'Claire has to drive back to London and I have to go back to Hall.'

'In Hall, are you? Dead place, full of straights.'

'Oh but – ' Claire began, and stopped. She thought of Mike's passionate voice as he read about the aborigines. This lot didn't seem to care about anything at all. 'I've met such nice people there today.'

Andy turned to Laura. 'Well, my girl, the sooner you get out of there the better.'

'Yes,' said Laura casually, 'I'm thinking of leaving next term and moving in somewhere else, so I can – you know – be myself.'

'Laura!' cried Claire. 'Is that true?'

'Oh yes.' Though actually she'd never considered it until now. Avoiding Claire's eye, she got up carefully. The room still slopped backwards and forwards, but once she was outside she felt better. Night had fallen and the rain had stopped. She took a deep, deep gulp of air.

'Do you feel high?' Claire was inspecting her with interest.

'No,' she replied, truthful at last. 'Sick.'

Laura being disinclined to talk, they walked back to the car in silence. With what pleasure had they walked down this street! But now the mood was spoilt. Passing the black railings, Laura wondered angrily Why? Why can't I just be myself like Claire? Why do I have to try to make an impression when Claire doesn't?

And later that night, having seen Claire off on her dark voyage, she wondered about moving out of Hall. Perhaps, if she lived alone, her character would tauten up and she would no longer find herself bending with every different person she met. Claire, in her charitable way, would call that being sympathetic, identifying with people. Not true. Even with Mike, Laura thought, nice friendly Mike, I was tilting my head at the right, thoughtful angle when he was reading that thing from the newspaper.

She was in bed now. She pulled the blankets up to her chin and gazed at her silent room, its washbasin glimmering in the moonlight. I'm a whole mass of people, she thought. That's my trouble. And none of them – except when I'm alone, or with Claire – none of them is convincing.

Somewhere out in the echoing night a dog barked. Outside these four warm walls there were real sadnesses, and real problems, and spaces and aborigines . . .

Laura snuggled down in bed, cosily wrapped up in her blankets and complexes.

SIX

Christmas Eve, and all along the Harrow avenue lights glinted in the windows; fairy lights, lanterns. Stretches of hedge, then fence, then stretches of hedge again; in between them, gates – The Lilacs, Woodland View, Greenbanks. Beyond the gates, pale in the gathering dusk, gravel drives and beyond them houses, similar but not identical, each with its shadowy double garage.

Out of the gate marked Greenbanks, a house whose double garage had Tudor eaves, issued a little party of three – two sisters and Badger, who was a border collie with a black and white face.

'Woods?' suggested Claire.

'No,' said Holly. 'I'm always going there.'

'Rec?'

'Shut. It's dark.'

'Oh yes. Well, what about that bomb site place Laura and I used to play in?'

'It's got a house on it now.'

The two of them stood on the pavement, thinking. Laura was usually the leader, but Laura had disappeared somewhere. Actually, it was rather a relief being without her. She had seemed so grumpy this holidays, mooning about and telling their parents how hideous their furniture was, things like that. One felt more Christmassy without her.

Badger looked up at them and waved his white plume of a tail.

'I know,' said Claire finally. 'The roofs.'

'What roofs? What roofs?' cried Holly.

They set off down the road, past the similar houses, past the large dark gardens, past the Rec with its closed iron gates. Holly, thrilled at this sudden sisterly adventure, skipped along the pavement. Now it was dark, there was that unmistakable Christmas feeling in the air, a sense of timelessness, a hushed expectancy.

At the bottom of the road they turned a corner. Here they passed a wrought-iron fence and Holly slowed down from a skip to a walk.

'What on earth are you doing?' asked Claire.

'Touching each of the twiddly bits. I have to when I go past.'

'Why?'

'So none are left out.'

Claire laughed. 'Do you know, I did that? At least, I used to run my hands along those bobbles at the top.'

'So you'd be sure there would be chocolate cake for tea or it wouldn't hurt at the dentist's.'

'That's right.' They moved off down the road. 'What else do you do?'

'Oh, I canter this bit when I'm being a pony.'

Claire looked down at the pavement. 'And you never tread on the cracks.'

'Of course not. You are, though.'

Claire looked down where she was stepping. She felt a vestigial tweak. Fear? Guilt? She started avoiding them.

With crack-avoiding strides they made their way down the street. They stepped in harmony. Soon they arrived at the block of flats with the roofs, the roofs where Claire and Laura had so often played. They crept through the shrubbery, past the rows of lighted windows; up the fire-escape at the back they tiptoed.

'This is super!' whispered Holly. Badger's claws made little scrabbling clatters as he followed them up. Claire gripped the iron railing; she peeped furtively into the lighted kitchens they were passing; she ducked when a shape appeared and closed a window. Her skin prickled with delicious fear, a feeling she thought she'd outgrown. Badger barked, once. 'Ssh!' hissed Claire. That exquisite, dry-throated alertness was still there, hardly blunted with her adulthood.

They tiptoed on to the roof. It was an interesting one, full of skylights and tanks and large strange air-ducts. Claire looked around; just for a moment she wished that Laura were there. Now they'd arrived she hadn't the faintest idea what they'd ever done. But she'd think of something; half of her was tingling with excitement. Half, the adult half, just thought of it as a nice view.

The skyline was jumbled with shapes; they were creeping past them when Holly drew in her breath. They stopped.

Holly pointed. 'Look!' she hissed.

Claire looked. 'What is it? I can't see anything.'

'Look at that shape. It's a person. It *is*.'

Claire stiffened. Holly was right: it was the hunched shape of a person. Someone was sitting there.

Just then Badger barked. The shape jumped up, suddenly familiar.

'Laura!'

They stared at each other, then giggled. 'Goodness, what a relief!' They laughed, each pretending they hadn't been frightened.

'What are you doing here?' Claire asked.

'Just thinking. Dreaming. Escaping from home for a while.'

They both looked at Laura. The surprise subsided, leaving the atmosphere changed.

'I came up here to breathe,' said Laura. She threw her head back and gazed up. 'To look at that beautiful sky. Amazing, isn't it.'

Holly frowned. 'What about our game?' she asked.

'We can look at those incredible stars,' said Laura.

Holly treated that suggestion with the contempt it deserved. 'You're not saying the proper things.' She looked from one to the other. 'Anyway, if you two are so feeble I'm going off with Badger. First I'm going to explore. Then I'm going to see where those pipes go. Then I'm going to try and get down one of those window things.'

Claire, with the faintest sense of loss, sat down beside Laura.

'Don't go near the edge!' she called to Holly, as boringly as an adult. Then she turned and stared down at the strings of street lamps.

'I feel so stifled at home, Claire,' said Laura. 'They don't realize I've grown up. All the nagging! *Why don't you give just a little tidy to your room, darling, if you've nothing else to do, and couldn't you possibly wear something a little more becoming, you know that Marion and her mother are coming for drinks and I do like you looking nice.* That sort of stuff.' She threw her head back and gazed at the sky. 'You know, even when I was younger my real reason for coming up here was to breathe.' To illustrate this she breathed in, deeply. 'You see, I needed space and freedom.'

Claire burst into laughter. 'Laura! You were as ordinary as me! You came up here to play! To boss me around. Don't you remember?' She looked at Laura's brooding profile against the night sky. Childhood was far away; it did seem a pity. 'Really, you do seem muddled.'

'I am muddled. And I analyse myself so endlessly I get into a worse muddle. I just think about what *I'm* doing all the time, how *I'm* reacting, what impression *I'm* giving. Very claustrophobic, it is. It's only when I'm alone that I can really relax and breathe again.'

'But don't you feel free at Bristol, with your lovely independent room and all?'

'Not really. It's different pressures there.'

'What like?'

'Oh, pressures to look as if one's got masses of friends and one's doing no work and one's sexy and careless. Insidious things, those.'

'So at home it's pressures to be tidy and in Bristol it's pressures to be messy. So to speak.'

'I never thought of it like that. And each is as bad as the other.' She fell silent. How was it that Claire, with her cramped flat full of landladies' cast-offs and Yvonne's tapestry pictures, with the difficult pressures of her teaching job – how was it that Claire seemed curiously freer than she, Laura, felt? For, even in mid-grumble like this, she knew that if she were honest she had all the freedom in the world – time, liberty, her own room – heavens, poor Claire even had to share a bedroom! And yet Claire in her unobtrusive way had managed to become much more independent inside herself than she, Laura, with all her gesturings, had ever done. Somehow she'd never had to be the loud one; there was no need. She'd grown up without a fuss, leaving home as naturally as fruit falls from a branch. No traumas, no complexes, no knots that had to be tugged against, then examined at length.

'Why were you always so reasonable at home?' she asked peevishly. 'Why did you never quarrel?'

'I was just more boring and obedient than you.'

'But you weren't. Underneath it all you were doing your own thing. You just didn't go on about it all the time. I make such a muddle of everything.'

'Still talking?' asked Holly, coming up and sitting down on the pipe next to Claire. 'You missed lots.'

'What sort of things?' asked Claire. Badger poked his nose into her hair and licked her ear thoroughly, leaving it wet. 'What did you find?'

'I got one window thing open but I couldn't get down, so I had a jumping competition with Badger over some pipes. They were very high, right up to my waist.'

'Who won?'

'Me, of course. He kept going under them instead; and then he looked so smug, silly dog!'

'Good old Badge! Shall we go back for tea?'

They both looked at Laura, who was sitting chin in hand. Badger went and sat in front of her, thumping his tail and gazing in his intent, flattering way into her eyes, but she was deep in thought.

'Laura?'

She roused herself and they made their way back to the fire-escape. Badger's claws made scrabbling noises as he followed them down.

In the street, Claire turned to Holly with a touch of the old spirit. 'Show me where you start to canter and I'll race you.'

'OK,' said Holly in the casual voice that showed she was pleased. 'We start here, actually. Want to come, Laura?'

'Not really,' said Laura.

Up the lamp-lit road they went, two cantering sisters, one barking dog, and one sister who was walking, her eyes on the pavement, not because she was watching out for the cracks but because she was feeling introverted.

Rosemary had watched the girls disappear into the dusk. 'Rum butter,' she said to herself. 'Sprouts, gravy mix.' She counted them off on her fingers. Tap-tap; in her high heels she crossed the room, drawing the curtains. Then she straightened some holly that had slipped sideways behind a picture frame – one of Dan's pictures. The house was full of his paintings now. They were mostly rather wavery still-lifes in watercolour and everyone was very polite about them. 'Stuffing.'

She gazed at the red rotating glow of the electric logs in the fireplace. Dan had protested when she had got rid of the real fire. *You can't gaze into it any more,* he'd said. But Rosemary had found it so dreadfully messy with all those bits of Coalite in the carpet.

'Ah, Holly's stocking! I knew there was something left.' She turned. 'Dan darling, could you be an angel and run up to the girls' room? See if you can find a thick pair of tights or something; I haven't filled Holly's stocking yet and it's a good time now she's out with Claire.'

Dan got up. Not being Father Christmas had made him feel inadequate once, but Rosemary had so obviously been more efficient at it that he had given up and left it to her. It had its compensations, anyway, in the shape of that second glass of whisky he could have after dinner; no longer was there the peril of tripping up on Holly's hearthrug and spilling a sackful of teddies and tangerines all over the floor.

Upstairs in Claire and Laura's room he scrabbled through the cupboard. Some wicked-coloured platform-soles were lying there all jumbled up with the sandals he remembered Laura wearing to school. He took the sandals out and looked at them; they were scuffed round the edges and had poignant bumps where her toes had been.

His feeling of loss returned; it was a familiar feeling and he shook it aside. After all, in a little while the downstairs door would slam and Laura herself would burst in, her cheeks reddened by the wind and her hair tousled.

But it wasn't quite the same Laura. Her hair seemed unacquainted with the touch of a brush, and she smoked. At least, he'd known she'd smoked before because he'd found her doing it sometimes, and he'd tried not to look too disapproving or she'd just have smoked all the more. But she'd never been so aggressive and open about it. And she was restless in the house, floppy yet irritable, lethargic yet pert, so very adolescent, criticizing everything yet never lifting a finger to help.

He stood up and went over to the chest of drawers. On the top was a pile of books, 'Evaluations of Personality', 'The Meaning of Pain', 'Stress and Duality'. All of their authors had impressive Middle-European names. He inspected them with awe. It seemed only last week that Laura had been sucking her Biro over her homework and it had been himself, Dan, who had bent over her and shown her how to do it. In his own small way he'd been able to contribute, and very satisfying it had been too.

But what on earth could he tell her about Duality and Stress? She seemed very far away now. He found some long socks and paused for a moment, gazing at the room with its twin beds,

Laura's surrounded by suitcases and scattered clothes. She hadn't even unpacked. How transient it looked! This grumpy, far-away girl had hardly come back home at all.

'Dan!'

He jumped.

'Dan *darling*!' She must be in one of her Bothers. He could tell by the 'darling'.

'Darling, what *are* you doing? They'll be back in a minute.'

'I've only been a moment.'

'You've been three-quarters of an hour.'

seven

When her parents came down to Bristol Laura, as she'd suspected, didn't quite know where to put them. They stood around awkwardly, her mother with her matching outfit and persistent voice, her father stooping from years of work. They seemed the wrong shape for the room. Restless too, and inquisitive.

'Darling!' cried her mother. 'Do tell us all about your friends. You've hardly said anything yet.'

'Ssh!' Laura glanced towards the door. 'Most of them are OK.' What else could she say about them?

'Shall we meet any?'

They should meet Mike, she thought. With his public school tweediness he was very suitable, and really she would like to please them if only they'd keep their voices down. He'd mentioned that on Sundays he often went to a pub called the White Hart; they'd go there and casually bump into him.

It was a bright January day near the beginning of term. They went out to the car and she got in beside her father. Seen from the passenger seat, Bristol took on the idealized glaze of a travelogue. They drove slowly, her mother stirring in the back seat. Always there seemed too much of her; too much hat, too many rings.

'That's the café we go to when we can't stand any more Hall dinners . . . that's the pub I wrote to you about that has the draught cider . . . behind those houses you can see the labs, and that's where I buy my books . . .' Pointing out each thing she felt it was simultaneously enshrined in her parents' memory, Monuments of a Golden Youth, Our Daughter amidst the Dreaming Spires. '. . . that's the fountain the cretins all fall into on Rag Day . . . and this is the Wills' Building.'

Above them rose the Wills' tower, huge, impressive, contoured with grime. Her father gazed up; then he looked at her. He wore the look he wore in church; soon he might say something embarrassing.

'My own little girl,' he said, 'part of all this.'

She laughed; it filled the car. 'Don't be corny! Anyway,' she added, knowing this was callous, 'it's all a sham. Built out of money from fags.'

They got out of the car and walked in the direction of the pub. The way took them along a curved street of peeling, beautiful terraces. There was no sound but the brisk tapping of her mother's heels. Her cherry-pink suit made the houses look shabbier. All around them was a Sunday hush.

'Where are they all?' asked her mother.

Laura said: 'During the week it's full of students.'

Her father stopped and gazed down the road. Laura knew he was imagining them in their black gowns: they walked in two's and three's; some laughed, some discussed with furrowed brow; some, blithely bicycling, their gowns black and billowing sails, called to friends as they sped by. She wished that one, suitably gowned, would appear. He'd like that. Sometimes – this moment, for instance – she'd like to please him.

Just then a front door opened. The figure in the doorway blinked, stretched its arms into the air and yawned, revealing a large area of greyish stomach. Slowly it scratched its long, stiff hair. Then it stooped, picked up a milk bottle and disappeared back into the depths of the house.

'That's one,' said Laura triumphantly, like a mammal-spotter.

There was a silence.

'They don't all look like that,' asked her father at last. 'Do they?'

'Most of 'em.'

'But you do wear gowns to lectures, don't you?'

She laughed crushingly. 'Heavens no! Hardly anyone does. It looks so silly.'

She heard him give a small grunt; a hurt sound. I like to please him, but I like shocking him even more, she thought. Why?

They walked around the corner and into another lovely street, all mouldings and balconies. From an open window Laura could hear a Bob Dylan song, as familiar as the thump of her pulse. Looking down into a basement window she could see rush matting and bookshelves. Looking up she could see, hanging from an upstairs ceiling, the sort of round white paper lampshade that no doubt she would buy when she left Hall and moved into a room of her own. The sense of a thousand identities the same as hers gave her that familiar obliterated feeling. If only she could talk to her parents about feelings like this! Then they wouldn't be walking along in rather boring silence. How different from her walk through these same streets with Claire, Claire who understood everything. Her parents, by contrast, understood hardly anything at all. Then she thought with sudden honesty: partly because I don't tell them.

They arrived at the pub. It was humming with voices; people spilled out on to the pavement. Mike was in there somewhere; he'd make up for that vision of grey stomach. She wanted to make up for it; there was something about that disappointed grunt that made her feel guilty.

'It looks such fun!' said her mother. 'All these young people.'

Inside it was packed; thick with smoke, hot with bodies. Laura searched for Mike's face but she couldn't see it. The three of them edged their way to the bar.

'Morning, Guv'nor!' her father shouted in his hearty pub voice. In pubs he changed; he also for some reason liked to call the publican Guv'nor. Why did he?

'What?' The man leant forward as far as his belly and the counter would allow.

'Anything on the old menu? Bristol specialities?' It surprised even his family sometimes; they could forget how different he became in public places. Not at all his usual, meekish self. 'Anything in the grub line?' Facetious too, oh dear.

The man said, as if only idiots would ask: 'No food on Sunday.'

'Goodness, not even a packet of crisps?' Oh how piercing her mother's voice was! Laura felt ashamed of being ashamed of her, and still she blushed. Next to all the grubby T-shirts her mother's hat looked so very cherry-pink.

'Never mind, Guv'nor,' said her father. 'We'll console ourselves somehow, won't we, ladies?'

Half of Laura wanted to disown the Guv'nors and the cherry hat and obliterate herself amongst the T-shirts. Yet half felt threaded to these two, fused with them. It made things so complicated, the fact that she did love them. The way, for instance, that now it was acknowledged that she smoked, her father would offer her a cigarette as he was offering her one now with a certain grave courtesy that she found in no one else; as if, regrettable though it was, she would honour him if she took one. And the way he cupped her elbow and steered her through the crowd. Somehow he always made her feel special. She liked his little ceremonies, for there was none of this ceremony about her friends.

'I must say, this is a charming place,' said her mother. 'So Olde Worlde.' She took her glass of sherry and sat on the window ledge, like a practised hostess, including everyone in her smile. Laura shrank yet perversely she was touched. In the face of the barman's indifference they were both so doggedly polite, so bright in the face of setback. How loyal she could feel towards them in sudden moments; yet she would rather die than ask that spotty specimen who was blocking her mother's view and waving his cigarette smoke in her face to move over just a fraction so that they could all be more comfortable.

Laura sipped her drink, watching her mother looking composed amidst the smoke, the sunlight slanting through the window on to her hair, her legs crossed in instinctive refinement. Her eyes, bright and interested, rested on each of the faces around her. Oh why couldn't she, Laura, be more sorted-out and just accept her fondly, without being so damned complicated about it?

She took a sip of cider, half of her tugging one way, half the other. Holly, she suddenly realized, was like this, too. Boarding-school had made two people of Holly; there was a Cliffdean one and a Harrow one. On the last day of the Christmas holidays the Harrow Holly had drained away; visibly it had drained away – Laura had watched, fascinated. By the time Holly had changed into her starchy school uniform, Sketchley labels still safety-pinned to the hem, the Harrow Holly had gone, leaving her face polite and absent. She had remained thus in limbo throughout the car journey across London and into Victoria Station. And there on the platform the absent face became inhabited again by a new Holly, the Cliffdean one. Her parents hugged her but her eyes had sought those of her friends, giggly friends wearing unbecoming school hats. And, unlocked by the sight of these faces, curious new words had appeared on Holly's lips, words like 'cripes' and 'nutcase'. Laura smiled. She wasn't alone in this, then.

'Anyone you know here, darling?' called her mother.

'There's somebody I'd like you to meet,' she answered. 'Can't see him, though.'

Her mother scanned the crowd. 'Tall? Short? What's he like, darling?'

Before Laura could reply her father said: 'There's somebody over there, Laura. He's looking at you.'

'Is it him?' asked her mother. Laura craned over the heads. And saw him. Sweat broke out all over her body. It was John.

Her mother smiled. 'Yes, he's looking very curious.' Laura saw with horror that her mother was giving him an encouraging smile. Oh, it was dreadful. How could she ever introduce them? It was unthinkable. The very idea made the sweat turn cold. The combination of him and her parents was too grotesque to contemplate. The innocent questions!

Perhaps he'd forgotten who she was; after all, she hadn't exchanged a word with him since that awful episode, though the Bosch book had been wordlessly returned to her pigeonhole. But no – he was easing his way towards them.

'Got your shoes on today?' he asked, half smiling.

Laura stared at him, mind busy. What was it he'd said about silly little girls running about barefoot?

John's smile lingered. His chin was still stubbly; at any other moment she would have wondered how he managed to keep it like that, neither bearded nor shaved. Then thank goodness he left.

Her parents looked surprised. 'What was that about, then?' asked her father.

'Oh . . .' Her mind raced. Then she had a brainwave. 'Oh, we, er, had a sort of barefoot race across the Downs once.'

Her parents laughed, pleased. Relief spread over all three of them.

'What *fun* you have!' said her mother. Her father smiled. The grey stomach had been forgotten, at last.

And why not, thought Laura. Far better like this.

Though they hadn't seen Mike, there was less reason for his presence now so Laura didn't make them wait for his arrival. Instead they wandered round Clifton, had some lunch and then returned to Hall, a slumbering Sunday-afternoon place. Passing the dining-room, Laura remembered her homesickness that first night. Never would she confess such a thing to her parents! Anyway, by now it was cured. Time had cured it, sheer familiarity had made it nothing more nor less than tame.

'Look, darling,' said her mother. 'Supper's laid.'

Branston Pickle and Salad Cream jars stood bunched in the exact centre of each table. Sunday nights meant cold meat and lettuce. 'Isn't it nice, to have everything done for you!'

'No, it isn't. I'm grown up now.'

'Darling, don't be silly.'

Laura looked at the jars, smug in their Sunday night routine. She knew the place so well, the people, the food. Nothing held tremor or excitement.

'It's such a lovely place,' said her mother.

Yes, and her saying that made it so boring.

eight

Claire enjoyed giving exams simply because, after a lifetime of taking them, it was a pleasure to sit back and watch other people doing the work. Relaxed in her chair, she gazed across at the classroom with its twenty bent heads and its twenty hands that scribbled, hesitated, then scribbled again.

It was February and mock C.S.E. time. These rows of fifteen-year-olds she knew well; each had a name, each had a face, she'd taught them for many months now, but just for three hours all were silenced into twenty busy brains and twenty busy hands. There remained small signs of individuality – Joyce's cheerful butterfly hairslide, Dave's alarming two-tone boots with their stacked heels, Elaine's chain bracelet that tinkled as she wrote and became silent as she thought – but so oblivious were their owners that such things were no more than emblems; poignant badges of personalities that, at twelve noon sharp, would return to them.

Another reason for her enjoyment was a letter from Laura. There had been no time to read it at breakfast, and no space on the bus (for Laura had the car this term), but now, with those bent heads in front of her, she had two whole hours.

Wait for it. Tomorrow I move out of Hall! Before you collapse with shock I'll tell you all. You know how I've been getting fed up with all its petty rules and things?

Claire, amazed, read on. Apparently Laura knew a girl who was fed up with her digs and wanted to move into a Hall. So Laura had gone out and found an advertisement in a newsagent's window – a bedsit. This other girl was going to pay the remainder of the Hall fees; a straight swop.

Dead simple. It'll be really easy moving, too, what with the car. Address: 18 Jacob's Crescent, Bristol. And it's furnished so I needn't buy any stuff. Longing for you to see it! It's a gorgeous room with its own little bathroom and an incredible view over the city. Hardly time to think of anything else, I'm so excited.

Claire put the letter down and gazed at the rows of bent heads. What on earth were her parents going to say to all this? She, Claire, would have to explain it to them. They'd think Laura had gone absolutely mad.

And they wouldn't be one hundred per cent wrong. Fancy Laura moving out of that satisfying little room! With only a term and a half to go, why didn't she stay? She was so very impulsive, that was her trouble. Suggestible too. If someone she admired like that rather feeble specimen in the overcoat – Andy, was it? – said something, then she'd go right ahead and do it. He was the one who had brought up the subject of Hall in the first place.

Somewhere where I can be myself, Laura had said that day. It hadn't sounded like her voice at all. *Be myself*; perhaps that was the trouble. Perhaps, when one had always been considered interesting and rebellious, to be suddenly plonked down amongst thousands of other interesting and rebellious people made one feel watered-down. Just one of a mass instead of one in particular; everyone the same, the same denim skirt, the same row of Penguin Classics on their shelves. So she goes and does something completely different. Mad.

'Of course,' boomed the lecturer's voice, 'the deprived child and the child of so-called low ability is often said, by and large, to have been given insufficient love by its mother. Mothers who handle their babies from an early age generate a security, through physical contact, with their offspring. A fulfilled and healthily-reciprocated physical relationship prepares the child, we are told, for a balanced and neurosis-free relationship with the opposite sex. *But!*' He paused, stared at them, then thundered, '*Is this true?* Can we take this so absolutely for granted? What, exactly, are the criteria involved?'

Laura's baby, pencilled on her sheet of paper under the lecture heading, had started to spawn its own varied offspring down the page. First, other babies, more or less human – some just blobs, other more successful ones shaded in. Once she tried to draw the physically-caring parents but couldn't get those enfolding hands right; she could never do hands, they were inclined to end up as sort of flippers.

But babies were too fat and similar to draw endlessly. Soon the page filled up with horses, which she was particularly good at – tiny horses garlanded round the babies, bigger horses for whose legs she couldn't find space at the bottom of the page, horses that on elaboration became unicorns and zebras. The lecture heading *What is Maladjustment?* at the top of the page became encircled by a horse's body and, when the horse turned out to be black, was finally engulfed.

'*You,*' boomed the voice, 'as prospective practitioners in the field, must learn to distinguish the healthily-communicative subject, unable to repress his instincts for social interaction, from the genuinely disturbed subject who . . .'

Laura's page was full up now, but it was not worth starting another as the clock showed five to four. The lecturer's final burst of rhetoric was rising to a climax. Wastepaper basket, she thought. Must buy a wastepaper basket. She wrote it down on the list that occupied the right-hand corner of her page . . . *dustpan and brush, paint things, tea, cockroach powder* . . . She gazed over the row of heads towards the window with its square of very bright blue sky.

The clock hands, with that institutional jerk, moved to four. Synchronized perfectly, the lecturer stopped, gathered his papers and with a flourish disappeared down some steps.

Outside in the street Laura hesitated. Across the road stood the library. What she really, what she honestly ought to do was to get out those two books he'd mentioned before she'd stopped listening and have a quick glance through them.

Oh, but the sun shone and her room waited! Round on her heel she turned and up the hill she strode, up towards Jacob's Crescent.

Near the shops she met Mike.

She said: 'I'm going to make my bedsit so beautiful.'

'Good. It's grotty enough now.'

'Mike! It's lovely. I'm going to paint it yellow.'

It had been four days since she'd moved in; he'd helped her. There was a silence. Was he going to offer to wield a brush?

'Well,' he said. 'I'd come along and slosh some on with you, but I'm rather busy with something we're doing at Hall.'

'What?'

'A sort of poetry recital with music.'

'Sounds fun.' Sounds corny, she thought. Much nicer to paint my room. Silly old Hall.

Still, she did feel a pang as he went away.

Down the hill she walked with her shopping, down towards Jacob's Crescent. It was one of the humbler crescents that curved round the hill, at the top of which stood grandest Clifton with its tall balconied houses, at the bottom of which stood the less grand Clifton with its river, warehouses and shabby pubs.

The front doors of Jacob's Crescent led straight out on to the street; many of its windows were net-curtained. Some of the net curtains, as she walked past them, twitched. She wasn't unnerved – no, of course not. It was fascinatingly real and working-class and unlike anything she'd ever known before. This was Life.

Number 18 was shamefully run-down. Its owner lived elsewhere and had done nothing to it. The ground floor was empty, with boards across the windows. Upstairs on the first floor the front room was also empty; it was the back room, with its landing bathroom, that Laura inhabited. Above her on the second floor lived a family whose sounds were becoming familiar but whose faces were as yet unknown.

She put her shopping on the floor and went to the window. The city was spread before her, its spires, its docks, its glittering office buildings and, faint on the horizon, its suburbs. Laura smiled to herself; she'd come a long way from suburbia now, hadn't she!

Down below she could see the strips of gardens that belonged to her neighbours. Number 18's garden was full of junk tangled up amongst thistles. Obviously upstairs never used it; she would, though. She'd sort it out somehow; clear it a bit.

She left the window and wandered round the room. How well she remembered those first few weeks at Hall and her feelings of freedom in her little room there. But this was a thousand times better. No more communal life, no more sheep-like shuffling from room to dining-hall, dining-hall to bar. Here she could really do what she wanted. No warden either.

It must have been a gracious room once, with its slender window and its moulded plasterwork around the ceiling. Since then, she had to admit, it had rather declined. Its flowery wall-paper had faded but for scattered unfaded rectangles where past pictures had been. There was a large bed, whose stained mattress she had tried to forget once she had covered it with her blankets, and a soggy armchair, a bald patch on it where unknown heads had rested. The cooker in the recess was encrusted from many hundreds of unknown meals.

She was still finding relics of the last tenant – a half-empty tube of toothpaste righteously squeezed from the bottom, a mouldy copy of Micky Spillane and (poignant, this, and slightly perplexing) one child's shoe beneath the mattress. All these things made her feel curiously like tiptoeing.

And today, cleaning out the sink drawer, she discovered a faded printed postcard saying, in red letters, *We need YOU! Urgently. Your blood could save a life.* Just write your address on the back, it told her, and pop it into the post; we will then make an appointment for you at the Bristol Blood Donor Centre. And why not? thought Laura, filling it in. To go and do something she'd never done before seemed apt.

Outside the sky had clouded over and it had started to rain. Laura shivered. It was cold in the room when the sun went in. The rain rattled against the window. Beyond the gardens her view was disappearing; Bristol was reduced to a smudge.

Someone upstairs coughed. How very silent it was in her room. She felt trapped in a spell of silence and was suddenly afraid to break it by moving. She didn't want to take a step and hear the boards creak; for some reason they'd creak too loudly and that would – well, not frighten her of course, just make her jump.

A gust of rain rattled against the window pane; she shook herself. She was being silly. There was much to be done. Before she started painting she ought to get rid of some of the more useless furniture, like that ugly little table with the cigarette burns round the edge and the small cupboard underneath. She could dump it in the passage downstairs to keep the prams and dismembered bits of iron company.

She lifted it up but it was heavy. There must be something

inside the cupboard, weighing it down. She pulled at the door which had warped shut. The silly little knob came off in her hand; she abandoned that and pulled with her fingernails at the edge of the door.

Straining and scrabbling, she wrenched it open.

Inside was a potty. Full.

'Ugh!' The hiss of her breath, the gasp, hung suspended in the silence.

Laura sat down heavily on the bed. Upstairs they'd switched on the telly; she heard laughter and then applause. For some reason she suddenly felt – well, not lonely of course, but a little solitary. More solitary, in fact, than she remembered feeling for a very long time.

She looked hopelessly at her half-unpacked suitcase, at the hideous carpet, at the empty fireplace which, if she didn't want to freeze for the fourth night running, she ought to fill with some sort of fuel. She kept her eyes averted from the potty; there was a dusty film on the top – she'd seen it. How was she going to *bear* to empty it?

It was the potty that made her feel lonely. No, solitary. Suddenly the room seemed a bit more than she could manage. Not dismal, not really; just more complicated than she'd bargained for. Had she realized just what she was facing? It had been so pleasant to sit in her Hall room with the candles lit and feel all individual. A comfortable solitude, with dinner waiting. Now she was here, and *properly* alone for the first time in her life.

Enough of this! She shook her head at herself; perhaps soon she'd start actually talking to herself like a mad old woman. She got up and started laying newspapers on the carpet, prior to painting. She wished now that she'd dropped a few more hints to Mike about coming around and visiting; he'd take her off to the pub and it would be so jolly. But then he was busy with his poetry thing at Hall.

If she were honest about it, that poetry thing did sound rather fun.

nine

What a very flushed face! thought Claire, inspecting herself in the mirror. Funny how a mere four hours' sleep always makes you look so radiant in the morning; have a blameless eight hours of it and you look all puffy and dissolute.

She inspected herself with interest. She rubbed some eyeshadow on to her lids; she put the box down and continued the inspection. Not for ages had she looked at herself so thoroughly; she wasn't in the habit of it. Nor was she in the habit of putting on eyeshadow, come to think of it.

Yes, she did look quite becomingly pink and she didn't feel at all hungover. Over the chair lay her dress, blue and crumpled. It looked far more weary than she felt. She gazed at it fondly. When she'd put it on last night she hadn't even met him. Already, after such a short sleep, her party clothes had become filled with memories. He'd encircled that dress with his arms, after all. It had a history now.

Can he possibly like me in daylight too? she wondered, rubbing foundation cream into her skin. On the other hand, will *I* like *him*? Perhaps he'll be all ashen and grumpy. Perhaps he doesn't like getting up at eight on a Sunday morning to take a girl he only met the night before down to Sussex. Perhaps – she stared back at her face, half powdered and half shiny – heavens, perhaps he won't come at all!

But that didn't bear thinking about. Carefully, so she didn't wake Yvonne, she eased her way out of the bedroom.

In the kitchen the picnic things waited. She'd prepared them before the party last night, of course, so there was only enough for herself and Holly. Now that Geoff – marvellous, virile name – now that Geoff was coming she'd better make some more.

As she stood looking at the food, looking at it through his eyes, she blushed. What would he think of it? None of the usual stuff was there; she and Holly never bothered about boring things like sandwiches. After all, when you were at boarding school there were certain things you craved; when you had a chance, then, you ought to devote all your energies to consuming as many of them as possible. It was a philosophy of which she, Claire, had become an expert interpreter and this Sunday she'd surpassed even herself. Home-made cake, two cream slices, jelly in a plastic container and – *pièce de résistance* – Gaz canister, bottle of oil, frying-pan and a tin of uncooked doughnuts. There seemed something very fascinating about those doughnuts. Claire actually forgot Geoff as she pictured Holly's face when confronted by them.

Still, grown men as debonair as Geoff seemed to be could hardly appreciate such things with Holly's fervour, so Claire made some regulation sandwiches to supplement this exotica. Buttering the bread, she could think calmly about the night before. About the dark noisy room and Geoff's sudden movement when she'd said she really ought to go home now as it was quarter to three. About the way he'd looked at her, a surprisingly intense look, and the way he'd kissed her right then and, almost better still, hugged her afterwards, both of them jammed against the kitchen door with people struggling past.

And about how, back in the flat, she'd lain awake for hours, caring little for once that Yvonne was snoring again, while across the ceiling and down the wall had swung, shivering squares, the headlights from passing cars. Such an ordinary party it had seemed before she met him.

A car stopped. She heard it in the street. One last throaty roar, then silence. Eight o'clock already; she felt quite trembly – she, Claire, usually so calm. Swiftly she threw everything into a carrier bag and ran into the hall.

Already he was at the front door; she could see the smudge of his shape on the other side of the frosted glass. What sort of face could she arrange?

She opened the door and thank goodness he was smiling.

'Hello,' she said. 'I'm all ready. I didn't really think you'd come.'

'Why not? I'm looking forward to it.' He opened the car door for her.

Claire wondered if he remembered just what they were going to do. 'I'm only visiting my little sister at school, you know. It'll probably be agonizingly boring for you. I feel guilty about asking you to come at all.'

How terribly dowdy the expedition must sound! Her parents'

Rover, borrowed for the occasion, stood on the other side of the road. Last night he hadn't asked if she had a car already, and she'd never thought of telling him. Too late now, thank goodness.

'I'll be happy to go,' he said. 'Do me good to get out of London for a while.'

'What a beautiful car!' She eased herself into the bucket seat and gazed along its red bonnet.

'Not bad,' he said, squeezing himself in beside her. 'Rather snappy, too.'

At this time of day the streets were empty. Up the hill they roared and across Clapham Common. Claire couldn't think what to talk about and yet felt, especially when they stopped at traffic lights and expectancy filled the car, that she ought to say something. Last night they had talked non-stop, she was sure; all about the party and who else they knew there, and what a lot they all, including themselves, seemed to be drinking, and about how once he'd had an old Austin something that he'd put a lot of work into. Not thrilling, perhaps, but it had seemed so at the time. Now, in daylight (and greyish daylight too, unfortunately) she felt that a different kind of talk was needed; more of the cementing kind, like had he any brothers and sisters and where did he live. Things like that. Somehow it was difficult to start on that kind.

Down Streatham High Street they roared, past shuttered Bingo Halls and shadowy Tescos. 'By the way,' asked Claire, 'do you know where we're going?'

'Eastbourne, isn't it?'

'Yes, but where in Eastbourne?'

'I don't know.'

'Cliffdean School.'

'Right. Famous, isn't it? You'll have to direct me, though, when we get there.'

Claire let out her breath in relief. One tiny hurdle over. He didn't disapprove of Cliffdean, then, like most people. Laura and Laura's friends, in particular, disapproved, what with it being so grand and expensive.

It became silent again in the car. The engine, though loud, was not quite loud enough to drown a conversation if they cared to have one, but what could she say to this handsome and impassive stranger? It had been so easy last night, what with all that music and everything. But today, with this grey morning threatening rain and a street lined with discount stores, what on earth could she say to this profile sitting beside her and driving so capably? Wearing driving gloves, too; brand new pigskin, they rebuffed her. Was it the same man who had embraced her so suddenly and, now she thought of it, so boozily? The same man who had clattered down the stairs after her, calling out for her address?

Just then he leant forward and turned on the radio. It was soul music, late night music. *You're the one I nee-heed, baby,* throbbed the voice, silky smooth. Inappropriate perhaps for these suburban streets, but reviving the magic of last night it suddenly seemed appropriate for them.

Without you-hoo honey I can't go on-hon. The heater warmed them; the seats seemed softer; they relaxed. The mood of the dark elastic music spread over and around them, filling the car and reducing their nocturnal separation to just a few minutes, a pause of no importance. Even the driving gloves looked friendlier.

The empty streets fled past. *Sockittome sockittome sockittome!* Geoff turned and smiled at her. What did it matter that the sky was grey?

They arrived in record time and drew up with a flourish. At the fortress façade of the school Claire could see many faces pressed against the windows, and was glad for Holly's sake that they were arriving in such OK style. After all, when most people arrived in shamingly posh and sedate cars, to be whisked off in a flaming red sports job . . . Holly, released by a shadowy matron, raced towards them.

'Hiya! What a super car!'

'Isn't it,' said Claire. 'This is Geoff. He's very kindly brought me down.'

'Squash in,' said Geoff. 'There's just enough room in the back.' Because of the threatening sky the hood was up, and Holly, waving goodbye to all those eager and impressed faces, scrambled on to the tiny back ledge.

Slowly they drove along the coast road. 'Well,' said Geoff. 'What are the plans? What's Eastbourne got to offer?'

'Last time,' said Holly, 'Claire took me on to the Downs and we found an old barn and jumped in the hay. And then she drew some pictures for me on the cover of her exercise book, then we had a *lovely* picnic and then we read *Beano.*'

'Oh dear!' Claire glanced at Geoff. 'How silly it sounds.' Put so baldly, such a lovely day did sound on the infantile side, but it had been fun.

'Yes . . . well.' Geoff cleared his throat.

'Oh goodness, we won't do that today,' said Claire quickly. 'What would you like to do, Geoff?'

'Yes, well, I can't quite see myself jumping in the hay I'm afraid.' He laughed, glancing down at his two trouserlegs, each with its centre crease. 'I don't think I'd be very good at it. What would Holly like to do?'

'Just muck about,' she said.

'Ah.' He pondered this one.

'She means just sort of play about,' said Claire, and stopped. Impossible to muck about with Geoff there, so adult and unknown. For he did seem like that; now that the radio was off and Holly was breathing down their necks and outside it had got so very much greyer and chillier, that warm car-spell seemed to have broken and she felt quite stiff with him again. She looked at her watch and to her relief it said eleven o'clock. Only an hour before they could reasonably have lunch.

'Let's drive around and look at the houses,' she said. 'And then we can go up on to the Downs and look for somewhere nice to have our picnic.' That solved that, then.

The picnic was not a success. Looking back on it, Claire realized that she should have abandoned the whole idea as soon as she knew Geoff was coming.

The weather didn't help, of course. It was drizzling now, gently but relentlessly, and they had to park beside a bus shelter, a cement edifice with mists on all sides, so that Claire could set up the apparatus inside it.

'*Doughnuts?*' gasped Holly. 'Real doughnuts?'

'Amazing, aren't they,' said Claire. 'Look, they come out of the tin all squishy. I can't believe they're doughnuts at all.'

'Er, are you going to fry them?' asked Geoff, looking chilly on a wooden bench. 'What happens if somebody comes along. I mean, won't it look rather odd?'

'We'll give 'em a bite,' said Holly. 'Lucky things.'

Claire laid the first lump of dough in the fat. It spluttered and hissed. Geoff, who'd approached, flinched back and wiped his trousers.

'Oh dear!' cried Claire. 'Has it splashed you?'

'Don't worry, they're old.' Geoff sat down again on his bench and gazed at the bizarre little ceremony.

'Ooh look!' shrieked Holly. 'It's puffing up!'

It was. Magically, it was puffing up into a real doughnut. Claire put the next lump of dough in the pan and stole a glance at Geoff. He looked cold and uneasy on his bench.

'Geoff, let's start on the sandwiches!' she called in the bright tones she sometimes used at school. 'Here!' She unwrapped them. 'And I've made us some coffee.' She uncorked the Thermos. 'Holly, you look after the doughnuts.'

She sat down next to Geoff. 'I'm sorry it's not very glamorous,' she laughed. 'I didn't know you were coming, you see.'

'Don't worry. It all looks great fun. It *is* great fun.'

He munched his sandwich, and as he munched he was thinking, she was sure, of a cosy lunch for two in some roadside pub . . . glowing fire, beer, chicken in the basket or perhaps steak . . .

'Quite a curious meal you're eating over there, Holly,' he said.

'Mmm,' mumbled Holly, mouth smeared with cream slice.

Afterwards they all sat in the car.

'What would you like to do now?' asked Claire. It was still drizzling, of course.

Holly suggested: 'We can always roll the tyres down the hill.'

'What?' asked Geoff.

'Just up the road there are lots of old tyres. They're at the top of a hill and we can roll them down.'

There was a silence, a long one. Then Geoff asked: 'Why?'

'It's fun. We can have races.'

Another silence. Then Geoff rallied, rubbing his hands and trying to look keen. 'Right then!'

'Of course not,' said Claire quickly. 'Let's, well, we can . . . there's lots to do.' But her mind was a total blank.

'We can do it in the rain,' Holly persisted. 'It's even better in the rain, so long as you're not a sissy about getting wet. They go faster, you see.'

Another silence. Out of the corner of her eye Claire could see Geoff taking a stealthy look at his watch. She cast her eyes over the Downs with their shifting veils of rain. They gave her back no answers. How annoyed she felt! Annoyed with herself for dragging Geoff down to Eastbourne and offering him nothing more exciting than freezing to death in a concrete bus shelter. She'd lost him for good; he'd never telephone her after this. And she felt annoyed that she'd spoilt Holly's day, because if they'd been alone then the bus shelter and the tyre-rolling would have been fun. Afterwards they'd have gone back to school and dried out in Holly's dorm. Then perhaps she would have helped Holly sew the pincushions shaped like mice that were suddenly and passionately fashionable amongst her friends. Difficult to imagine Geoff sewing pincushions.

She gazed along the red bonnet, glistening with moisture. And if I were alone with Geoff, she thought, we could have driven to a pub with confidential lighting, and held hands under the table, and talked like we talked last night. Just for a second she actually resented Holly.

'Oh well,' she said briskly. 'It is awful weather, isn't it. Perhaps we'd better take you back to school, Holly.'

Geoff started up the car and they drove back across the Downs, through the grey and shifting rain. Oh dear, thought Claire, a sister's day and a lover's day. Both so nice, but how stupid of me to think they could possibly mix.

But surprisingly enough, when they'd said goodbye to Holly and she'd disappeared back into the fortress, things relaxed in the car. Perhaps it was relief at being alone; perhaps it was that, now Geoff had seen her messed up in the rain with wind-purpled hands and all that careful eyeshadow smudged, the last shred of unreal party glamour, which was nice but which didn't really suit them, was washed away, revealing something more durable underneath. And perhaps, too, it was that Geoff had entered, brief and un-satisfactory though that entry had been, into the closed world of the two sisters – a strange place rarely glimpsed even by their parents – and so had entered into a secret.

Whatever the reason, they talked. As the trees loomed up out of the mist and flashed by, he talked about his job (an accountant), his flat (a nice room in Bayswater), his family (just a mother), and about how he'd once wanted to do all sorts of things but had some-how ended up doing a business course instead.

And when they'd arrived back in Clapham and stopped outside her flat, the rain that blotted out the landscape no longer seemed a depressing backcloth. Instead it seemed to enfold them in their own cocoon of murmuring heater and sudden closeness, and to prompt them at last to stretch out their arms and kiss each other, cold noses and all, across the difficult bucket seats.

ten

Because Laura had never given her blood she felt alert and uneasy when the morning came. She had no idea what the day had in store, no idea at all. In fact, as she stood in her room, one arm in and one arm out of her coat, she nearly gave up the whole plan. If she had, the next few months would have been considerably different. But she didn't. Don't be feeble, she told herself, doing up the buttons.

Outside it was densely foggy. Nothing was visible but the pavement in front of her. It was one of those days when you can't see the houses that surround you, you can just feel them in your bones, as you can feel it in your bones when there is someone standing behind you and not speaking.

Iron gates loomed and she was in the park. Pavement was replaced by grass; sounds faded. First-gear noises from cars grinding up the hill grew fainter, muffled in mist, and were replaced by birdsong ringing in the air around her. She met no one. Looking up she could make out the glow of the sun and, very faintly, the web-like branches of the trees. Like the red webs inside her body.

Dreamlike, it seemed. She, Laura, usually so substantial with coat and shoes and money in her pocket felt vanished away, leaving only a miraculous body, blood vessels under the skin; complex busy blood vessels, webs of them. As if I'm a sacrifice, she thought. Perhaps they felt like this on the way to the blood-stained altar, walking in their white robes through a silent world. This day seemed portentous.

'HOI! Wotcha think you're doing!'

A car brushed by. Laura leapt back on to the pavement, dreams scattered. The main road. The fog was lifting, the street busy and the clinic, when she arrived, quite unsacrificial.

'Good morning, dear,' said a pleasant plain receptionist. Laura was shown into a waiting-room which looked quite ordinary really – potted plants, a stout woman making tea, piles of *Punch* and *Woman's Realm*. But she still felt odd, what with the fog, and the fact that she was missing a whole morning's seminar and, above all, the unknown in store for her behind that closed door. And also odd because, since some time yesterday morning, she hadn't said a word to a living soul. It startled her to realize it. Living in her bedsit, she had not used her voice for twenty-four hours. Long silent afternoons, long silent evenings.

'Miss Jenkins?'

Laura grabbed a *Woman's Realm* as a sort of reassurance. Whatever took place behind that closed door, she could always bury herself in 'Cakes for that Festive Occasion'.

She was in a room full of motionless figures on beds. She didn't look too closely. Clutching her magazine, she lay down where she was told. She thought of Tony Hancock and closed her eyes.

Once the thing had gone into her vein, she felt able to open them again. She stole a glance down. There it hung, a plastic sack, reddening already and rocking ever so gently from side to side. As if becoming just a touch tipsy with her blood. Ugh.

To avoid this she looked at the other people who lay like beached whales on either side of her. Her two neighbours, in particular, she inspected with curiosity. Were they surviving? On one side lay a gaunt leathery woman, her eyes closed. Not a flicker. She looked definitely yellow. Perhaps she's dead, thought Laura. Perhaps they've forgotten to stop her pump thing and it's just going on and on till she's drained.

She turned to the left. He was younger and he looked relaxed yet somehow incongruous, as if someone had put him there by mistake. Perhaps it was the way he was wiggling his toes in their holey socks. Plus his wild hair spread all over the dainty white pillow. Not what *Woman's Realm* would choose for a hero.

She was thinking this when a nurse approached him and released his arm. He sat up, scratching his head and saying something to the nurse that made her laugh in that humouring nurse-like way, as if he were a silly child.

Once he had left the room she could concentrate on her arm, which after all wasn't half as bad as she thought. To be absolutely honest, it didn't actually hurt; just a benign firmness, a smiling pressure in the grasp of the rubber round her vein. Against the wall stood a fridge. The nurse opened it and Laura glimpsed a row of fat red sacks, each smug with its treasure. Her neighbour's sack, identical to them, was placed at the end of the row and the door was closed.

Five minutes was an awful long time to do nothing in. She tried to turn the pages of *Woman's Realm* but they were too floppy to be managed with one hand. So she listened to the tactful little hum of the machine busy at her arm, and gazed up at the ceiling.

'All over, dear.' The nurse stilled the swinging bag and dismantled the apparatus. It relinquished its vein with a sigh.

'Now sit up carefully, dear, just in case you feel a little dizzy.'

Laura hoped she would feel a little dizzy, as proof of her loss, but she didn't. She watched her sack being put into the fridge next to his, touching it. This made her feel odd, as if he and she were already acquainted.

He hadn't left. He was still in the waiting-room, sitting in a chair and rolling a cigarette.

'Reckon we deserve a Guinness after that,' he said, looking at his cup of tea. 'Could manage a pint nicely.' He was growing a moustache, Laura noticed, a tentative moustache; its shadow on his face looked curiously mannish.

The stout woman set down another cup of tea for Laura and turned to him. 'Now you *know*,' she said, shaking her finger, 'that there's no smoking for half an hour after giving blood.'

'It's me nerves, me nerves,' he said.

She chuckled. However corny they were being, everyone got pampered in this room just for five minutes.

'Well, be it on your own head,' she said. 'Don't ask me to catch you if you faint.'

'*She* will,' he replied, looking at Laura. 'Won't you?'

Yes, thought Laura. She smiled into her teacup.

The stout lady went back to her urn. Now they were alone, Laura wondered what she could say. He looked content enough, idly turning the pages of her *Woman's Realm* and raising his eyebrows at some pictures of Princess Anne. Nice eyebrows; humorous, quizzical ones. She would ask him a question.

'Have you been here before?'

'Yeah. It's me only good deed for mankind.'

'I was terrified at first, but there's nothing to it, is there?'

'Right. And they give me time off, too, to come here. If there was Guinness it'd be perfect.'

He stubbed out his cigarette, pocketed a couple of biscuits and stood up. Laura stood up too, perhaps because vistas of his less good deeds intrigued her. She would leave at the same time.

Outside it was sunny. He stood still and considered for a moment; then he turned to the right and wandered along the pavement. Why shouldn't she turn to the right also? The only alternative was turning to the left. She looked at his back view; he was ambling along as if he didn't mind her catching him up. Ah, now he'd stopped; he was munching a biscuit. Why not, Laura? The sun's shining; be bold. Fifty-fifty chance you'd be walking this way anyway.

She caught him up.

'Have a biscuit,' he said, offering her the other one.

It startled her, how pleased she was. She took it and they both ambled along, munching. One biscuit each; it was nice.

Outside a supermarket she stopped. She had some shopping to do. She also had the desire to test the bond between them. Would the thread snap? She mumbled something and went in.

For a moment she was pleased that he had followed; then she was gripped by her usual paralysis. She always felt like this in supermarkets; it was something to do with the pitiless lighting and long perspective of little packets. She never knew what to choose. The packets dismayed her too; the earth's fruits dismantled and reassembled into economy-sized plastic squares. Masses and masses of them, rows and rows.

Clutching her wire basket, she hovered. There were only a few people about, preoccupied and boring-looking, like people usually look in supermarkets.

He held up a tin, eyebrows raised hopefully. 'Have these,' he said. 'Such a classy label.' Marron Purée, it was; its picture was embellished with leaves. He dropped it into her basket.

Hands in pockets he shambled along the row of frozen meats, looking as incongruous here as he'd looked in the clinic, enquiring and messy, altogether rather cheering in the sterile aisles. Definitely not preoccupied and boring.

'Could you find me some sausages?' she dared to ask.

He rummaged amongst the frosty packets and found her some – beef ones, she didn't like those, and far too many just for one – but she took them. He went off, eyeing the shelves.

'Treacle you must have,' he called out. 'Reminds me of me youth.' He put the tin in her basket. 'Hey, and a bottle of this. What a kitsch colour. I like it.'

'But *I* don't like it. It's raspberry cordial.'

'Put it on your mantelpiece and admire it. Give it a home.' He put it into her basket and wandered off again. She looked down at her odd little collection.

He was holding up another tin. 'Must try these.'

'Why?'

'Because I've never tasted them before. Whole Guavas. From Malaysia. Somebody must buy them after all that; think of them bumping about on donkeys, and packing cases, and – '

' – stick 'em in, then.'

She was enjoying this. Inspecting her list, comparing prices – how dreary all that seemed now! As dreary as the other people here with their empty faces and heavy baskets.

And to hell with money, she thought, standing at the checkout and watching the paper strip of mauve numerals lengthen. *I* don't care what Marron Purée costs. Anyway, there's lots of grant left. 'Five pounds, eighty-five pence,' said the girl at the machine, uninterested whether guavas came from Malaysia, uninterested whether they came from Mars.

Laura put the things into her carrier bag while he stood, hands in pockets, and still looking somehow as if he shouldn't be there. His muddy plimsolls had left marks on the floor. As she put in the Weetabix (for she'd added things too) she felt the bond between them thicken; thicken with something domestic, a suggestion of breakfast. Now he knew she ate Weetabix in the morning, could they any longer be strangers?

They stood outside for a moment. Somewhere a clock struck twelve. 'How about a quick one, then?' he asked.

At the doorway of the pub she summoned up her courage. 'What's your name?'

'Mac.'

They went inside; she sat down, he went up to the bar. No longer nameless, his ensuing Mac-ness filled her with pleasure; the way he fumbled for money in the frayed back pocket of his jeans, the way he said something to the man behind the bar and the man chuckled, the way he came back with the brimming glasses, raising those eyebrows at a girlie calendar on the wall and then raising them at her. She liked that. She smiled; they shared the nude; the bond thickened. There was something easy and natural about him; by comparison she felt fussy, the way she thought about how much things cost, the way her carrier bag kept spilling its contents when she moved in her seat.

'What's yours, then?'

'Laura.'

'That's nice. Know what? You're the first fanciable bird I've ever seen in that blood place.'

'Am I?' She didn't know what to say to that. Gladdened by being fanciable yet taken aback by its simplistic sort of solving, she gazed into the timeless amber of her cider. The pub was empty and dimly lit. She was thankful about that, for words could trail off into the semi-darkness, they could even be left unsaid, yet suggested by the shadows.

'Fancy a cigarette?'

'Yes, but I can't roll them.' She liked watching him do the rolling; his hunched shoulders, his whole concentration, when she'd seen it in the clinic, had been the first thing about him to move her.

'I'll show you.' He put his tobacco tin on his knee and took her hand in his. One by one he laid out her fingers and in her palm placed a paper; into its crease he fed a slim roll of tobacco. She looked with distaste at her hands, clumsy and red compared with his calm beige fingers which worked despite her own stubborn ones springing back and getting in the way. Finally it was finished and lay, a simple offering, in her palm.

'We'll share it,' he said. 'It's the last of me baccy.' He lit it, hand cupped, cradling the flame the way men on street corners cradle the flame. He *is* different, she realized with a small thud. What sort of thud? Excitement?

They sat back in silence, an easy natural one on his part, she was sure, but even with this lighting she couldn't quite relax. Such an unfathomable silence, that was why. A silence as yet with no complexion, for knowing him but an hour she had no clue how it would finish, and it is the words around a silence that create its complexion. Had he broken it with 'Do you go to university here?' it would have been confirmed as an enquiring, nervous silence; had it been 'How about seeing "Oedipus Rex" with me tonight?' it would have been confirmed as a constructive one. How analytical and selfconscious I am! thought Laura. Can I never shake it off? He's probably just enjoying his Guinness.

When what he actually said was: 'I planted twenty-four fir trees this morning,' she was pleased. What a relief; it had been an easy, companionable one.

'Where?'

'On a grassy bank. It looks quite Norwegian now, if I'd ever been to Norway, that is. Each one I put in I prayed to Thor that it would grow.'

'Who's Thor?'

'Some Scandinavian almighty. I read about him somewhere. Remarkable bloke, Thor.' He relapsed into reverie. Laura, though, was curious.

'Are they for you?'

'No, I'm a gardener. Work for the university. Up at Addison Hall.'

'Heavens! That's my Hall – or it was until last week. I wonder if I ever saw you.' She was almost certain now that she'd seen him working in the flowerbeds. He didn't look like a student, now she thought of it. He didn't have that cultivated scruffiness; he looked as if he'd been born with his.

'I wish I'd known,' she said. She passed him the cigarette. 'How long have you been there?'

'Since last summer. It was good in the summer.' He fell silent. Was he reminiscing about the girls; seducing classy birds in the rhubarb patch? She could imagine him doing that.

'What do you like doing best?' she asked.

'Shit-shovelling. That and mowing. No hassles, nobody bothering you. Practically breaks your back, though. But I like that once in a while; makes my body feel good.'

Laura thought of his body and surprised herself by blushing. Was it slender and graceful, beige as his hands were? Today, anyway, it was linked with hers with its missing pint and now its added one. He passed her the cigarette; it was intimate, their sharing it like this. She felt so drawn to him; why?

'You a student, then?' he asked.

'Yes, psychology. But I've moved out of Hall. I live in a room on my own now.' She liked saying this, it made her sound different from the others. 'I've got a garden too, but it's a bit messed up at the moment, full of rubbish and stuff. The family upstairs have about twenty children and I'm sure they chuck stuff out of the window.' She passed him the cigarette. 'I want to dig it up and plant it and make it really lovely.'

'If you like, I can borrow a spade from the works. You know, dig it for you.'

Laura sat back. The faded roses wallpaper, the girlie calendar, the back view of the barman who was polishing glasses, all were irradiated with the most surprising joy. She felt dizzy; she couldn't look at him. Suddenly it seemed as if everything today had been leading up to this; she was amazed.

'Oh yes, please do.'

'What's better than today, then? After work.'

He stood up and finished his glass. She stood up beside him. He gave her the cigarette. 'The rest is yours,' he said.

'Strange, that draught cider. It makes me feel all loose round the edges.'

'Good protein. Puts hairs on your chest.' He smiled at her, and for a moment she thought he was going to touch her, he was so near. But he said: 'Must be pushing along. They only give me time off for doing me blood.'

They went out into the street with its dazzling sun. She told him her address.

'Be seeing you, then,' he said. He went.

She leant against the wall. Quite apart from the cider, she felt intoxicated. Almost glad, she was, that he had gone, so that she could recollect everything that had just happened in detail.

The sunlight flashed on the windows of the buses as they turned up the hill; even the spittle-gobs on the pavement winked.

eleven

On the evening of that same day, Dan was painting. He was painting in Laura and Claire's bedroom. He liked it up there; since his solitary visit on Christmas Eve he'd found himself drawn to his daughters' rooms, still redolent, as they were, of the girls – Holly's with its mantelpiece menagerie of glass animals and its poignant pencil notice on the cupboard door MUSEUM – OPEN that she'd forgotten to change to CLOSED; Claire and Laura's with those childhood shoes.

He looked round. Laura in particular he felt he was experiencing in theory rather than in her often exasperating practice; perhaps that was why he liked it there. The pictures and the books declared she was a girl with interests. Nothing was spoilt by the clothes all over the floor and the unmade bed that, once she herself was in occupation, reminded him that she could be also an irritating or a disappointing one.

He was painting a still-life. It consisted of a shawl-draped table with various objects on it. The objects were all right; it was the shawl that was giving the problems. A crocheted thing of Laura's, he'd said it was terrible the first time she'd come downstairs in it, swathed like a granny. Tonight, on further inspection, it had turned out to be rather prettily intricate. Infuriating, though.

The thing was, how could he suggest lots of little holes without covering it with dots; and how could he cover it with dots without it seeming to be just that – covered with dots? A spotty shawl, in other words. How on earth did one turn a dot into a hole? Damn shawl; he dabbed jerkily on, but the shawl just got spottier. Even the folds didn't look right and he thought he'd got the hang of folds. But the spots inside the folds were too bright, so it looked not so much full of shadows as full of stains. Stained and spotty, not shadowed and holey. And getting worse every minute!

Dan threw down his brush. It was a mess; he had to admit it. How it irritated him. He scrumpled up the paper and threw it into the wastepaper basket. Bloody shawl.

He got up and put his painting things away. Tonight he was very conscious of it being a hobby. Terrible word, hobby. Vacant hours that had to be filled. With the girls there, he'd never had time for a hobby. To his surprise he remembered complaining about it. Endless interruptions, packed hours through which one fought for a moment's peace. Nowadays there was nothing to have a moment's peace *from*.

Downstairs Rosemary looked up from *Good Housekeeping*.

'All right?' she asked.

'Bloody awful.' Dan poured himself a whisky; he'd feel better after that. 'Never mind. Time for the dog.'

Every night before they went to bed they took Badger round the block. It could hail, it could thunder, but they always did. Whisky then dog. And whatever the weather they always wore the same shoes, Dan his brown gardening ones, Rosemary her old boots. Dan opened the hall cupboard and fished them out. Together they bent down and put them on.

Outside the air was sharp and Rosemary put her hand through his arm. 'Chilly, isn't it,' she said. 'I do hope Laura's got lots of blankets.'

'Hmm. Wonder what she's doing now.' Dan looked up at the sky. At least he shared that with his girls. Perhaps one of them was glancing up at it now.

'Tucked up in bed, I hope.'

Down the familiar street they walked, Rosemary's arm nice and warm in his. Badger, purposeful, trotted on ahead. Dan loved these nightly strolls, Badger's tail a jaunty plume ahead of them, other people's evenings in the windows.

They had a comfortable rhythm, those three. It was just that, occasionally, he could welcome those old interruptions.

twelve

Laura had indeed been tucked up in bed. In fact, she still was. When she woke the next morning Mac's arms were still around her. She lay still, not daring to move, not wanting to wake him; not quite yet. Nor did she dare look at him.

Instead she looked out of the window. The bed was close to it and from where she lay she had a view down into the garden. Amongst the matted grass and thistles she could see the small brown square of earth he'd dug yesterday. His fork still stuck out in the middle of it.

Proof, then. Solid fork; real mud. Real skin too, next to hers. It had happened, and outside she could see the sun shining on the newly turned soil.

She still didn't like to look at him; easier to look around the room. Their clothes lay scattered on the floor; his underpants and jeans near the bed, her skirt abandoned in front of the fireplace. They'd found some wood and built a fire last night; later he'd undressed her beside the flames.

On each side of the bed, altar-like, a candle stub stood in its saucer of wax. The candles had been his idea. And in each saucer lay the cigarette ends from when, long after the fire had died down, they had lain back on the pillows. How damp, how marvellously mutual they'd been, lying there, blowing into the darkness their twin plumes of smoke!

He stirred. She stiffened. He grunted and stirred again. She lay rigid.

She didn't dare look at him. She stared up at the ceiling. How very much easier to kiss someone, to do anything with their bodies, in the thankful dark! Much, much easier than to meet their eyes so close and in such very glaring sun. With one's greasy face and smudged mascara.

He must be disappointed. He'd be polite and have a cup of tea and then say he'd better push off now. Heavens, she couldn't have been much good compared with all those girls who'd had it a lot, or even had it a little. She thought of those heavings on the cinema screen; it looked so accomplished when those sort of girls did it.

Just then she felt her hand being taken by his. He grunted and turned his face towards her. 'Hello, my sonner.' He blinked through his tangled hair. Then he smiled. 'You look really rosy.'

She buried herself in his arms.

'My nice, rosy, morning girl,' he said.

With her face in his hair she asked: 'What's my sonner?'

'Old affectionate Bristol talk. My friend, it means.'

She ran her fingers along his straight eyebrows to feel what they were like. She was his slave.

'Hey, you were laughing last night,' he said. 'I was amazed.'

'It was so funny.'

'Why?'

'I don't know. After all that thinking about it, I suppose. All those huddles in the cloakroom at school. Such a relief.' She laughed, pressed her face into his hair and kissed his warm, buried ear. She ran her hand over his shoulder and down his hard beautiful back. Goodness, what a relief. He wasn't being polite and cool. Nor, though he was kissing her, was he trying to do it again, because she didn't think she could manage that in full daylight. Not quite yet. Not looking down and seeing her limbs and his and everything. He was kissing her though, slowly, oh so slowly, sleepy mouth against sleepy mouth. She twined the sheets around them; they lay there, their hair mixed. Could anything be more satisfactory? she asked him. No, he said, nothing.

'I've got you and the view out of my window,' she said. 'Do I ever have to get out of bed?'

'Never.'

They lay in the nicest of shared silences, the sort of settled silence which before today had been possible only with her sisters. Better than the lonely silence that had filled this room before he'd come into it. For she had been lonely, of course; twined cosily in her sheets, she could admit it now. Frightened too; not by anything solid, but by something intangible from which all her life she'd been sheltered. The poverty upstairs had something to do with it, so had the emptiness in the rooms below, and herself trapped in the middle, glimpsing desolation.

'Come to think of it,' he said, 'I wouldn't say no to a cup of tea.'

'Nor, I must say, would I.'

She disentangled herself and walked all white and bare across the room. She was very nearly unselfconscious; he made it natural to be bare. How different from those episodes with John and Mike, the one so phoney and the other so muddled. Mac accepted her nicely, without fuss. Was that why she'd found it somehow silly to stop him last night? One of the reasons, anyway; he'd just presumed they would. Another was that great big bed being there and no one to stop them.

'To think,' she said, putting on the kettle, 'that I haven't known you twenty-four hours yet.' She cleared away the empty tin of guavas. They'd had a curious meal last night: guavas and sausages – that way round, too.

Down in the street she could hear children shouting and the far plaintive tinkling of an ice-cream van. She had no idea what time it was. Mid-morning? Lunchtime? Odd to think of a humdrum day going on down there, people slamming doors, clocks chiming.

She took the teacups over to the bed. He propped his head up and lay there on the rumpled sheets, sipping. Lacking brothers, she had never looked unabashed at a full-grown, calm male. And she still couldn't. Not really; not *all over*. She might have come a long way since yesterday, but not that far. In a film, if she'd been one of those heaving girls with their mascara still intact, she would be gazing into his eyes now and caressing him. In real life she lay down, careful not to slop her tea. He hooked her foot round his. 'Let's do it sixty times a day,' he said. 'Again and again, everywhere, all round the room, all round Bristol.'

'You couldn't.'

'It'd be nice, though.'

There was more talk of this kind when they were interrupted

by a chime from the university tower. One o'clock.

'Oho,' he said, unhooking his foot. 'Long past opening time.'

It was the strangest feeling to walk down the street with him and realize that nobody who looked at them *knew*. Could no one tell? Her tingling skin, her smile? In the pub they sat close together, his knee against hers under the table. His fingers, which had been everywhere, clasped his glass. She worshipped his hands. They sat side by side saying nothing, silent with their large secret.

'How's the Cortina running, then?' boomed a voice behind them.

'So-so, Alec,' boomed another. 'Bit sticky these cold mornings, you know.'

Two bulky men holding pints. They stood inches from them. The jacket of one of them almost touched Laura's hair.

'And Dot? Bearing up, is she?'

'Bearing up, yes. Touch of flu last week, Alec, nothing much. Lucky the twins were away at their grandma's.'

Laura gazed at the split seam down Mac's jeans. She knew the skin in there. She felt warm.

'Excuse me.'

She jumped. An arm stubbed out a cigarette in the ashtray, brutally near.

'Quite frankly, Alec, I advised her to let them stay away a bit longer. Never know with the flu, especially with the youngsters.'

'You're right there. Doesn't do to take chances, does it?'

She gazed at Mac's fingers, calm round the handle of his glass. She longed to touch them.

'Daphne well?'

'Oh, fighting fit, Jock. You know Daphne, always on the go.'

'Beats me how she manages it, what with her old mum and all.'

She couldn't bear it any longer. She took his hand and felt each of his fingers in turn, the nails, the tips. Wherever had she been as bold as this before?

'Must be toddling.'

'Rightio, Alec. Don't do anything I wouldn't do.'

Laura watched the two men leave. Despite herself she couldn't help feeling fond of them, for hadn't they shared this charmed space?

'I'm starving,' she said.

Mac got her a hot pie with a dollop of brown sauce. 'Aren't you eating?' she asked.

'Plenty of protein in this.' He held up his new brimming pint.

She was to discover that he seldom ate, saving his energies for booze, cigarettes and when he was rich enough (which was seldom), hash.

She munched her pie; he swallowed his beer. 'Isn't it funny,' she mumbled between mouthfuls, 'I don't know anything about you. You might be an escaped convict for all I know. And you don't know a thing about me.'

'Doesn't worry me. It's nice like this.'

'Oh, but I want to know all about you! Every detail.'

'Hmm.' He scratched his head. 'I've got a rhinoceros skull; found it in a junkshop.'

'Yes, but what about your parents, things like that? Do they live in Bristol?'

'Yep.'

'Hmm.' A silence. 'Do you want to hear about me, then? I have two sisters and a dog.'

'Wow, a dog.'

'He's all of ours, really.'

'I like dogs.'

On this pronouncement they got up to go. It was true; he wasn't concerned with the things around and behind her, her past, her background. Only – for he was taking her hand and smiling at her – only with her. She hoped. How could she tell?

It had turned into a mellow, sunny afternoon. They wandered through the streets, past terraces and crescents, and after a while found themselves outside the university buildings. Students were everywhere – emerging from the library, gossiping in the road, disappearing into the Berkeley Café. It surprised her, seeing them. How irrelevant they looked, as irrelevant as the fact, now she remembered it, of her double seminar this morning and practical this afternoon. How senselessly busy they seemed! They resembled the mice in the lab going round and round on their little wire wheels.

Arm in arm, she and Mac left them behind. Down the hill of shops they wandered, and through the little park she had crossed only yesterday on her way to the clinic. Not yesterday, a hundred years ago. Passing some flowerbeds she asked: 'Shouldn't you be at work today?'

'Yep.'

He smiled at her, collapsed on the grass and, a neat package, rolled down the bank. He lay at the bottom, bundled up She went down and sat beside him.

'I'm an artist, really,' he said, his face still hidden. 'An undiscovered genius. You should see me masterpieces.'

So he wasn't just a gardener. There was much to discover. A chink opened; she glimpsed vistas.

He lay back, hands behind his head, and gazed up. Suddenly she went cold.

Had he just stopped like this because it was the end of their day? Was this charmed feeling, this timelessness, something that she alone felt? He looked so very self-sufficient lying there, gazing beyond her at the sky, the limbs she'd touched clothed now and no longer hers. Was this it; just his casual way of coming to a full stop?

He wasn't moving; it was late, the sun slanted across the grass. She didn't know whether to move or not, and sat gazing at a nearby bush which was already sprouting; on its branches veined bundles had split, and from them hung tassels and damp young leaves. Painfully green, those leaves.

Just then he got to his feet, looked around, stretched and started walking away from her. Her heart froze.

But now he was stopping beside the bushes and stooping down. Picking something up, then something else.

'What are you doing?' she called.

He straightened up. In his hand she could see a bunch of sticks. 'Nicking some kindling,' he called. 'Don't want to freeze tonight, do we?'

He filled his arms with sticks, and then straightened up again. 'Why are you smiling, my sonner?'

Then he smiled too.

thirteen

Once she'd become a teacher, Claire thought that her childhood feelings towards school would change. But after a whole year there was still that same mixture of dread and excitement, mostly dread, that settled on her as she walked through the gates each morning, through the entrance hall and into those chilly corridors that smelt of disinfectant and murmured with the hum, always the hum, of children. Metaphorically, she could hear the gates clanging shut behind her, closing her into this big grimy building. Behind walls, scuffling feet, the sudden mass scraping of chairs and the single sad note of a piano.

There was the childhood feeling, too, of being in a different world, sounding differently, smelling differently, even divided differently, with its five periods before lunch and three after, from the outside world. All sealed in. Ordinary outside sounds, street sounds, lorries changing gear as they turned into Clapham Junction, the hoarse chant of the *Evening Standard* mid-day edition man, motorbikes revving up outside the Honda showrooms – all drifted into the classroom with a peculiarly intense normality, rather as they drift into the windows of a sick room. Lost, weekday world. When at lunchtime she crept out, as she sometimes did, for a bar of chocolate, she felt the thrill of the truant in this place of housewives and noisy cars, a place which, in her non-school hours, she took so amazingly for granted.

And, most simply of all, once she was inside school she never had time to think of anything else. Even Geoff – it was four days since the Eastbourne outing and still he hadn't phoned – even Geoff could only be dwelt on in a snatched moment as, with the other teachers, she paused in the Staff Room at nine o'clock. Once she was in the classroom signing the register –

'Please miss is that a new sweater miss?'

'Please miss it's ever so nice. Did yer buy it down at Dawlins miss?'

'Miss! Clive's pinched all me crisps!'

Desk lids banged, chairs scraped, children shouted, and underneath it all was the furtive rustle of sweet bags. Poor stammering Victor sidled up, urgent with words, but she couldn't hear.

'SHUT UP!' she yelled, helplessly watching desks being pulled across the floor. Every night the cleaners made them symmetrical; every morning they were ruthlessly shoved into the same groups, the same faithful huddles – Roy, Clive and Kevin's huddle, Tracy, Susan and Maureen's huddle.

'Look what I've brought miss. Special for you miss.'

'Miss 'e won't give 'em back. 'E's eatin' 'em miss!'

'Please miss you've got a 'ole in yer tights'.'

'ONE AT A TIME!' she yelled.

She was still trying out new theories because that was what

teachers were supposed to do and anyway she was only just out of college. Occasionally still, in backward flashes, she caught glimpses of those intelligent seminars. Occasionally.

'Today,' she said to her first class; they were twelve-year-olds, 'today we're going to have slow-worms.'

It was an idea she remembered from one of those seminars, and probably wouldn't work. Those sorts of ideas, she was discovering, didn't. Still, as a teacher of English shouldn't one try? Words, sensations, communication, that sort of business. They were always going on about that in those seminars.

She'd brought the slow-worms in from the biology lab where they spent their days lying lethargically underneath their vivarium straw. The biology master had been surprised and then gallant when she'd asked for them.

'I beg your pardon. Did you say you were going to *handle* them?' Then he'd rallied. 'Well, Miss Jenkins, it's nice to see one of the lady teachers with a bit of spirit.' He lived a lonely life amongst his fauna and test tubes.

She looked at the expectant faces. 'Now, I'm going to give them out. There are only four, and I want each of you to feel them, so don't hold them for too long.' She looked at them brightly. 'Really feel them. Close your eyes. Are they smooth or rough, warm or cold, hard or soft? Then pass them on – gently – to your neighbour.'

She held out the limp amphibians. Hands grabbed. One boy, chin jutted, snatched the nearest and pushed it down Maureen's neck.

'*Clive!*' Claire shouted. Maureen screamed. It dropped down her dress and out at the bottom. Six boys lunged for the floor.

'*Gently*, I said!' Hector, author of *Jap Doom*, picked up the slow-worm and took it to his desk. She could see him carefully taking out his penknife.

'HECTOR!'

Goody-goody Jonathan, author of *My Hamster*, glanced at her, understood and scrambled across to rescue it. Shrill-voiced, the familiar sweat breaking out, she groped from child to child. Easier with old theories. Definitely easier. 'Just *feel* them!'

Really, she thought, with my subtle ideas it's like trying to cover a volcano with tissue paper . . . or tying a bull down with cobwebs . . . or . . .

She sat down heavily. Curiously enough, as so often happened, the children suddenly all subsided too and started looking quite thoughtfully at the slow-worms. She leant back in her chair.

And at that moment there was a tap at the door and on the threshold stood Geoff.

GEOFF.

She stared. Her heart lurched.

He stood there, hesitating. She jumped to her feet. In a flash she thought Am I wearing one of my dowdy schoolmistressy outfits today?

Thirty pairs of eyes were glued on her; four slow-worms dangled, forgotten. She felt a blush spreading as she made her way to the door.

'Come outside,' she murmured to him, and closed the door behind them. 'Fancy seeing you here!' Her voice sounded quite calm, really; calm and confident, she thought. 'No one ever visits me at school.'

'How are you?' he asked. He really was extraordinarily handsome. 'I happened to come by this way so I thought I'd give you a surprise.'

'You did.' Soon she'd start trembling or something silly.

'I'll be quick,' he said. 'How about coming out on Saturday?'

She controlled her face. 'Oh, that would be lovely!' Then she remembered. 'Oh, bother. What a bore. Holly. She's got a long weekend home and I said I'd take her to "Twelfth Night". It's one of her set books, you see.' Heavens, he must be sick of Holly.

'Oh.' There was a pause. 'Well, I must say, I wouldn't mind seeing some Shakespeare myself.'

'Ah, why don't you come, then?' She *was* trembling now.

'Would you mind? I mean, would I be butting in?'

'Geoff! Of course not!'

Admonishing him like that suddenly relaxed them; perhaps it was the use of his name. They both smiled and then they hovered. Unthinkable to touch in this echoing corridor, as unthinkable as in church. Yet some sort of gesture seemed essential. So, surprising themselves, they shook hands.

After its initial stunned silence the class had worked itself up into a busy hum. It stopped dead as she opened the door. In a deathly hush she walked back to her desk, thirty pairs of fascinated eyes fixed on her.

She stood at her desk and after a moment remembered what

she'd been doing. 'Now!' she said, with something of the old briskness. 'How many of you have *not* touched the slow-worms yet? Put up your hands.'

Silence. She met their multiple stare. No one moved. Then Roy, who was the boldest, spoke. 'Who was that, miss?'

'Who has *not* touched the slow-worms yet? Hands up, please. Come along.'

'Is he your boyfriend, miss?'

'Come along, hands up. Karen, have you held one?'

'Are you going to marry him, miss?'

'Gloria, have you?'

'Are you, miss?'

'*Right*. Everyone stay sitting except the four people with the slow-worms. Those four bring them up here. Quickly now! I haven't got all day.'

Three of them got up and came to her desk clutching their dangling slow-worms. 'Where's the fourth?'

Blank looks. 'Children, where's the fourth?'

Nobody seemed to know. They all started vaguely to look under their desks. She joined them, hunting around on the floor, trying not to listen to the words which, now they were bending down, they dared whisper to each other. . . . 'I betcha they was kissin'; yer, betcha they was snoggin' out there' . . . 'think he was givin' 'er the old feel, you know, feelin' 'er up?' . . . 'yer, 'course 'e was, you see 'er face when she comes back? Red as a bleedin' brick, 'course 'e was touchin' 'er up . . .'

'Miss, here we are!' It was Jonathan, always ready to oblige. He picked the slow-worm out of the wastepaper basket and carried it over to her, holding it in front of him as though it were going to burst into flames.

'Oh, thank you, Jonathan!' At moments like this goody-goodies were a support.

It was not until four o'clock that she had a moment to think of Geoff, and by then it was difficult to believe he had come at all. The very incongruity of an outsider – let alone him – appearing within the high school walls lent the whole episode a dream-like air.

Back in the Staff Room she sorted out her books against the usual chorus . . . 'less bloody able, ha bloody ha' . . . '*motivation, motivation*' . . . 'socially disadvantaged, ha bloody ha' . . . 'behind the counter at Woollies' . . . 'those IIIb's, I ask you' . . . 'filling the dole queue' . . . 'not surprised, seeing his father' . . . 'that Roy, could anyone be like Roy?' . . . 'theories, theories' . . . A chorus of monologues, identical but for the names of their villains. By four o'clock nobody listened to anybody else.

Claire sat down for a moment. She heard nothing of the voices. The biology master approached her. 'Well, Miss Jenkins, and how did you get along with my – ha, my *charges*?'

'Oh hello!' She focused. 'Not too well, actually. I don't think my lot is really up to them yet. Or perhaps *I'm* not.'

He unlocked his cubbyhole and brought out his special tea-bags. His using them rather than the large staff canister spoke of many years of solitude; a bedsitter finickiness, a painstaking self-absorption. But today, due to his tenuous connection via slow-worms with Geoff, his dreariness fell from him. The other staff faded away; she was drawn only to him.

'Thank you *so* much,' she said warmly, 'for letting me borrow them.'

Walking down to the cloakroom she found that the injection of Geoff into the school had changed it; he had walked through the door, spoken to the secretary and then passed along this same corridor with its cream-above, chocolate-below walls. It was unsettling, how it had changed.

Going past the boys' cloakroom she saw a familiar group standing in a circle. From the noises, they were engaged in a belching competition. Roy, she could hear, was the best. He would be.

In the staff cloakroom she shut the door behind her; the coats that hung on it rustled and swayed. In the mirror she inspected her face. All aglow, it was. Then she pulled on her woollen school-teachery beret she'd bought herself the day she'd heard her exam results. She paused, listened to the comfortable murmurings of the hot-pipes, thought for a moment of her utter joy, and opened the door.

As she passed the boys' cloakroom the belchings stopped and were replaced with perfect timing by unmistakable kissing noises. As she hurried up the corridor towards the outside world, towards that glimmering rectangle of daylight, they echoed behind her mockingly. Roy's, she knew, would be the loudest.

fourteen

Far from finding her a bore, Geoff actually found Holly rather a help. For a start she did most of the talking, so he didn't have to think of anything clever to say as they sat waiting for 'Twelfth Night' to begin. Even though Claire was separated from him by the intent figure rustling through the box of chocolates he'd bought (90p, what a con!), somehow he felt much easier than if she'd been sitting next to him, touching. He might look relaxed; he was quite good at that. Someone once had even called him suave. *Suave.* But no one knew, of course, how very inadequate he so often felt underneath it. All in all, wooing was better with a sister there to loosen things up.

'Do find me a coffee cream,' Claire said to Holly, leaning towards the small bent head that was studying the chart like a gourmet studying the wine list. 'I don't want any dreary hard ones.' She turned and looked at him with a dazzling smile. Lovely, she looked. 'Perhaps *you* like hard ones. Can we fob you off with a nut crunch?'

'My favourite,' he said, and held out his hand. It wasn't true of course, but how he wanted to fit in somewhere amongst those bent sisterly heads!

'And a montelimar?' asked Holly hopefully.

'Yes please. I like that too.'

'Wow,' she said, turning to Claire. 'He's useful. Perhaps he likes the ones wrapped in gold stuff. Nobody likes them.'

'*I* do,' he said. 'The harder the better for me.' He examined the box with them. This was rather fun. Much better than saying 'Er, do you think "Twelfth Night" the best of the comedies', or something like that. 'That looks like a hard one,' he said.

Claire laughed. 'How convenient you are!'

'And here's another!' he said.

But just then the lights dimmed and they had to sink back into their seats. He lost sight of Claire.

They were sitting in the front row because Claire's father had insisted on paying for the tickets, and the curtain towered above them. Geoff took a breath. He must concentrate so that he could think of something original to say in the interval; it was difficult, because as far as he remembered he'd never actually seen any live Shakespeare. Not since school, anyway.

'Look, there's Viola!' he heard Holly whisper to Claire. 'Still looking like a lady.'

'Isn't she pretty,' whispered Claire. 'With her elfin face.'

'Yeah, but I want to see her change to Cesario. I want to see how she does it.'

He was impressed. There was something definitely cultured about these two, what with the grand school and their knowledge of Shakespeare and all. As far as he could remember, the only literary matter back in his mother's house had been a stack of *Reader's Digests* and a virgin volume called 'Your Hundred Best Loved Poems'.

Holly was whispering again. He leant discreetly sideways; perhaps he could learn what was happening on stage, where one fat man and one thin one were engaged in the telling of incomprehensible jokes.

'I can, honestly,' Holly was whispering.

'Can what?' whispered Claire.

'See the join.'

'Ssh!' hissed Claire. A pause, then: 'Where?'

'Look, on the ugly one's forehead. It's obvious as anything.'

'But they're both ugly.'

'The skinny one, dope. Sir Andrew Thingummy. You can see it's a wig.'

A pause, heavy with concentration.

'Gosh!' came Claire's whisper. 'You're right. You can even see globs of glue.'

'Oh look! You can see the fat one's join, too.'

Really! thought Geoff and leant back again. He felt quite shocked. Giggling like that (for they *were* giggling now) about *Shakespeare*. It seemed wrong.

He tried to concentrate. Somebody entered the stage with various men in tights around him. Geoff squinted down at his programme. Must be the Duke. But all the time he was pressingly conscious of the small figure next to him straining forwards, rigid with fascination. And stupidly enough, *his* eyes too couldn't stop straying up to those damned hairlines.

When the lights came on for the interval he decided to take

charge and suggested going outside for a spot of fresh air. And once outside he was intrigued anew by them, by the casual way that Claire sat down with a sigh on the nearest doorstep and smiled up at the luminous London sky.

'Well,' she said, turning her smile to him. 'Do you like it?'

'Oh yes,' he said.

Holly sat down beside her and put Claire's handbag around her neck. 'I thought it was jolly good, too.'

That was that, then. No need for cleverness at all. Standing rather than sitting because he was wearing his pale trousers, Geoff relaxed and lit a cigarette. The three of them gazed in companionable silence at the deserted doorways on the opposite side of the street. Names were written over the shops.

'What does a Bespoke Tailor mean?' Holly asked suddenly.

'I've never known,' said Claire. 'But Geoff can tell us, I bet.'

'It's a tailor,' he replied, pleased, 'who makes your clothes specially for you. Not ready-made, in other words.' At last he'd contributed.

'Ah,' said Holly, a new fact digested. They chatted a bit then, about sewing and then about something – pincushions, was it? – that Holly was making at school. Easy natural chat. It really was a help, Holly being there. Alone with a girl, he'd always found it difficult to know where to start, so to speak; that drive down to Eastbourne, for instance, he knew he should have been saying something. But Holly got things going; they could leap over the awkward beginning bits.

The bell rang; they returned to the theatre; they waited for the lights to dim. Trouble was, having had no brothers or sisters, he'd missed out. Missed out on that easy Saturday-morning informality with friends of sisters, friends of brothers, who giggled on the landing or borrowed one's bike or were caught plucking each other's eyebrows in the bathroom. In other words, who were generally being themselves. Ordinary. Sometimes he'd glimpsed it but never had he been amongst it. He'd missed all that, he realized, sitting here in his theatre seat.

As a result girls had been relegated to the evenings where they had to be prepared for and then, when the evening was over, perhaps prepared for again. In the evenings their hair was neat and their eyebrows plucked; one felt obliged to converse about subjects. But in the daytime, their hair in curlers, lunch plates rattling downstairs, one didn't feel obliged to converse about anything. One just chatted.

The curtain lifted. Their heads bent towards him, whispering a question. He was included; they were a threesome.

This second half was altogether better. He'd worked out who was who by now. Knowing he needn't be clever, he even started enjoying it. Behind him he was conscious of the vast Aldwych audience, brainy and intent, familiar with every word. But at least – comforting thought – not in such expensive seats.

And when it was over, and the audience was shuffling out through the Exit doors and Holly was stacking the corrugated cups in the empty chocolate box, they chatted. Sitting in their seats as the theatre emptied, they chatted about silly family things. The girls' dog, called Badger, and his old age pills; things like that. And he realized with a start: their giggling didn't irk me because it was Shakespeare and they shouldn't, but because it was sisterly giggles and I couldn't join in. There's something so self-contained about two sisters, damn it. But it's better now.

Afterwards he took them home. Claire, it seemed, was staying the night at Harrow with her parents, so he could take them both together. He led them through the streets to where his pride and joy sat beside its dead meter. His Lotus! Not for the first time it crossed his mind that cars were a good deal easier to tackle than girls. No soul-searching; no trying to impress. Just stick in the key, put the old foot down and you're off, roaring through the empty streets of Covent Garden.

'It's jolly kind of you,' shouted Claire.

But he wanted to take them home. He didn't want to say good-bye to Claire so early. Besides, he was keen to see the background to these oval-faced girls; make his presence felt there; glimpse for a moment something he'd so far missed.

A prosperous home, definitely. Detached, mature garden, forty thou at least. They scrunched to a halt outside.

Indoors, small lamps glowed in the drawing-room and Claire's mother approached with outstretched hand.

'Hello!' He could see her taking in the situation at a glance. 'You must be Geoff. Really, you shouldn't have brought my daughters home. I hope they tried to stop you.' Without waiting for a reply she called out in a sing-song: 'Dan! Come and introduce yourself and bring this kind young man a whisky!' She smiled at him and gestured to a chair. She was very well-dressed; in fact the whole room was most tasteful. 'If only my other daughter, the one at university, didn't have the car, you would have been spared the bother.'

'No bother, really. It was a pleasure.' He turned conversationally to Claire. 'I didn't know you had a car – or another sister, for that matter.'

'Half a car, really. Laura – my other sister – and I share it.'

Mr Jenkins came in. He managed, Geoff knew, an electrical firm. They shook hands, man to man. 'Nice piece of machinery you've got out there.'

Geoff felt himself glowing. 'Yes, it's a good old banger.' His car, he had suspicions, was to some people the major part of his identity; the thing that made him memorable. Never mind; he loved it, he was grateful to it.

The spell, his threesome with the sisters, was broken. He was now a stranger to whom one was polite. A low-voiced argument began about whether Holly was to go to bed now or later, and he wandered off, glass in hand, to look at the photos dispersed in silver frames around the room. He saw one of Claire, plumper of face in a Brownie uniform. The same body he'd actually dared caress at that party. He blushed and passed on to a girl seated on a horse.

'That's Laura,' called out Claire. 'Pretty, isn't she. Her hair's much longer now.'

'And messier,' said Mr Jenkins in a voice full of feeling. She was indeed pretty, despite the riding-hat.

He turned back. Holly had been sent to bed. Claire, settled into her home, was nice, even nicer. But it was late; that family hesitation was there; he was not without sensitivity.

He drained his glass. 'I'd better be pushing off now,' he said, and despite polite exclamations he pushed off. In the hall Claire smiled at him, tantalizingly near, but he couldn't touch her.

Alone again with his Lotus he roared back through the sodium-lit suburban streets. It had been a good evening. He had been near Claire; nearer, in a way, than he'd been when she was in his arms at that party. And for an hour he'd been part of her family. Holly had aided all this.

Sisters, he was beginning to realize, didn't get in the way; they helped.

fifteen

Dear Claire.

Laura couldn't think how to begin. *At last I have a lover?* Too pretentious. *I've just met a super marvellous person?* Too squeaky. *I've just fallen in love?* Too *Woman's Realm*ish.

They were all true, of course, but how difficult it was to write even to Claire about such a vast event. Nobody, surely, could feel the way she felt. It couldn't have happened to anybody the way it had happened to her. And yet, annoyingly enough, every word she thought of seemed to have been used before. Like discovering a secret wood and then on closer inspection finding lots of little picnic benches everywhere.

How could she lift it from the cliché of girl-and-boy to the rare realms, the breathtaking heights, of Laura-and-Mac? Difficult. Much easier to see Claire, to grasp her arm and flood her with the news. However much she enlarged the letters and underlined them, they had a definite secondhand look. Big and secondhand, perhaps, but still . . .

I've just been swept off my feet by a marvellous person called Mac. That would have to do.

He's an artist but he's been doing gardening since last summer – much more romantic than being a painter, don't you think? He's done one year at the art school here but he dropped out because it was teaching him nothing. We met at the Blood Donor Clinic of all places. And tombé dans le lit that night.

He lives in an extraordinary house full of interesting things. The people he lives with aren't students, they're a couple called Hal and Min who have two children. Hal doesn't seem to have a job but plays the harmonium, wheezily, into the small hours and generally enjoys himself. The children sleep in a room full of murals of toadstools and caterpillars. I wish you could see it all.

I've known him for two weeks exactly. Everything's changed now. Somehow he's such a relief from all those pseuds and weeds, more real than student life with all those tame rituals like Rag Day and ghastly parties, and all those intense discussions which are exactly the same as everybody else's intense discussions, and all those safe little rooms where one could pretend to be rebellious.

. . . and all those safe little rooms where one could pretend to be rebellious.

Unfair, thought Claire. Laura was as bad as any of them; worse perhaps.

Enough. Please come and visit. I'm dying to see you and haven't heard any news for ages. Something exciting must have happened. Don't leave me out of it.

Claire folded the letter. *Tombéd dans le lit*, eh?

'Why are you smiling, Clary?'

'Am I?'

Yvonne nodded sagely, knitting on lap, sturdy ankles; a virgin still. A virgin, perhaps, for ever.

It was another evening alone together, Yvonne with her knitting, Claire with her pile of exercise books. Outside, the orange glow on the houses opposite, the empty street bathed in shadowless light, and no Geoff. He hadn't phoned since the theatre outing. The suspense of waiting!

She got up and drew the curtains. What, she wondered, would Laura think of him with his neatly-pressed trousers and settled career? With his lack of murals and wheezing harmoniums? The sort of person about whom one could say nothing remarkable in a letter. She'd probably think he was terribly boring, though for Claire's sake she wouldn't say so. She'd just be extra polite.

'Gosh,' said Yvonne, closing the letter. 'She really goes in for the wierdos, doesn't she. I wonder if they're hippies. Mr Crawford calls them The Great Unwashed.' Mr Crawford was her boss. She looked at Claire, eyes bright. 'He always has such a clever way of putting things, don't you think? He sometimes says this country's going up the spout and somebody ought to take the kettle off.' She hesitated. 'D'you know, Clary, I've got something *so* exciting to tell you. I've been dying to tell somebody all day.'

'Out with it.'

'Well, you know what I told you last week, about Mr Crawford coming back from lunch and sitting on the edge of my desk. You know he asked me if I had any boyfriends?'

'Yes, I remember.'

'And I told him I'd got lots – you know, just to make him feel jealous. That was clever of me, wasn't it. Well, today . . .' She looked at Claire. She glowed. 'Guess what he did, Clary. Go on. I bet you'll be green with envy when I tell you.'

'He screwed you on the office floor.'

'*Nikki!*' cried Yvonne. Nikki had just walked in. Yvonne looked as if she'd been shot.

'You have a filthy mind,' said Claire.

'Just realistic. Anyway, no more tasteless remarks from me, girls. Just off. Anyone seen my hairbrush?' She rummaged amongst the cushions. 'Never mind, I'll just mess it up and pretend it's an Afro.'

She swept out. They heard the front door slam, then a man's low laugh and finally the roar of an engine. Nikki never stayed in to correct exercise books.

Yvonne turned to Claire, her brow puckered. 'Honestly, Claire, she drives me bananas!'

'Don't mind her. Go on.'

'Well, you see, he was giving me some papers to type and when he came up to my desk he stood quite near me . . .' Her voice trailed off.

'Go on.'

'Would you guess, he put his hand on my shoulder! Oh Clary, I'm sure I didn't imagine it. Honestly, I was all collywobbles inside.' She gazed at Claire. 'Do you think if I drop a gentle hint, just a *teensy* hint, that – well – I'm quite free and happy-go-lucky really, do you think he might, just might, ask me out?'

'I hope so.' Claire smiled encouragingly.

'Gosh.' She sat back in her armchair, radiant. Then she rallied and, picking up her knitting, said: 'Anyway, I mustn't go on about my own silly little life. Tell me about *your* Man. I'm dying for a peek.'

'He's not my man. I hardly know him.'

'Oh, but he is, Clary. I can tell. You've got that far-away look in your eyes, and sometimes you don't even hear what I'm saying.'

'Heavens, I'm sorry! I didn't realize.'

'Don't worry. Us girls in love, you know – '

With a yelp she jumped up.

'My pie!'

'What?'

'My Low Calorie Peach Delight! I've left it in the oven!'

She disappeared. From the kitchen Claire could hear flustered rattlings but here in the sitting-room silence reigned. She sat at the table, momentarily swept by a wave of the usual maddened poignancy produced by Yvonne's presence.

She opened the first exercise book. She tried to concentrate on the pencilled words but her eyes kept sliding away from the page and resting on the walls, the curtains, the tapestry milkmaid it had taken Yvonne six months to stitch. She couldn't settle. To think that it was just because Geoff hadn't phoned was the easiest way of putting it – the nearest peg, so to speak, on which to hang her heavy clothes.

No, it was more to do with Laura, and with her own certainty that Laura would dismiss Geoff as boring. It wasn't for Geoff's sake that she was uneasy – after all, in some deep way she was more sure about her feelings for him than she had been sure of anything for a long time (if only he could be sure of *her*). It was just that it pointed to something in Laura that for the last few months Claire had been noticing; a snobbishness, a withering dismissiveness that created areas of people or things, packaged them and bundled them aside as middle-class and suburban. Perhaps Mike had suffered this same fate; neutered somehow by hailing from Norbiton instead of a houseful of drop-outs who played harmoniums at three o'clock in the morning.

Just then the phone rang. Claire's speculations were cut short; indeed, all thought of Laura vanished from her mind, for it was Geoff and he was asking her to come out with him the next Saturday night.

sixteen

Holly's school dorm, occupied as it was by girls who were nearly thirteen, bore witness on its walls to their momentous transition. The school had started to allow posters to be hung ('But girls, only pins. Absolutely no Sellotape!'). The result was that the girls with bosoms had their beds down one end of the dorm and had hung up pop stars, while the girls who still possessed flat chests had their beds down the other end and had hung up horses.

Holly's bed was firmly down amongst the horses. Her neighbours, though outnumbered (and as the months went by, increasingly so) by those with bosoms, had a fine collection between them – horses with their foals, horses jumping, horses just standing with their manes floating in the wind, agonizing close-ups of beautiful intelligent horses' heads with eyes that understood everything. Most girls, too, had photo frames beside their beds containing blurred snapshots of their own pony, or their cousin's pony or, failing that, *any* pony.

Above Holly's bed hung the best picture of all, a huge colour photo given by Claire of a lot of white horses splashing through the sea. Fancy anyone preferring boring old pop singers to that! thought Holly, gazing at it as she put on her clothes. Crikey, they even wore *make-up*! Men with make-up, I ask you. Nutcases.

At about the same time that Claire got Laura's letter in Clapham, Holly got one too. She couldn't read it at breakfast because if one's attention was distracted, all the toast disappeared. Breakfast, with twenty of them fighting for one blob of marmalade, required concentration.

But after breakfast they had Free Time for ten minutes. Holly threw herself on her bed.

It was lovely seeing you at Christmas. I've found that bottle-opener you gave me jolly useful lately, having a rather boozy friend. We went out for a picnic the other day and I brought along some wine and used that nifty corkscrew thing on it. Afterwards we had fun climbing trees but he fell down and tore his jeans which, being full of holes anyway, I spent a whole evening mending when we got home.

How's school? I feel such a bond with you, us both being away in institutions for the first time. Does yours have lots of awful rules like mine? Are they a bore? Mine were, so I moved out and now I live in a lovely room which I've filled with yellow daffodils. I have a garden too – sort of – and I've planted lettuce and broad beans and cornflower seeds in it. It's only a tiny patch but I hope it'll be dug a bit more soon by my friend with the mended jeans.

                    Lots of love,
                          Laura

Holly's friend Ann, also at the horsey stage, plonked herself down beside her on the bed. 'Who's it from?'

'My sister.'

'The one who came in the snazzy car?'

'No, the other one.'

Joyce, who had passed the horsey stage and was getting lumpy, sat down next to them. 'He was a *dish*,' she sighed.

'Who?'

'The one with the car.'

'Oh,' said Holly. She must mean Geoff.

'Didn't you think so?'

'Dunno about dishes. He didn't like the same sorts of things as me and Claire. We couldn't do them with him there.'

'Of course,' sighed Joyce, turning round and gazing at a poster on the wall, 'nobody, just *nobody* could compare with Dave.'

Holly and Ann looked at Joyce pityingly. 'Here we go again,' said Holly. 'David Essex, I ask you!'

'Honestly, Joyce,' said Ann, 'you can see all his mascara and stuff. He's just like a girl.'

'Worse than a girl,' said Holly. Really Joyce was a different species, what with all the things she and the others down the dorm giggled about after lights out. There were so many more interesting things to giggle about.

'Oh, you just don't understand!' said Joyce, gazing dreamily in the direction of the poster, her chin already bumpy with the beginnings of acne.

Just then the bell rang for the first lesson. It was English.

Whatever differences they had in the dorm the entire class was united during the English lessons. They dreaded them. Last term it had been all right, but this term they had a terrible new teacher called Miss Withrington. She was young and extremely friendly.

'Call me Margaret,' she had said at that now legendary first lesson. 'That's my name, after all. Much nicer than Miss Withrington, don't you think?' She had smiled down at them. 'You see, I'd like us to be people together rather than pupil and teacher. Not you and me. Us.'

They had sat petrified. Down the class she'd walked, between the desks. 'I think I see some puzzled looks. Don't worry, I understand. I expect it's all rather a surprise for you, even a shock. After all, it *is* rather shocking when one's suddenly treated as a person, isn't it. Especially in an environment like this one, where rules sometimes seem in danger of engulfing us as individuals completely.'

Silence. She paused. 'Well, enough about me. This is *your* class. I want you to feel that it's a special place where you can express those rather special thoughts. One thing we must never feel,' she smiled at them, 'is embarrassed. Now, is that a promise?'

Her steps had taken her to Holly's desk. Her hand was on Holly's shoulder. Holly froze.

'And what's your name?'

'Holly Jenkins, Miss Withrington.'

'Now Holly, I know it might be a little strange for you to get used to this new franker way of speaking, but it's Margaret, OK?'

Holly couldn't get her mouth to answer.

'Anyway Holly, why don't you tell us a little about yourself. Any interesting events in your life, something that's made you happy or sad. Don't be shy. Whatever you say we'll all find it special because it's *you*.'

Holly's mouth went dry. It was a nightmare. She clenched her palms together, clammily. Nothing; she could think of absolutely nothing.

Never had her mind been blanker. She sat there, every muscle in her body urging Miss Withrington to pounce on somebody else. A hundred years later, she did. Smiling still – she always smiled – she went over to another girl and Holly sat back, flooded with a relief more exquisite than she'd believed it possible to feel.

After that first lesson the classroom buzzed. 'Cripes, what a nutcase!' . . . 'poor old Holls having it first' . . . 'she's bats!'

But words couldn't really do it justice. Nor could the giggling quite cover up the acute and humiliating embarrassment of the thing.

One of the bosomy girls, more articulate than the rest, heaved a deep sigh. 'My God,' she said. 'She's *unspeakable*.'

However often she reminded them, smilingly, Miss Withrington could never get them to call her Margaret. But curiously enough, nor could they bring themselves to bestow on her a nickname. Withers, they might have called her behind her back, or Old Withered (she was definitely bony) or even, if they were really witty, Shrivel. If she'd been anyone else, they would have.

But somehow Miss Withrington's very informality, her un-flagging closeness, had taken the wind out of their sails. She defied nicknames; she terrified them too much. Amongst themselves they could only call her, in tones of dread, Miss Withrington.

On this particular day, the day of Laura's letter, they trickled into the classroom even more slowly than usual.

'You know what we're doing, don't you,' said Holly.

'That Spring Thing,' answered Ann.

'Just think. We've got to do it in front of the whole Junior School! Just imagine! They'll think we're nuts.'

The Spring Thing was called by Miss Withrington *Rebirth: An Event*. It was all very confusing but seemed to consist of four girls reading poems on the subject of spring while the rest chanted. 'It's all very *free*,' Miss Withrington had explained. There was supposed to have been a little dance, too, but even Miss Withrington had had to admit that the rehearsals for that had not been a success.

Holly, because of her long wiggly hair, was one of the chosen four. 'The image of Flora,' Miss Withrington had said, smiling down.

Today she dropped the bombshell.

'Our four young readers,' she said to the class, 'should, I've decided, wear something a little more appropriate than their school uniforms, which after all have little of the spirit of spring about them. Buttons, collars and those crippling ties . . .' She reached down and took something out of a carrier bag. 'So I've run these up.' She held out a thin muslin robe, grass-green.

'But you can see right through it!' one girl gasped before she could stop herself.

Miss Withrington looked tolerant. 'You'll all be wearing underclothes, won't you? So where's the problem?'

Holly sat back aghast. How *could* she wear it? She'd have to wear her vest underneath, but her vest was so dreadfully babyish. The other three girls already had bras, she knew, but she hadn't. Everyone would see. How *could* Miss Withrington not understand?

'Never mind,' whispered Ann, who didn't have to wear it. 'I know it's awful but it'll soon be over.'

'But . . .' Even to Ann, her oldest friend, she couldn't quite bear to talk about the vest. 'But . . . nobody's ever done anything like this in Assembly before. They'll think we're mad. It's so long, too.'

That was another point. Although every Friday one class was given the task of contributing something to Assembly – the bit between the hymns and the headmistress's stern notices – it was an unspoken rule that this consisted of just five minutes of a girl reading from something dull or perhaps playing the piano. Any longer and it meant that the Senior House, who went to a different Assembly, would get to breakfast first and finish all the marmalade. No one had quite dared to explain this to Miss Withrington. Anyway, to dress up and *chant* . . . they'd look so *stupid*.

'Now, remember that I'm not going to tell you what exactly to chant,' said Miss Withrington, putting the robes away. 'I'm just going to give you some words which you can use in any order you like. The impression, as I've told you, should be a mass thing, suggesting all at once the richness, liberation and yet, somehow, the *painfulness* of spring.'

'We'll suggest that all right,' muttered Ann.

'All right? Just scribble down the words then . . . Green . . . thrust . . . burst . . .'

Holly looked down at the poem she had to read. It was all about daffodils. She would have quite liked it at any other time, but of course she'd never be able to read it again after this.

Daffodils reminded her of Laura's letter. In a moment of introspection (perhaps she *was* growing up, despite not liking David Essex) she thought: Laura might hate her rules but I like mine. This beastly Spring Thing is against all the rules; it doesn't make me feel safe at all.

'. . . rustling . . . blooming . . .'

Miss Withrington finished and looked at the girls with that understanding smile, that bright, hectoring smile. 'It'll be very beautiful,' she said.

Holly felt lost. School was so vast and unnerving that rules helped; and anyway, wasn't half the fun breaking them? But to have a grown-up go and break them for you – it was all wrong. Laura could say what she liked. It *was* all wrong.

seventeen

The next Thursday Laura returned from a seminar not one word of which, now she was back, could she remember. She closed the door behind her. What had it been about? It was different with practicals; setting up labyrinths for the long-suffering rats, transporting mice from one box to another, that sort of activity occupied her hands and left her mind pleasantly free. Anyway, she enjoyed it. With the exception of slugs she liked all animals;

mice and guinea pigs had been her companions since childhood. It was odd, of course, seeing them in a lab, like meeting an old friend in hospital, but at least she knew where she was with a practical.

Seminars and lectures, though, were less successful. The professor's voice droning on about patterns and theories and empirical situations struggled to compete with what Mac's supple body had been doing to hers the night before. Not surprisingly, it lost. Invariably, after the first few words the voice faded to a hum, a far murmur like the noise of the sea. A pleasant sound. She just sat there, skin singing, limbs warm, mind busy with recollections. Probably she was smiling.

It wasn't just Mac, either. Her room, her garden, what she was going to buy for supper, how she was going to get that pipe fixed, all the mechanics of her fascinatingly real and adult life filled her head and left no space for anything else.

She dumped her shopping down on the draining-board. She gazed at the plug-hole and tried to remember even one word. Impossible. Gone, like the washing-up water, for ever.

In a way she knew her father had been right. *You may have found Hall irksome,* he had written, *though I am amazed if you did. But it left you free from normal day-to-day things, free to develop your mind, make friends and readjust. Believe me, you have the rest of your life to do things just as you wish. I find it disappointing that you have suddenly decided to do it now.*

Daddy had obviously taken great pains with this letter. With extra-neat writing and no crossings-out it had certainly been copied from a rough draft. Laura preferred his chatty ones, about the peculiar people at his evening class and how Badger chased a cat right through Mummy's crocuses. That word *disappointing* stuck. She could bear almost anything but Daddy's disappointment, which made his shoulders droop and his manner, always courteous, grow achingly polite. She always pictured him in his faded green cardigan when he was disappointed, it made him look so sloping-shouldered and old.

Also, it had continued, *there is another reason. Hall protected you in many ways. It's worrying to think of you on your own. Why did you have to be the special one like this? In October you would have all moved out anyway.*

These words slightly nagged, too. *The special one.* How much did she admit this as part of her motive, and how large a part?

Upstairs as usual a baby was crying. Someone swore, she could hear the actual word, and then the television was switched on. Sounded like the afternoon racing; the tedious hysteria of the commentator, rising and falling, invaded the room. To drown it out she fiddled with the radio knobs.

. . . and here we have a card from Vera, Vera Scannel of Laurel Drive, Swanage. Hi Vera! You say you'd like a card for the best Mum and Dad in the world and for all the gang, that's Jim, Piff, John, Mo, Sue, Ned, Barney . . . Goodness, thought Laura . . . *Babs, Gruggs and a very special hello to Dave . . .*

What a lot of friends that Vera seemed to have. Laura thought of Hall; mid-afternoon and they'd all be trooping back from their lectures, dumping their books, making tea, chatting.

It was all right when Mac was here, of course. But when he wasn't the solitude pressed in on her more than ever. No longer was it a stillness about the furniture; now it was a solid, weighty need. Part of the trouble was there being no one around to distract her – upstairs the large upset Irish family, downstairs the derelict spaces, nothing else. Standing here in the middle she felt so exposed. *Hall protected you*, her father had written. There was no protection here, no bar to go to, no friends to drop in, no warden to fear. Just her own body. No wonder she'd succumbed to Mac that first night. Lovely to succumb, of course; it was just that she was so vulnerable here.

Today she felt more vulnerable than ever because of the diaphragm.

Trouble was, she had no one to tell. At Hall she could have told somebody; it was just the sort of topic for the hour before bed, hour of dressing-gowns and confidential mugs of Nescafé. Here there was just a draining-board of drying plates.

And here she was lingering over it, spending ages wiping them, even washing out the dishcloth, a thing she'd never done in her life. Anything to delay opening the door and walking up the road to the chemist. All by herself.

Funny how she and Mac could be so bold with each other's bodies but so shy about this. In the end, though, she'd taken it into her own hands and gone to a doctor. His trolley had been full of domes, surprisingly roomy things, whose shape was familiar from line drawings in 'Young Marrieds'. Years before, she and Claire had discovered this intriguing volume in their parents' bookshelves and countless nights had giggled over it with a mixture of fascination and unease. Each drawing had been thoroughly inspected until they knew it by heart. Finally their father had found it under Laura's pillow, and in a moment of wit for which she was eternally grateful had written a note saying *Really!* and slipped it between the pages. He could surprise sometimes.

So yesterday she had seen them in real life, rubber objects laid out like exhibits. The doctor, rolling on his crackling membranous gloves, had foraged inside her with one cap after another. Stiff she'd lain, comparing his rummaging with Mac's midnight welcome, until finally he'd unpeeled the membranes and written down her hidden number – the circumference, she supposed, of her womb.

All that remained was to go out to the chemist and buy one. Then mention it casually to Mac. Silly to be selfconscious about such a very sensible and adult thing as this, but she was.

She bundled the rubbish from the sink basket into a plastic bag that was bursting at the seams. The trouble was, there seemed to be so much sheer apparatus piled up round this business of being free. So much she had to take care of herself – rubbish bags that kept splitting, pipes that got blocked, complicated things like diaphragms to be organized. Hall lifted off the burdens, her father had said. He was right.

Down the stairs she went, past the pram – bulky result of a union that was dome-less. Up the road she walked.

Outside the chemist's shop some workmen were digging up the pavement. They gave her a bold look. She felt even more self-conscious. She opened the door.

Her heart sank. The shop was full of customers and there was only a male assistant in sight. She realized she'd expected a woman. Waiting for her turn, she scanned the shelves hoping to see a discreet package so she could just point. Behind her she could hear more customers joining the queue.

Her turn. 'Good afternoon,' said the man.

'Er, hello. Er, I wonder if you possibly have – ' With a cough and a splutter the road drill started up outside, deafeningly.

'What did you say?' shouted the man.

'An Ortho Diaphragm!'

'I beg your pardon?'

'An *Ortho Diaphragm!*' All those people behind her! She felt her face reddening.

'A diagram?' shouted the man. 'A diagram? Of what?'

'A diaphragm!'

'I'm sorry, could you speak up please!'

'I said, an – ' Suddenly the drill stopped. *'Ortho Diaphragm!'* The shout hung in the dead silence. Someone behind her cleared his throat.

'I beg your pardon,' said the man in a normal voice. 'What size?'

Hell! She'd forgotten that. She fumbled in her bag and found the doctor's piece of paper. She could have just given it to him wordlessly, she realized. No need to speak at all.

'Here we are,' he said, fishing out a package. 'And would you like cream or jelly?'

'Cream or what?'

'Jelly. Spermicidal jelly. Cream or jelly.' Eyes bored into her back. The whole shop was dead quiet, listening.

'Jelly!' she hissed.

Thank God she could escape. The door swung shut behind her. 'Wotcha Boobs!'

One of the workmen was resting on his drill, grinning at her. 'Nice,' he called, eyes on her chest. His grin widened.

Laura stumbled across a mound of sand, tripped over a pipe and walked up the road as fast as she could without running. She was blushing, she knew. Never, ever had she felt so completely *exposed*.

According to the clock above the jeweller's it was 4.30. She would go and see Mac; he'd be back home at Hal and Min's house by now. Being a gardener, he ended work at four. Perhaps she could tell him about this awful episode so that, amidst the laughter, the fact that she'd actually done something as sensible and boring as buying such an object would be less of an event.

He was back. She found him in the kitchen eating something from an open tin and drinking something from a brandy glass. Over its rim he smiled and her heart turned over.

'What peculiar meals you have,' she said brightly, 'at peculiar times.'

What she really longed to do was to kiss him, but he was scraping out the tin – Heinz Vegetable Salad – and anyway, still blushing from the chemist's, she was too selfconscious. So she perched beside him on the kitchen table instead and felt his nearness all up her right-hand side.

Mac took a swig from the brandy glass. 'You look bonny,' he said. 'Quite pink.'

She didn't tell him why. Instead she looked round the room. Hal and Min's kitchen was most un-kitchen-like, its atmosphere far removed from the spotless Formica of Greenbanks. Much, much nicer. In one corner rested a heap of leeks and potatoes, smuggled by Mac from the university vegetable garden. In another corner stood a moose's head that stared at them glazedly. The walls were covered with scribbles upon which, the first time she'd been there, Laura had congratulated Hal and Min's little daughter. She'd indignantly replied that they weren't *her* drawings; she used her drawing book of course. They were Daddy's.

A disembowelled bicycle, a hookah, a tuba . . . the room was hardly recognizable as a kitchen. Except, that is, for one neat row of baby food tins, a reminder of the orthodox needs of the baby to keep growing.

'What did you do today?'

'Oh, climbed a tree and had a snooze, did a bit of the old shit-shovelling, raced a couple of snails. They had amazing striped shells. A healthy sort of day.'

How he charmed her! How the whole household charmed her, so casual and disconnected from the outside world with all its silly rules and conventions. She looked at the scribbles on the wall. They were like children. Almost.

Mac was tapping his feet to some inner song. Never, she was discovering, did he ask her about *her* day, or her past, or anything like that. Never, it seemed, did he feel the need. He just smiled and drained his balloon glass and existed, amiably. How his very casualness tantalized! Here she was, longing to hold him; and there he was, slipping from her whenever she tried to get a grip.

Mac wiped his mouth. 'Hal's just got his dole,' he said. 'So it's piss-up night tonight.'

'Marvellous,' said Laura untruthfully. The Heinz Vegetable Salad, combined with the piss-up, meant he wouldn't eat the stew she'd made for tonight – but what a dull housewifely thought! She blushed. Never ever would she let him know that such terrible thoughts existed. He, who never showed the slightest urge, in contrast to her shamefully strong, shamefully *ordinary* impulse, to do any possessing at all.

Looking round at the communal belongings, at the car keys Hal always left dangling from the moose's antlers for anyone to use, how she admired their ease, their lack of demands, the way everything was shared. Every day seemed a delightful surprise to be drifted through unhampered by dull things like jobs and routines and blush-making little awkwardnesses like buying a diaphragm. Unhampered, too, by the desire she was trying to hide of having Mac all to herself, in her own little room, surrounded by her own things and eating the stew she'd so painstakingly prepared.

Just as it took weeks to dare buy it, it took weeks to dare produce her little package, tell Mac about it and creep from the firelit bedroom into the chilly little bathroom on the landing.

The first time she dared struggle away at it with her clumsy hands, she felt a wave of nostalgia for the innocent, giggly days of 'Young Marrieds' when such things remained safely on the printed page. Easier on the page than all rubbery and springy in the fingers. Also, she felt a pang for Claire. Funny to want a sister now, of all times. But Claire would understand better than Mac.

And yet, when she grew better at it she got to enjoy her solitary bathroom preparations. They grew to be the one unfailing moment of order in the day, and she had to agree that, like Holly, she needed a little order, somewhere. She had more in common with Holly than she was prepared to admit.

eighteen

Geoff's next hurdle was Nikki and Yvonne. Claire couldn't help thinking of them as a challenge, Nikki being so very pretty and Yvonne so extremely plain. Most people coped badly with this. Would he?

On this particular night Nikki happened to be in. From the sounds and scents a general overhaul of face, nails and body seemed to be taking place. As Claire ushered Geoff into the living-room Nikki's gay singing voice could be heard through the bathroom door; fragrance wafted through the cracks.

'That's Nikki,' Claire told him, gesturing towards the door. She led him to a chair. 'And this is Yvonne.'

Yvonne, plump and sedate in her dressing-gown, sat on the sofa.

'Pleased to meet you.' She gave him a significant look. 'Clary's told me all about you.'

'Really?' asked Geoff. 'Hope it wasn't too bad.'

'Oh no, I should say not.' She gave him another meaningful look. 'But you aren't quite like I expected.'

Claire stiffened.

'Why not?' he asked.

'Well, Claire said you looked a bit like Paul Newman. He's my favourite actor, you know. He makes me feel all whoozy inside.' She stopped her knitting and inspected him. 'But you don't look as much like him as all that. You have brown eyes, for a start. His are blue, a sort of deep gorgeous blue. Baby-blue eyes, that's what I call them.'

Claire asked quickly: 'Would you like something to drink?'

'Let me.' Yvonne put her knitting aside. 'You two just stay there and I'll make you a nice cup of tea.'

'Not tea,' said Claire briskly. 'It's seven o'clock. How about some sherry, Geoff?'

Claire escaped into the kitchen. She could hear Yvonne's voice carrying on in the living-room. Oh, to live alone! She scrabbled about in the cupboard, pushing aside the awful cracked coffee mugs. Panic-stricken, she could feel things slipping out of hand. And soon there'd be Nikki too.

She didn't meet Geoff's eye when she came back with the sherry glasses. She set them down. 'Would you like some, Yvonne?'

'You know me. I'm a good little girl.' She put her knitting aside. 'What I prefer is a nice cup of tea.' At the door she stopped and wagged her finger roguishly. 'I'll leave you two alone then, but no hanky-panky, mind.'

Rigid and wordless, Claire and Geoff sat still as she padded out and closed the door behind her. Hanky-panky seemed a long way away. Claire stared into her little sherry glass and carefully lifted it to her lips. Out of the corner of her eye she could see him doing the same. They took a sip each. They put the glasses down. Then she stole him a glance.

He turned to her, raised his eyebrows and smiled conspiratorially. 'Goodness,' he said.

She went limp with relief. They were confederates. He smiled at her with a new intimacy and took her hand. 'Here's to us.'

With their free hands they clinked glasses.

They were just finishing their sherry when the singing stopped and Nikki came in.

'Hi,' she said. 'Is that your super car outside?'

Geoff looked pleased.

'I *adore* Lotuses,' she said. 'A touch of your actual class. What's it do in top?'

'Oh, about a hundred on a clear stretch.'

'That's cool. It's an Elan, isn't it?'

'Right.' He looked at her with respect. 'You seem to know a bit about Lotuses.'

'They're so beautiful. When did you get it?'

'Oh, when I was just starting college. I'd taken a holiday job . . .'

Claire listened. Never had she heard Geoff sound so interesting or talk so eagerly about himself. She had no idea he'd once had a holiday job in a Bird's Eye factory. How did Nikki manage it?

'. . . so I felt I could afford it,' he finished. 'An Elan, anyway. When I'm really flash I'll buy a Europa.'

'Nice, yes. But I love Elans. So light and powerful to ride in.'

Claire tensed, waiting for him to say the obvious, which was 'Well then, would you like a light and powerful ride in it?' But thank goodness he didn't.

'So you're Nikki,' he said instead.

'Excuse the hideous curlers. This is my homely evening.'

She rearranged herself in her chair, looking far from homely, and smiled at him. She was wearing a sort of towelling turban. Geoff offered her a cigarette; she took it; there was a tiny shift in the balance of the threesome as she and Geoff lit up and Claire didn't.

'What are you drinking?' she asked, leaning over in a cloud of smoke to look in his glass.

'Sherry.'

'Goodness, how ladylike! Such a tiddly glass too. Fancy a whisky?'

Geoff brightened. 'Well, now you mention it . . .'

She was wearing a thin silky caftan. They watched her as she shimmered out and returned a few moments later with a bottle, glasses, ice and a bowl of olives. She sat down and switched on the cosy table lamp. 'On the rocks?'

There was a certain air about Nikki; half transient, as if she was going on somewhere exciting very soon – even in a turban she managed to convey that impression – and half intimate, as if just for the moment she couldn't bear to drag herself away. Claire had always admired this.

'Cheers,' she said, smiling at him as Claire had smiled. They clinked glasses. She turned to Claire. '*Sure* you don't want any?'

'No, I don't really like whisky, thanks.' She wished she did; she felt prissy drinking sherry now, even though Geoff was pouring her out another.

Ice clinked; they sipped. Nikki smiled dreamily and said, almost to herself: 'I just feel like going out tonight. So dreary staying in.'

'That reminds me,' said Geoff, turning to Claire. 'We'd better get a move on.'

Claire sighed with relief. There had been no hesitation, no asking of her to join them or, worse still, no moment's thoughtful silence as he worked out how he was going to ring up Nikki next time and suggest some little jaunt in the Lotus. Claire glanced at him; he looked particularly stolid. The danger was over; she knew it. They chatted, they finished their drinks. He was behaving perfectly; he was neither ignoring Yvonne, who was back with her tea now, nor becoming, well, rather silly with Nikki. Most people did both. He was just being polite; in a kind way to Yvonne, in an appreciative way to Nikki.

And in a few moments they would drive off, just the two of them, and drop in at a riverside pub for a drink and be at last alone. They hadn't been alone at all yet, what with Holly and everything.

Then perhaps they'd go for a meal, the sort they should have had when they went to Eastbourne. And after that . . . sitting next to him, she didn't dare look at his face, only at his hand, such a beautiful brown hand that was reaching out for an olive. She would do anything he wanted.

'. . . you see,' Yvonne was saying, 'we have this kitty, and we all put in a pound a week, just for milk and things. But then, of course,' she rolled an eye towards Nikki, 'some of us aren't here for breakfast and so that puts everything out.'

'Sounds interesting,' said Geoff gallantly.

'I mean, I don't like to *interfere*, but – '

The doorbell rang. Claire got up. Who could it be? She walked down the hall. No doubt some stud for Nikki.

'Laura!'

'Hello,' said Laura. 'I've brought the car back.'

'Heavens, you've come all the way from Bristol? Just like that?'

'I thought it was time for your turn.'

'That's nice, but how unexpected.'

They were in the living-room now. 'Hi, Nikki and Yvonne,' said Laura, 'and hello, er . . .'

'Geoff, this is Laura,' said Claire. Laura looked at him; he must be Claire's friend then, if she introduced him.

In the general pause that followed Claire thought, fleetingly, of her evening with Geoff. Much as she loved Laura, she thought of it. 'Er, are you staying the night? I mean, can you?'

'Yes please. That OK?'

'Of course. You can sleep on the sofa.' This romantic tête à tête business would just have to wait for another night. Never mind. Anyway, it was good to see Laura; interesting too, because there was something on her mind. This sudden arrival – even Laura wasn't this impulsive – and now a restlessness about her, a fidgeting.

'What on earth are you wearing?' asked Nikki.

'It's a jumble sale dress,' Laura answered. '5p, it cost. Isn't it nice? I feel like somebody out of a Steinbeck book.'

'Oh yeah?' Nikki raised her eyebrows. 'Anyway, tell me all about ravey Bristol.'

While she talked, Geoff looked at Laura. Yes, she was pretty, he could see that, but what a mess she'd made of herself! All that hair and that terrible droopy dress that made her look like a tramp. She ought to smarten herself up; make the most of herself, like Claire did.

Claire spoke. 'Well, Geoff and I were just off for a drink.' She stood up; she hesitated.

It was for Geoff to say, and he knew it. He was nothing if not polite. 'Are you coming, Laura? I'm sure you and Claire have a lot to talk about.' Hmm, if it wasn't one sister it was the other. But still, if he were honest it wasn't entirely unwelcome.

From her position wedged into the back of the Lotus, Laura inspected the two heads with interest. Obviously they knew each other quite well or they wouldn't be sitting there in such a settled silence. But how well? And were they, perhaps, just shy? It must be recent, this Geoff business, or Claire would have written to her about it. He wasn't bad-looking, she had to admit, but on the dull side. In that sports jacket and those dreadful cavalry twill trousers he looked like an advertisement for Player's Senior Service. Manly and dependable; that scene.

They found the riverside pub and sat down with their drinks. A large number of people stared at Laura's peculiar dress. She stared back at them, half gratified and half embarrassed. Such a bourgeois lot! But she wished she didn't blush so damn easily.

'Well,' asked Claire. 'What news? Still seeing Mac?'

'Yes.' A silence. Then Laura said: 'I'm living with him.'

Claire's eyes widened. 'Really?'

'Uh-huh.' She tried to sound casual. 'He moved into my room a day or so ago.' There! Now she'd told her. She watched for Claire's reaction. Geoff, she saw, was fiddling with his glass.

'Goodness,' said Claire. 'I must meet him now.'

'Do. Come down and visit me – us.'

'He just moved into your room?'

'Yep.'

Geoff felt dreadfully in the way. He pretended not to listen and gazed out over the glittering river.

Laura went on: 'You see, everybody was chucked out of the house he lived in. They'd never paid the rent. So he came in with me.'

'Simple as that?'

'Yep,' said Laura. Geoff, she noticed, was looking most disapproving. He was the sort that would, of course.

'He simply dropped in,' insisted Claire, 'and sort of stayed?'

'Just about.' She picked at the holes in her sleeve. Actually, she had to admit that she was feeling rather uncomfortable. The ease with which it had happened had rather taken her by surprise. No discussion, no arrangements to speak of; he wasn't that sort. One moment he wasn't there and the next moment, amiable and plimsolled, there he was. Nice, of course; lovely, in fact. But almost *too* easy. And here was Claire harping on just that; irritating of her.

'Well, what are you going to do about it?' Claire asked.

'Oh, I don't have to think about that yet,' she said airily, studying her sleeve. 'The present's enough for me – us.'

'Don't be so silly, Laura. Lovely to have him, but are you sure you want to close yourself off? It's mad in your first year. Think about all the other men you could be meeting. Such a waste.'

Laura suddenly thought: Was it so easy because I was lonely?

'Claire!' she snapped. 'Stop playing the big sister. I know what I'm doing.'

'You're talking in clichés.'

'Well, it's a clichéd situation, isn't it. All this disapproval – '

'It's not disapproval. Don't you understand one bit? I'm just worried about you closing the door on everyone else. Anyway, who's supporting who?'

Laura fiddled with her sleeve again; the holes were getting bigger. 'He is, of course,' she said carefully. 'His gardening didn't pay enough, so he's a bus conductor now.'

'What?' Geoff couldn't stop himself.

'A bus conductor.'

'But you say he's an undiscovered genius,' said Claire. She looked at Laura; Laura's face was closed and defiant. Geoff's presence was making her take up a stance; she would be different if they were alone. Just for a moment Claire resented Geoff being there; then she thought of the candle-lit supper and resented Laura. It was just like Eastbourne all over again. 'Anyway,' she said, 'let's talk about something else.'

But everything else seemed rather flat after that and their voices kept trailing off in mid-sentence. In fact the evening didn't last long, and after a swift and muted meal Geoff dropped them off at the flat.

Laura disappeared indoors; Claire lingered by the car.

Geoff spoke. 'Well I never,' he said. 'Is your sister always like that?'

'Like what?'

'Sort of rebellious. You know.'

'Yes, she was always wilder than me. She does silly things sometimes.'

'I can see that.'

Claire was stung. 'What do you mean, "I can see that"?'

'Oh. Well, I mean, rushing off with young men she hardly knows.'

'How do you know she hardly knows him?'

He battled on. 'If *you've* never met this Mac – '

'That doesn't mean anything. It doesn't matter if I've never met him. They're obviously deeply, passionately in love.'

'Yes, but you yourself were telling her that it was a bit silly – '

'I might tell her, but I'm her sister. I'm allowed to. You're not.' She shrugged. 'She knows what she's doing.'

Geoff gazed at her, astonished. 'Well,' he said at last. 'I'd better be pushing off.' He got into the car. 'I didn't know, well, you'd get like this. Goodbye.'

'Goodbye,' she said. Her voice faltered but the door was closed now.

She watched the tail lights disappear down the street and leant against the wall, exhausted and angry. Angry with Laura for spoiling everything with Geoff, for surely he would never come back after this. Angry with herself, and angry with Geoff for saying things that she as a sister could say but he, an outsider, couldn't. Yet he wasn't an outsider; she didn't want him to be. And of course he was quite right, dammit. Loyalties pulled at her from all sides.

She sighed and went indoors.

But Geoff drove away exhilarated. This was marvellous. Angry looks, confidences, family secrets, a real live quarrel. Lovely not to be polite for once; what a relief. How close they'd come to each other, shouting. He knew her better than twenty, *thirty* well-mannered evenings would have made him know her. When he phoned her up, which would be tomorrow, they would be breathlessly apologetic, *real*.

He was involved now; that was it. And he'd found it so very difficult to be involved with anyone before.

nineteen

I should be doing my Jung, thought Laura. She should too. There in front of her lay the notes, lit by a ray of sunshine. Every day she would reshuffle them, hoping that something would happen, a stirring in her brain perhaps, a click and a whirr and the whole mechanism would start up as it hadn't started up for several weeks now. And then perhaps the essay would get written.

But nothing clicked, nothing stirred and ah! how nice it was just to lean out of the window and let the warm spring sun seep into her skin. She lifted her arm to her nose; already her skin had that warm biscuity scent of summer. Time stood still. Since Mac's arrival she'd found herself caught in a trance of inactivity.

Down below she could see her garden – *their* garden – half-dug but nevertheless satisfying, its dandelions starring the grass and peeping out from the coils of rusty iron, its square of earth already showing the broad beans she'd planted. Stout greyish plants; more real, somehow, than Jung. Soon perhaps Mac would dig the rest of the garden and she could plant some more things. She had plans, but nothing seemed to get done.

The room, too, was still only half-finished. Mac, when prodded, said he'd finish painting the walls with her but he never did. She could do them herself of course, but something stopped her, the need perhaps for them to be more of a couple, for them to do ordinary tasks together, solid workmanlike everyday tasks. After all, she thought, heaving about under the sheets binds us together very nicely, but so would painting side by side, our hands speckled with emulsion. In its different way.

Not that he didn't try to embellish the room. Sometimes he would bring home strange objects to put on the mantelpiece – bits of curly wood or an intriguingly knobbled potato. Nothing useful, just little treasures that he brought to her as a child would.

When he left the gardens and became a bus conductor he still found objects, though of a more urban nature – matchboxes with camels on perhaps. It pleased her, his way of noticing things. Most people at university only noticed things inside their heads. Her parents, on the other hand, only noticed things that had to be done. A pile of leaves in the gutter meant, for them, a blocked drain. For Mac it meant a nice pattern. Sundays with her parents were an exception; Sundays were holidays and one was then at liberty to lift up one's eyes to admire the trees or cast them down to remark how pretty the snowdrops were and how early for this time of year.

But Mac noticed things. She liked wandering about with him. The fluster of life – telephones ringing, cars hooting – meant nothing to them as they ambled along the pavement. Perhaps they'd stop to watch a dog, purposeful and jaunty, trot past; perhaps an old man sitting on a bench, rustling inside his carrier bag while the pigeons waited. Small things, nice ones.

In fact, he often didn't go to work at all and spent all day just doing this. Now she didn't disapprove of this – heavens no! It just might be nice to see him get down to a painting, perhaps, for wasn't he an artist? Or at least help her with the garden. Sometimes he did look rather *aimless* in his frayed plimsolls. Content, though.

During the last weeks of the spring term he was put on to the early shift. That meant getting up at 5.30, and for a few days he was actually quite good. Laura had bought him an alarm clock. With a grunt and a moan he would roll over, thump his fist on it, roll further and land on the floor with a thud. Laura would stretch out an arm, switch on the light and just lie there, bathed in her tenderness for him and the warmth of the sheets. Who couldn't love him now when he looked so utterly at a loss, all bare, searching amongst the trail of clothes across the room (he'd had a few last night) for his underpants? So young he looked from the back, with the skin stretching over the necklace of his spine as he bent down (ah, he'd found them). So slender and classical he looked, such a perfect animal, as he stood poised. He scratched his head, bemused, wondering where he'd left the next item; then he turned round, focusing on her.

'Hello, my love.' He smiled. How she longed for him to come over and kiss her, but he was rummaging in his pockets, now he was dressed, for a cigarette. Then he looked at the clock.

'Wow, it's getting on. Never make it in time, my sonner.' He was wandering vaguely round the room. 'Anyway, can't find me hat.' He lifted up books and looked under them, he looked behind his latest little heap on the mantelpiece. 'Hmm.' He lifted up the saucepan lids. Then he straightened up and she knew what he was going to say. 'Hmm, hardly worth going in now, is it.' He wrinkled his brow. 'Anyway, don't feel up to it. Me brain's sore.'

She looked at him in his uniform, his crumpled jacket and those unbelievable regulation trousers she'd tried to taper. Now he was dressed he looked quite comic. Then she looked around the room, at its overflowing ashtrays and its half-painted walls. She looked at it all with a familiar, faintly sinking feeling which she was trying not to define. Even his moustache had never really grown.

'It's not *that* late,' she said. 'I'll take you.'

The most sensible thing to do was to ignore the feeling, ignore those walls and ashtrays, find his hat, struggle into her raincoat which slapped her skin with its chill, and drive him to the bus depot. Which she did.

But they had some beautiful days; they did. One really sunny morning they took the day off – yet another day off – and drove to the seaside. How marvellously free they were, speeding along in the Morris! Claire had refused her turn when Laura had brought it to London; the reason, perhaps, was not unconnected with Geoff's ownership of a car.

It was April now and the last day of term. Laura would soon go back to Greenbanks just for a while, to put in a holiday appearance. She didn't want to stay in Harrow longer than the minimum necessary.

'But listen, Mac,' she shouted above the rattle of the engine. 'Why don't you come up? My parents are going away for a weekend, they've just written and told me.'

'Me come to London?'

'Well, why not? Apparently they're having some dreadful cocktail party that they want me to come to, and the next day they're taking Holly off for the weekend. It's Easter, you see. They're going to some posh hotel in the country.' She glanced at his profile as he scratched his hair. Mac in Harrow! It would be amazing. 'So why don't you come? When they're away that weekend. We can have Easter together in that great big house.'

And why, thought Laura, don't I ask him as a normal guest when my parents are there? Because she knew exactly what would happen. The gin-and-tonics in the drawing-room, the polite questions about his background. In dreadful detail she could imagine it. Under such a grilling he'd start shifting about in his chair and being deliberately stupider than he was, tremendously stupid, saying things like 'People with more than one car ought to be shot', though Laura knew he'd seen the double garage outside. And then he'd not have cleaned his nails, and he wouldn't stand up when her mother came into the room, and Laura would feel that of course it didn't matter but slightly wishing he *had*, and then Daddy would ask him about jobs and there would be that slight pause, no, that long pause, when Mac had told them . . . And then of course the tentative little enquiries about him after he'd gone. And her father's cardigan shoulders. Oh dear me, no.

The sea. The beach. They slammed the car doors and ran down towards the waves. The pebbles clunked and rolled underfoot. Laura flung herself down on her back. She swept aside those complicated thoughts. She just lay there and felt the sun seep into her face, hearing nothing but the suck and rattle of pebbles at the water's edge.

She heard Mac sitting down beside her. She sat up and looked at his ankles. In the gap between his jeans and his plimsolls she could see the bare skin, just a narrow band of it. She had a strong impulse to cover it up.

She picked up some pebbles and heaped them over his ankles. He squirmed. 'Don't move,' she said. 'I don't want you to move.'

He lay flat on his back, smiling, the sun in his face. She hesitated, hand poised. 'It's so fascinating,' she said. 'Let me do more.'

'Go ahead.' He closed his eyes. 'Don't be shy.'

She began logically at his feet and very gently heaped the pebbles on to them. His feet pointed skywards; she had to heap the pebbles in two large mounds to cover them up. Then, very gently, she began to scoop the stones and heap them on to his legs, higher and higher. The undersides of the pebbles were cold and damp, she could feel them as she picked them up, and she was touched that he didn't complain but lay there for her, his eyes closed. His outstretched hands looked helpless, their pale palms and pale fingers. They didn't flinch as she covered them up.

It took rather long. Stones kept sliding off and revealing pieces of Mac. Doggedly she replaced them and patiently he lay. She liked the way he didn't question her.

Finally only his head remained. She hesitated. 'What about your face?' she asked.

'You're very gentle, my sonner.'

Carefully she began to place the pebbles one by one on his face. It twitched, it couldn't help it. With fascination she watched the warm and loved skin, his living face, disappear pebble by pebble. The pebbles themselves were skin-smooth.

'Can you breathe?' she asked, before she covered his mouth.

'Uh-huh,' said the mouth. It looked exposed.

With the utmost care she placed the last few pebbles over it and he was sealed up. Cancelled out. Just like that. Her doubts cancelled out, all her uneasiness about him sitting in the Greenbanks drawing-room cancelled out. As simple as that. Just a longish mound of pebbles amongst the other mounds of pebbles that stretched down the beach as far as the eye could see. She stood back to look at her workmanship. Mac obliterated. Her darling Mac gone. Why did it give her such strangely mixed feelings?

After a moment she began to feel uneasy in the silence. She leant over the tomb-like mound. 'Are you sure you're all right?' she whispered. What was he thinking under his mantle of stones?

Was he smiling perhaps? Was he at peace there under his primeval hood?

'It's nice,' she heard him mumble. 'But dampish.' He shifted himself; the stones slid off. He sat up, white-faced as Lazarus, his hair sticking up round his head in wet spikes.

He looked at Laura. Yes, he said, he would like to bury her.

So he did; then they drove home, their clothes sticking to their bodies and their shoes full of pebbles, just little ones. And what, thought Laura, would Jung think of all that?

twenty

'They'll never eat all this,' said Laura.

'But it's nice to have little nibbly things,' said her mother. She laid out the specially small and specially dainty sausage rolls on a plate. 'And it's so much more welcoming, don't you think?' Her mother always made these most obvious statements with great emphasis, as if she were the first person ever to think of such things. 'It's *so* tiresome when the car breaks down,' she'd been known to say, as if everyone else in the world found it first-rate entertainment. Sometimes the family found this pleasingly naïve and sometimes they found it annoying, depending on mood.

Laura arranged slivers of gherkin on slivers of egg. 'How many people are coming?'

'About fifty.'

'Heavens.'

'Some of them haven't seen you since you were *so* small.'

'Um. They'll have a shock. I say, this isn't *real* caviare is it?'

In half an hour the guests were due. Together Laura and her mother took the trays of food into the drawing-room. It was full of flowers, large red tulips and large yellow daffodils. On the tables bowls of nuts and ashtrays were placed. The french windows were open and a carpet led out into the garden. For those who wished to sit, chairs faced each other in confidential circles. And in the midst of it all stood her father polishing glasses.

Laura gazed round. 'Wow, it's all so organized!'

'Compared to your parties, I bet it is,' said her father. He was in a good mood. 'It's not just a crate of beer and an open door here, you know.'

'Yeah, I can see that.'

'I do like to make an effort,' said her mother. There was a tiny apology in her voice; very occasionally this appeared, but Laura chose to ignore it.

'The thing is,' said her father, 'all you lot – you young lot – you're afraid for things to look as though you've taken any trouble. You think you'd look silly.'

Laura opened her mouth to argue then shut it again. She shut it because the room really did look rather nice – glittering and expectant. Beer-puddled Bristol kitchens . . . she remembered her lost feeling at that party. Somehow such parties didn't make one feel exactly cherished. This room did. She could almost forgive things like that hideous cocktail cabinet.

Her mother spoke. 'If only that man would come and fix the verandah light, everything would be perfect. It's a beastly curse; he promised he'd come before five and it's nearly six now.'

Just then Claire, who had been upstairs changing, came into the room. She wore a soft red dress, very simple. Dan smiled.

'You look very nice,' he said. 'Er, what are you going to wear, Laura?'

'This, of course.'

A silence.

'But Laura,' said her mother. 'I mean, it's covered with repairs. I can see the stitches.'

'It's beautiful,' said Laura. 'It's tremendously old.'

'Yes, I can see that.'

'It suits her,' said Claire quickly. 'Jolly evocative. She looks like somebody out of "The Great Gatsby".'

Dan said: 'Actually, that was before our time.'

Rosemary looked at Laura. 'Oh dear, I wish you could have made an effort. Just for our friends, so I can feel proud of you.'

'Don't be silly. It's one of my nicest dresses.'

'But – '

'She *has* made an effort,' said Claire, being loyal. 'It's Laura's sort of effort, that's all.'

Laura tossed her head. She stopped thinking the room looked nice. Pretentious chandeliers. Stupid, false cocktail parties.

'As if it's important what I wear.'

'Ah, but you think it's important too,' said her father. 'Else you wouldn't have worn that particularly extraordinary dress.'

Laura paused. 'Oh,' she said, and then she laughed. She thought of her mother in her cocktail dress hating looking odd; and herself in her tatty one, liking it. She shrugged cheerfully. She could never decide which way she was going to feel. Couldn't she even *rebel* consistently?

The moment was over; the irritation subsided. The four of them stood, poised in the room that was fragrant with flowers. They could hear the clock ticking.

'Well,' said Dan at last, rubbing his hands. 'There's no reason why *we* shouldn't start. Shall we?'

'Let's!'

Dan poured out their drinks. Holly walked in and was wordlessly handed a cider. Usually she had to argue to get a cider but tonight was special.

Drinks in hand, they sat down and looked out of the front window.

'Do you feel we're doing something forbidden,' said Rosemary, 'having this little drink first?'

'If somebody knocks on the door,' Claire replied, 'I'll leap up as if I've been caught smoking in the lavatory.'

'Or reading under the bedclothes,' said Dan.

'Reading "Young Marrieds",' added Laura. Dan looked at her and chuckled, remembering.

They sat in a companionable silence. They hadn't been all together like this for ages, just sitting still in one room.

Rosemary said: 'I have a sneaking wish that nobody was coming at all. Even though I love parties. Wouldn't it be fun!'

'We could stuff ourselves with all the caviare.'

'And then watch the telly all cosily.'

'Or play Scrabble . . .'

'. . . in our nighties.'

'We haven't played Scrabble for years. Wonder where the board is . . .'

The doorbell rang. The spell broke. They tensed; they looked at each other.

'I'll go,' said Rosemary. She got up and smoothed down her dress. She cast a last look at her girls sitting in a row on the sofa. She wished she saw more of them but they only seemed to meet for functions nowadays, never for Scrabble.

She cast a quick glance at herself in the hall mirror. She straightened her brooch; then she opened the door. The first guest.

When Geoff got there, the room was full. He'd deliberately come a bit late because it was such a strain, being one of the few. Mrs Jenkins greeted him warmly, he thought; someone put a drink into his hand and he launched himself amongst the heads, searching for Claire. How very impatient he was to see her! He really could hardly bear it – he, Geoff, usually so calm.

The fact was, the basic big surprise was, last night he'd suddenly realized he wanted to marry her. As simple as that. He really, truthfully did. There was nothing he wanted more; in fact, everything else dwindled away compared to this large need imprisoned, bulky, in his ribcage. It must be love, love for the gentle sensible girl somewhere – dammit, where? – in this room.

Someone brushed past him; someone in a tweed jacket blocked his view; some unknown woman smiled at him, or through him, with glistening red lipstick. Faces, faces, all he could see were faces, every one of them a strange face and not one of them hers.

And the noise! Deafening. Where was she?

'Hello.' A voice at the level of his chest. 'Would you like a sausage roll?'

'Ah, Holly! Hello. Have you seen Claire anywhere by any chance?'

'Not really. I can't see much, everyone's so tall. She might be out in the garden, though.'

He pushed through the bobbing heads. Outside were more people talking and drinking in the evening sunshine.

And there she was. He spotted her at once. Her head was on one side; she was listening to an elderly man, smiling and then, at something he said, breaking into laughter.

He hesitated. How dared he approach – especially now, with everything so changed by his discovery? So absolutely changed, his skin a different fit – how could it not show? She could see, surely.

She was listening to the man again. He looked at her in her new role, that of the desired wife. Again she broke into laughter, and he couldn't bear to wait. He, Geoff, usually so controlled!

'Claire!' he managed to say, walking up. 'Hello.'

'Ah Geoff, how lovely to see you.' She took his arm in a light, cocktail-party hold and turned him to face the man. 'Geoff, do meet Uncle Tim.'

Oh, but he didn't want Uncle Tim.

Laura was trapped with old Miss Price from next door. They were sitting on the verandah, and over the grizzled head she could see all the people standing around in the garden. Actually it was rather peaceful with Miss Price, because one didn't have to make an effort.

'. . . so I tried the green ones,' Miss Price was saying, 'and quite honestly they were the size of saucers. Never was anything so huge. Two whole glasses of water it took to get the wretched things down. Three after meals, and then the capsules with my glass of milk.'

'And did they work?' Laura asked, a quarter of her listening and three-quarters thinking of Mac arriving tomorrow and the amazing time they'd have in the house all alone. By the time her parents had got to their posh hotel he would be here. *Here.*

'Did they work? My dear, you've no idea!' Miss Price shook her head sorrowfully. 'My tummy just acted and acted. Quite honestly, dear, I was scarcely out of the bathroom all day. But of course I pulled myself together this evening because it was such a special occasion and I just had to see my dear Laura and Claire again.'

'Heavens, couldn't you stop taking them if they make your, er, tummy act?'

'Well, dear, I could stop, but – '

Laura stiffened. She clutched her glass. She stared out into the garden, she stared out through the people, her eyes glued on a figure standing near the gate. It was talking to her mother.

It couldn't be. No, surely not. Not *him*!

Rosemary was enjoying herself. Many people had complimented her on her daughters and her decor, and though she knew they were just gushing she couldn't stop feeling pleased. And then the food was disappearing fast; it pleased her to feed people; she'd missed that since her daughters had gone. She thought: I wish I'd made more of those little gherkin biscuits, though.

Rosemary hovered a moment and looked at the room; she moved out into the garden.

'Ah! Colonel Ray.' Such a dear, and such a nice-looking young man with him. His nephew, it must be, but how he'd grown! Just right for Laura.

So where was Laura? She scanned the faces for her. But her eyes came to rest on someone else who was standing over by the gate. A scruffy youth, it looked like, with a bag over its shoulder.

She turned to the colonel. 'Marvellous to see you, but could you both excuse me just a moment? I've seen the man who's supposed to be fixing our verandah light.'

She hurried over towards the figure. Yes, it must be. Even scruffier in close-up.

'At last!' she said when she was near him. 'We thought you were never coming.'

'Pardon?' said Mac.

'Well, I did ask you to come before five, you know. I rang up specially.'

'Er.'

A long silence; Mac, glassy-eyed, looked at her. 'Erm,' he said at last. 'Are you Mrs Jenkins?'

'Of course I am.' She looked at him with distaste. He looked so dirty and everyone else looked so clean. 'Look, what you'd better do, I think, is just to fix it as quickly as possible without disturbing anyone. Really it is *too* bad that you had to come so late. I told you, you know.'

Mac fiddled with his bag. 'Erm, I didn't know you were, like, having a party.' He gazed helplessly at the mass of faces and then at hers, puckered with irritation, in front of him.

'But I *told* you! That's why I needed it fixed before six. Honestly!' She looked at him. Really he did look half dotty, his mouth hanging open like that. Quite stupid. 'I suppose you don't know where the light is.' And his shoes! She'd just seen them; heaven help her carpet if he went into the drawing-room. 'You'd better follow me. Come along.'

Ah, there was Laura. But why was she rushing up so breathlessly? Had something happened?

'Hello!' panted Laura. She looked from one to the other; several expressions passed over her face. 'Have you introduced yourselves?'

Rosemary froze. There was a silence, a very long one.

At last she whispered: 'What did you say, darling?'

'This is Mac,' said Laura brightly, over-brightly. 'A friend of mine from Bristol.'

Rosemary stared at him, speechless. Then she laughed. It was the only thing she could do. 'Good heavens!' she cried, extending her hand, 'I'm dreadfully sorry. How absolutely idiotic of me! I had no idea.'

Mac started chuckling. It was his sort of situation, this.

'Who on earth did you think he was?' asked Laura.

'The electrician, actually. I think it was that canvas bag that did it.' No wonder he'd looked gormless, poor thing. 'Do come along, Mac, and have a drink.'

'Yeah, I'd like that.' Mac hitched up his jeans and followed her. Laura walked behind, her mind busy. And when her mother had left them on the verandah she sat down beside him.

'Gosh, Mac!' she hissed. 'This is a turn-up! Why on earth didn't you wait until tomorrow when I told you they'd all be gone?'

'I forgot,' said Mac. Then he leant towards her. 'Hello, my sonner.' Before she could flinch (all those people!) he'd given her a big kiss. 'I've really missed you.'

Her confusion melted away. She gazed at him. He'd missed her! He'd actually said he'd missed her.

She watched him as he reached over to the table, poured a bowlful of nuts into his palm, threw back his head and swallowed them in a gulp. So relaxed he looked, but underneath it all he needed her. He'd said so.

Mac munched for a moment, gazing with interest at the decidedly kitsch fountain in the middle of the goldfish pond. 'So this is Harrow,' he said. 'Your nest.' He looked at the pond. 'Your spawning-ground.'

'That's right. Comfy Harrow.'

By and large she'd been enjoying this party more than she'd expected. But now he was here everything had changed. He showed it up somehow with his insouciance, the way he'd swallowed the peanuts as if he'd been starving for weeks, the way he was now yanking up his socks with their great gaping holes. He was so real compared with everybody else. They were both so burningly real, sitting here side by side. Everybody else looked suddenly cardboardy.

She must get Claire to meet him. Claire was the only one who wouldn't seem cardboardy. Where was she?

Claire hadn't noticed the Mac episode. There were so many

people, so many faces from the past. And of course there was Geoff. He wasn't beside her at the moment; instead he was walking around with a bottle, refilling glasses. She didn't have to see where he was; as he moved about she could feel him with some sixth sense. And funnily enough his helping like this made him closer, more of an ally, than if he'd been standing right beside her.

And those snatched glances! Glances over people's heads, glances when she was going into a room and he was coming out . . . so rich, those glances were. They confused her.

At the moment she was talking to Mrs Varley, a figure from her childhood. She hadn't seen her for years. All she remembered of her was an extraordinary laugh at dinner parties. In those days she and Laura, chilly in their nighties, had leant over the banisters for hours and listened to the noises that wafted upstairs. Mrs Varley's laugh had been the best; a bray that ended, abruptly, with a snort.

She wasn't laughing now, she was talking. 'You know, Claire, I'm simply consumed with admiration! You being a teacher. And in such a frightful area. Doesn't everyone get – well, knifed in the cloakroom in schools like that?'

At her own facetiousness Mrs Varley exploded, the same bray-and-snort that flicked Claire back in time. In fact, when she was a child Mrs Varley had been little more than a fascinating noise buried in an otherwise blank adult. But now she was grown up she, Claire, was noticing other things; the way for instance that Mrs Varley's hand fluttered nervously to her mouth, and the way that an unexpectedly kind smile followed the bray-and-snort. The way, in fact, that she was filling out around her laugh.

This was happening to everyone tonight. Odd to stand here, gin-and-tonic in hand, and see how all the old familiar adults were filling out. Years ago they'd just been towering shapes, each characterized by something – an intriguingly hairy mole, a funny laugh. And they'd been so easily divided, too. She'd known by a sort of scent which ones would and which ones wouldn't help her with her Meccano.

Holly, wandering round with her tray of sausage rolls, looking up at faces – did Holly still see them like this? Mrs Varley left and Claire stood for a moment, longing for enough time to talk to everyone, all these half-remembered faces of her childhood. Faces in the drawing-room, faces on the verandah . . .

Who was that? Laura on the verandah sitting huddled with

somebody who, Claire knew instinctively by the way they were leaning together, must be the celebrated Mac. She didn't recognize him and he looked marvellously out of place, so it must be Mac.

But what was he doing here? How intriguing! She must investigate.

'Extraordinary things, cocktail parties,' Laura was saying. 'Stick a bunch of people in a room, wind them up and buzz, whirr, they're off. Gabble gabble. Just look at them. They've all got that fixed stare; nobody's listening to anybody else.'

Mac gazed into the garden whose twilit trees were becoming pleasantly blurred after his third glass of wine. 'Mmmm.' He stretched out his legs.

But Laura was feeling uncomfortable. Mac must be sneering at it, surely. After all, what could be more sneerable than this bunch, so comfortably suburban and so comfortably middle-aged? She had nothing to say to them when she was little and she certainly had nothing to say to them now. Not now Mac was here.

'Just look at them,' she said, focusing on Geoff who looked so bland and polite chatting to someone in the garden. 'Nothing's really happening to that lot at all. Nothing's real.' Compared to me and Mac, that is.

But things were happening. Things were real – unbearably real for Geoff. He paused and looked up through the trees. Though the garden was darkening, the sky remained radiant with a flame-like sunset. It caught at his throat. It looked just like, well, streaky bacon.

Fancy thinking of comparisons! But probably he'd got it from a book. He knew he was the least imaginative person in the world. It was just that tonight he was noticing things; everything had grace. Not just the obvious things like the lovely fountain in the pool and all the flowers, but things he didn't usually bother much with, like the branches of the trees and the colour of the sky. It was something to do with Claire being so very near him and yet so far. Even the people, these strangers, even they were enveloped in a kind of glamour. It was as if they were all here especially for Claire and himself, especially for this tremendously important moment in his life. Everything, down to the last biscuit on the plate he was holding, seemed *significant* somehow. If only he could express himself better.

He could see Claire. She was walking over to the verandah where, as far as he could make out, Laura was sitting down with somebody. He must go over and talk to her. About anything – it hardly mattered.

He drained his glass, murmured some excuse probably rather abruptly to the man beside him, and launched himself into the crowd.

'Hello, Geoff,' said Laura. 'This is Mac. We're just discussing,' she lowered her voice, 'how to smuggle him away.'

'Ah,' said Geoff. How very confusing. 'Why?'

'Because he's coming for the weekend while Mummy and Daddy are away. But they don't know he is. And if he spends tonight here – well, it would make him too apparent. I'd have to explain him.'

'Ah,' said Geoff again. He ought to say something, but what? So difficult to concentrate with Claire so close beside him. 'Well . . .' He looked at Mac who was blowing a succession of smoke rings, grey and quivering, into the darkness. 'Why doesn't he go to a nearby hotel?'

'Too expensive,' said Laura.

'A friend's house?'

'Don't have any. Not real friends. Not round here.'

'Hmm.'

They all looked at Mac as if he were some stray puppy that had suddenly landed on the doorstep. Appealing, but a problem. The smoke rings – expert ones, they were all admiring them – shivered and dissolved. No one had any ideas.

'I say,' said Geoff suddenly. 'It's dark out here. What's happened to the light?'

'Bust,' said Laura.

Geoff didn't like things not working. He climbed on to his chair and fiddled with the bulb socket. Suddenly they were flooded with light.

'Well done!' Claire was smiling at him as he stepped down and dusted his trousers. 'We can think much better in the light.'

She looked at him. He got things done, did Geoff. She liked that. She glanced at his capable hands and then at his face, which was smiling at her.

Now that they were illuminated Laura felt uneasy. People could see them; she must think quickly. 'Tell you what!' She turned to Mac. 'It's very warm tonight. Why don't you go down the road to the Rec – I mean the park – nip over the wall and wait for me in the shelter there? It's not far.'

Mac considered this. 'You mean, doss down there? Well, why not? Just snitch a bottle of the old – ' he lifted his wine glass, 'to keep me company.'

Laura got up. Funny how she didn't want him to stay in the house while her parents were there. He could, quite easily. She could act as if he were an acquaintance; they could make up the spare bed. It was just that she didn't want to bring the two halves of her life together. Simpler to wait until her parents had left.

They dispatched Mac out of the side gate and watched him as he ambled quite happily down the road, a bottle of Dan's 1969 Côtes du Rhone under his arm. The darkness swallowed him up.

'He seems nice,' said Claire after a pause. 'Nice and gentle.'

'Oh he is!' cried Laura, willing her to say more. But she didn't.

As they returned to the house Geoff, emboldened by being in on the sisterly secret, linked his fingers through Claire's. In front of Laura and everything. Claire flashed him a smile – an encouraging one, he thought.

The guests were thinning out when they got back. Soon the room was emptying and the hall echoing with goodbyes. Geoff and the sisters started clearing up.

A hush fell on the hall and Mrs Jenkins returned. Geoff helped her stack some glasses on a tray.

'Whatever happened to that strange young man?' she asked Laura over her shoulder.

'Oh,' Laura's voice was casual, 'he just dropped in.'

'How odd.' Geoff and Claire exchanged looks over Mrs Jenkins's head. He felt quite giggly – he, Geoff, usually so *ungiggly*.

Suddenly Mrs Jenkins stopped. 'Goodness, who on earth got the verandah light working?'

Geoff looked modest.

'Geoff did,' said Claire.

Mrs Jenkins turned to him. 'How *very* clever of you! My husband couldn't get it to work at all. Whatever would we have done without you tonight!' She went on: 'You're staying to supper, aren't you? You must. You've been such a help.'

Geoff gladly accepted. Tonight his wooing was being done, as it were, at long distance. But it was easier like that. Scintillating conversation, he knew quite well, wasn't his forte. How much easier to fix the light and get Claire to smile at him for *that*. Much easier.

Thoroughly into his role, he was enjoying clearing the drawing-room when he couldn't help but hear hissing whispers from the direction of the kitchen. In no way did he linger as he passed the door, but angry whispers are so much more penetrating than their whisperers think them to be.

Mrs Jenkins's voice: 'Honestly, Laura, it really was a bit much! Mrs Wilson *so* wanted to talk to you. Marion's planning to go to university, you know, and Mrs Wilson was *so* keen to get your views on Bristol.'

'Well, I gave her them, didn't I?'

'Hardly! A few curt words and then you turned back to your odd friend. Really, at least you could've been polite. I felt so ashamed.'

'I was polite, but Mrs Wilson was such a drag. Everyone was. They either bored me to tears with their stomach pills or else they spent their whole time throwing up their arms and screaming "How charming! I'm sure psychology must be *fascinating*!" '

'Goodness, you're so intolerant. It's us, darling, who are supposed to be that, not you.'

'Ha ha. Honestly, it infuriates me how you both get angry if I say what I mean, if I'm honest, if I don't gush away all the time. You think the most important thing in the world is to say the right thing, never disturb anything ever. It makes me sick.'

But both Geoff and Laura felt better after the quarrel; Geoff because he could communicate more, Laura because she could communicate less. For Geoff, hearing these hissed hostilities made the whole Jenkins family less perfect and therefore more approachable. And now, consuming scrambled eggs off canapé plates and finishing bottles of wine made him feel so included; the meal's very informality made him feel less of a stranger. And Claire . . . smuggling Mac out had left her disarranged, her barriers down, less of a cocktail-party girl. He dared approach her now. In fact, he was driving her back to Clapham after supper. He'd ask her to marry him then. Or anyway, he'd edge towards the subject. He could do that tonight, after all this.

Laura felt better because the sharp words had sorted every-thing out. Silly, those untidy feelings, that uneasiness about having Mac to stay, those sudden moments of warmth towards her parents. Silly to see-saw about, not knowing on which side she stood. But now she knew, for weren't her parents hopelessly in the wrong, stupid and social?

What a relief that was! She felt quite calm now. Free, too. Funny how unsettling moments like that Scrabble moment could be, when they all seemed just right together. Well, she wasn't going to be friendly now, not when they'd been so bourgeois about the party. She could sneak Mac into the house tomorrow without feeling peculiar about it. Guilty and things. Not her.

After supper she crept out to visit Mac and bring him a blanket and cushion filched from the drawing-room. Wild she felt, wild, free and deliciously cleansed of uncertainties. She could see Mac sitting on the grass, a blacker shape in the blackness. She ran across the Rec and flung herself into his arms.

And full of Daddy's Côtes du Rhone, warm and sensual, delightfully lawless, they struggled together on the damp Harrow council turf while the lights from the neighbouring houses looked down on them sternly. Trembling, they fumbled each other's clothing apart; it was thrilling, it was unspeakably uncomfortable, it was shameless.

And serve them right, thought Laura as she walked home later in her damp and crumpled dress. 'Serve them right!' she called out loud to the stars and the ordered silhouettes of their street, not realizing how pleased she was to reach such a neat conclusion.

twenty-one

'Now Laura, if the light man calls, tell him we've fixed it – at least, kind Geoff has. And remember to water those seedlings over by the pond, darling, and bolt the back door at night, oh and don't try to open that funny window that's jammed and your father says – says – he's going to unjam. And, let's think, feed the dog and put some of that Baby Bio stuff on the plant in the hall if it looks feebler . . .'

'Good grief,' laughed Laura, 'you're only going away for two days, you know.'

Her mother looked up at the house doubtfully, fussily. 'I'm just worried about leaving you all alone. Do remember to lock up.'

'Perhaps a mad rapist'll get in,' Laura chuckled. Perhaps he will. 'I am nineteen you know.' She felt so cheerful this morning.

They seemed to take a hundred years to leave but at last they were gone. Badger stood beside Laura and wagged his tail at the departing car that in a few seconds would be passing the Rec. Passing its shelter. Little did its passengers know it had a swathed and chilly occupant. Swathed in their blanket, too. Laura smiled.

She watched the car turn the corner and then she was off. Down the road she ran, her feet thudding on the pavement. Birds sang, the sun shone, Badger danced and barked around her, excited at her sudden energy. He wasn't used to her running.

At that hour the Rec was deserted. Deserted, that is, except for the rows and rows of daffodils, her yellow conspirators, her rustling witnesses that whispered together as she ran past them over the grass. The dew sparkled and the birdsong rang out loud enough, she was sure, to deafen all Harrow and shake up every suburban slumberer. Let them be shaken up! She laughed out loud. The most radiant of mornings and she herself, free at last.

Actually, the shelter was empty. Or was it? In the sudden gloom she could see nothing distinctly. Perhaps the whole thing had been a dream. Now she thought of it, it did seem most unlikely – Mac in the shelter; Mac in Harrow at all. Could yesterday really have happened?

It had. She could see the blanket now. At its bottom lay the empty bottle.

Then a whistle behind her; a rustle of bushes. Mac's face appeared behind the foliage. She looked at him, sunlight haloing his hair. He stepped out. 'Top o' the mornin',' he called, zipping up his jeans. 'Nature called.'

Carefully he stepped through the bed of daffodils; he picked his way through them, for he liked plants. Their yellow heads nodded.

'Hello,' she said, awe-struck at her Easter vision. It was going to be a strange weekend, she knew.

'And hello dog,' he said.

She introduced them.

'Wotcha, Badger me lad.'

They fetched his things and walked back, arm-in-arm across the grass and past the asphalt place where as children she and

Claire had played for hours and hours on the swings.

'Were you all right?' she asked.

'Bit on the chilly side, but some intriguing night sounds. Cheeps and patterings. I got up and watched the spiders this morning in their webs all sparkling; it was nice.'

This park, the Rec of old, whose tiniest crack in the asphalt was etched in her memory, whose most secret tunnels through the bushes had been her commonest route, today it was as if she'd never set foot in it before. He'd known it too, but in such a different, Mac-like way. Familiar old Harrow; today it was the strangest of countries.

They walked up the street. The day was starting. From the houses, Saturday morning noises . . . from the Hacketts' the sound of a vacuum cleaner; from the house where those new people had moved in, the buzz of an electric drill and the sound of some-one trying to start a lawnmower; from Marion's house (here she hurried) the noise of a transistor from the downstairs room they called the den. How busy everybody was, busy and blameless! Sounds from the sunlit vista of Saturdays, reassuring in their known-ness. Whatever was going to happen in the tranced house known as Greenbanks, the rest of Harrow was carrying on as usual. Soon the corner Co-op would be full of faces, housewives weighed down with necessities, neighbours inspecting the bin of Special Offers. They were all the same, Miss Price, Mrs Hackett, Marion's mother: Saturdays to them were a list of tasks. More brightly coloured, perhaps, than the monochrome weekday ones, but chores all the same. Things to be Done.

Not like us! Laura hugged the stolen cushion.

Indoors, though, it was different. Just slightly so. The whole place was silent in rather a stealthy way. Dark too, because her parents hadn't drawn back the curtains before they left.

They hovered in the shadowy hall. Though she'd only run out of the house ten minutes before, she felt a different person now she'd returned with her uninvited guest. Outdoors they were free; indoors they might be thieves. Who on earth could be watch-ing? Of course, nobody.

They both hesitated. Could he be thinking the same? Surely not.

'I'm starving,' he said.

'Heavens, I forgot you haven't eaten for days.' She took him into the kitchen which was sunnier and less watched somehow. More a normal room. But it still looked odd with him sitting on top of the washing-machine – would he break it? – swinging his legs.

'Posh, isn't it,' he observed, gazing round at the gleaming surfaces. 'Straight out of a colour supp.'

'Is it?' Yes, it must be to a stranger – no, not a stranger: Mac. She wished it were all a bit humbler; she felt impelled to apologize for everything.

'All those gadgets. Wow.'

'But they often go wrong,' she said.

'Any leftovers? I fancy some more of that caviare stuff.'

'No, we finished it all.' She remembered the quarrel then, and felt reassured. 'Let's rummage around for something.'

'Hey, what about this?' Mac was crouching at a cupboard now. He lifted out a tin. 'Prawn Curry and Rice. Just Heat 'n' Eat, it says.'

He inspected it, curious as a child, reminding her of that first day in the supermarket. For the slightest thing he did she adored him. The way he held it up, brows quizzical. But today they were at Greenbanks and she felt uneasy about him rummaging about like that as if they were stealing. Ah, but it thrilled her too!

'Prawn Curry at nine o'clock!' she laughed, stirring the saucepan.

They sat down on the back steps while they ate. Nobody ever sat on the back steps; they either sat in the kitchen or on the lawn. She surveyed the garden from this low and novel angle. 'Shall I show you things?' she asked. They finished their curry and wandered out into the garden.

'This is the sandpit. We played here for hours. We made little towns for my Dinky cars.' She liked to volunteer childhood facts, she realized. Despite herself she wanted to link Mac to this garden and her former life. The thinnest thread perhaps, but she needed to join them somewhere. 'I had a huge box of Dinky cars. Wherever you dig here I bet you find one. Dinky cars and Badger's turds.'

Mac didn't dig for the Dinky cars, though. Instead he made swirly patterns in the sand with a stick. When they got up the sandpit was swirly all over. It looked different now.

'And in these hollies,' she went on, 'I threw away secret things, like stuff I didn't eat at lunch and threepence I pinched once. Nobody could ever find them there.'

'Uh-huh.' Mac peered into the depths and flicked his smouldering butt-end into the leaves. It disappeared and she thought of it lying amongst the half-eaten bits of cauliflower, surely fossilized by now, and that ancient threepenny-bit. Odd to have Mac with her, flicking butts into her wood, putting swirls into her sandpit. It was altering her childhood.

But she'd grown beyond sandpits now, hadn't she? Grown out of this house too. Mac didn't fit here, but then neither did she. Misfits, rebels, the pair of them! As they walked to the house she squeezed his arm.

Back in the darkened drawing-room Laura didn't bother to open the curtains. It was mysterious like this. It wasn't right, but it was mysterious. What could the time be? Who cared?

Mac pulled some cushions on to the floor and lay down, leafing through *Good Housekeeping*. ' "Tempting Roasts for Your Man to Come Home To",' he read out. 'Hey, why can't you make me a tempting roast, Laura?'

'Because you'd never eat it, stupid. You'd never come home at the right time or you'd be pissed or – '

The phone rang. They froze and stared at each other with sudden surprising guilt. For a moment they couldn't move, either of them.

Laura pulled herself together. Why should I feel guilty? She rolled over and picked up the receiver.

'Rosemary darling!' A voice crackling down the line.

'Hello. Actually it's Laura here.'

'Oh, *Laura* darling! It's Mrs Wilson here, you know, Marion's mother. I was just phoning to tell your dear ma what a really super party it was.'

'Oh, I'm so glad you enjoyed it.'

Mac had rolled over behind her. He started to run his hands up the inside of her jumper, up the back. 'Mmm,' breathed Laura.

'Sorry? I didn't catch that. Anyway, Laura darling, your dear ma always does things so very well, I think, don't you? Perfect company, delectable food . . .'

Laura spluttered something. Mac's hand was edging round to the front of her jumper now, inside it, all warm and groping. And he was making little hissings and nibblings at the back of her neck. It was agony not to giggle.

'. . . and she'd taken so much trouble with the house and garden, hadn't she. It looked so delightful . . . charming . . .' The voice was trailing off. 'Anyway Laura; Rosemary's not there, is she? No. Well, I *do* hope you'll come round and see us very soon. Marion's awfully looking forward to seeing you again . . .'

'Ha!' Perhaps an odd reply, but that was all she could manage, what with Mac's hands now zeroed in on target. Whoops.

She put the phone down and rolled over, giggling. 'An idiotic friend,' she told him, 'of me mum.' Mum? She never called her Mum, always Mummy. Until today, that is. Why did she feel the need to call her Mum today?

'Actually, I suppose I'd better write that down.' She disentangled herself and reached for the pad under the telephone directories. The pad was there as it always was. So was the pencil, 'A Present From Bangor' it said up the side, it had been hanging on its string there for years getting shorter and shorter. A wooden sliver of family history, that pencil. Despite everything she was still part of it, this house with its pencils and pads and tiny routines. Despite Mac lying back on the cushions, fascinatingly inappropriate, despite her jumper rolled up like a woolly necklace, this *was* her home.

She wrote the note, she went outside and wedged it into the curl of the banisters where such notes were always put and then, in a flurry of normality, she watered with Baby Bio the plant in the hall. Her mother was right, feeble was the word for what it was looking.

'Hey.' Mac poked his head round the door. 'How about a drink for *us*, then?' An endearing hopeful look.

'What? At eleven o'clock?' She paused with her watering-can.

'Well, why not? I ask myself.'

Back in the drawing-room they opened the door of the cocktail cabinet. They gazed in awe at the rows of bottles, a radiant panorama lit from the back. 'Pretty hideous object, isn't it,' she said. 'Vodka? Campari?'

And just for a moment they hesitated, both of them. They looked at the proud and neat rows, at the silver shaker, at her father's special little thing for chopping up the lemons. Both of them faltered.

'Shall we, my sonner?' Mac asked at last.

Laura rallied. Wasn't she the reckless one, heedless of shadows? 'Of course we should. He can afford it.'

She reached for the Campari. It felt like stealing the church wine but she wasn't going to feel doubtful, no. No little tugs.

She wouldn't even open the curtains; it was so tranced and twilit like this, so wicked to be islanded in the middle of the floor, sipping, in the half light, their bright pink drinks.

Badger sat on the floor beside them and, courteous as always, thumped his tail whenever they looked in his direction. He was an old dog now and had taken care of Laura through her youth. Now he was taking care of them both, and when Mac got up he too heaved himself to his feet with a creak and a grunt. Respectfully he followed as this new occupant of the house wandered round the room.

'Hmm.' Mac had come to rest in front of one of Dan's watercolours.

'What do you think of it?' asked Laura. She didn't tell him her father was the artist.

A pause. 'Well,' he said. 'It's a bit, like, on the corny side.'

Quite true. It was! She knew there had to be a word for it. It was dreadfully corny. Nobody had ever dared admit that before. All his paintings were.

She jumped up. 'Let's not look at any of them any more,' she cried, and walked from one little painting to another, turning them round so they faced the wall. Quite calmly she did it, not stopping to think.

Badger sat on the floor thumping his tail at this new game. Always courteous he was, and pleased with anything, but then he was a dog.

'Ah, that's better.' Laura threw herself down on the cushions. She kept her eyes away from the walls with their rectangles no longer of cottages amongst hills but of cardboard backing with Winsor and Newton printed on them. Daddy couldn't watch them now.

And his paintings really weren't much good; she'd always known that.

Funny how playing-fields are always muddy, Claire thought. Or else iron ruts. And always those rows of poplars. Funny, too, how she'd been roped into taking the girls' team for a netball practice. Was there something about her face that made her so obviously the sort to agree, on Easter Sunday, to trundle off in a coach to these nameless suburban playing-fields and skid about in the mud vainly blowing her whistle? Obviously there was. Who cared, though? He'd proposed.

Geoff had proposed.

'Miss!'

The ground thudded.

'Watch out!'

Bodies hurtled past. She blew her whistle.

What a day! Sun, blue sky, a mist of green on the poplars and a brighter, more determined green on the grass that had escaped being turned into mud. And he'd asked her to marry him.

Keep your mind on the game, Claire. But she'd had no idea it was coming. A complete surprise. *Did* men propose any more? Today, in the sunshine, it seemed such an unlikely thing to have happened.

'Miss! It was 'er fault, wasn't it. You sawl'

'But miss, she pushed!'

Claire joined them where they stood, stamping and steaming like ponies, filling the air with girlish sweat and Woolworth's 'Affair'.

'I didn't!'

'You did!'

'Didn't! Just lost me balance!'

'Oh yeah? You pushed. Didn't she, miss.'

'Girls! Don't be babies. Here, Elaine, you take the ball.'

They surged off, their aromas lingering. Claire stood in the mud, lost in thought. What had she replied? So dazed she'd been, sitting there in the car. She hadn't looked at his face, just at the cracks of light between the curtains all down the Clapham street. Slivers of light. *Do you really mean it?* She had a suspicion she'd said that. How very stupid. And then *Oh dear, just let me think for a bit, give me a few days*. How ungracious that must have sounded. What a dope she was.

Thud! The ball landed at her feet.

''Scuse me, miss!' A gasp, a whiff of 'Affair'. The others surged round. 'Janice! This side! Quick!' A muddy struggle and then they were off, bobbing up and down for the ball. She liked them like this, when for an hour their dull adolescence slipped from them and revealed their faces shiny and alive. Their bodies revealed too, with such mauve and childish knees. Just for an hour they were children again, freed from the selfconsciousness that usually weighed down on them, their communal burden.

But back in the changing hut the selfconsciousness was re-applied with the make-up. Max Factor Pan-Stick was applied to glistening faces. Pink legs disappeared into smart flared trousers. Friendly plimsolls were taken off and replaced by ferocious black platforms that resembled surgical footwear. Mirrors were produced.

Standing there with her whistle, Claire suddenly felt rather solitary. How she longed to talk to somebody. There was a phone in the hut; why not try Laura? It would be nice just to hear her voice. She wouldn't tell her about Geoff – not yet, and not by phone – but they could gossip about the party and perhaps just mention his name; talk *around* it. That would be enough.

'Laura? Hello. I say, how are you getting on there? Have Mummy and Daddy left?'

'Oh yes,' came Laura's voice, faint as from Australia. 'Goodness, they left aeons ago. Aeons.'

'And you're having fun without them.'

'Telling me. It's fantastic, doing just what we like with no one to boss us around. Isn't it, Mac?' Muffled mumbles. 'We're just about to grub about for some lunch. What are you doing?'

Claire told her.

'Gosh, poor Claire. How tedious, and keen of you.' More mumbles. 'Mac says you're the kind that keeps Britain great.'

'What have you been doing?'

'This and that. Mac had a weird time in the park, didn't you Mac.' More mumbles.

Claire felt shut out. She couldn't talk about Geoff now, not even indirectly. Not with them both mumbling together like that. She liked Mac but she couldn't say anything with him there. And they didn't even call it the Rec, they called it the park. That made her feel more shut out than anything else.

The girls were ready. They lounged around, their faces no longer shiny and pink. Now they were matt and orange. She felt a pang for them.

And on the coach back she thought of Geoff's words. They still seemed unlikely – more unlikely than ever; as a snapshot by long perusal loses its resemblance to its subject and becomes a mere emblem, so Geoff's words, after a morning's repetition, had become a mere chant going round and round in her head. They had been said, hadn't they?

'Where are we dossing down, then?' asked Mac that night.

Laura hesitated. She'd been thinking about this. In fact,

she'd been thinking about it all afternoon. 'Well . . .' she began. 'My bed's ridiculously narrow. We couldn't possibly squeeze in there. Not possibly. We'd be hanging over the edge. We wouldn't be able to breathe.' She paused. 'So I thought we might just as well use, er, me mum and dad's.' A silence. 'After all,' she went on, 'it's just sitting there all empty, just waiting to be used. It seems immoral for us to be all squashed up when we could be, well, not squashed up.' She kept her eyes on the wall, hoping to convince herself.

'Sounds logical,' he said.

Of course it was logical, Laura told herself as they walked upstairs. Of course it was, she thought as she pushed the door open and hesitated on the threshold.

The room was immaculate, as it always was. The bed, large and inviolate under its quilted satin counterpane, stood squarely between the two windows as it had stood for as long as she could remember. It had creaked with her conception and the conception of her sisters. It had stood there before she was born, before she even existed. It was the very centre of the house, its secret heart. How could she?

Easy! thought Laura, plonking herself down on it and feeling the satin sighing and settling around her. She threw herself back on the pillows and, twisting her head around, gave a challenging stare to the photos in their silver frames on the wall. One was of her parents' wedding day, war-time uniforms and her father looking innocent and Adam's apple; another showed herself as a baby, fat smile and nothing to hide.

She went over to the dressing-table and sat down. Behind her Mac had washed and was climbing into bed. She switched on the lamp whose frilly shade matched the curtains and she started brushing her hair with her mother's brush. A dab of scent? She picked up the bottle and then, after a moment's pause, she put it down. To actually use her mother's smell . . .

In the mirror she could see Mac's wild hair against the pillows. He looked as incongruous here as he'd looked in the blood clinic. But it was not as simple as that any more, not in this house. She looked at the hairbrush, at her mother's dark hairs mingled with her own. How complicated it was! She put the brush down.

Conscious of his eyes watching her from the bed, she pulled off her jersey. For a moment she sat there gazing at her breasts. Beyond the angle of her shoulder she could see, in the mirror, his face and his soft brown hair that she would soon be touching. Her eyes returned to her breasts. He was looking at them too, she knew. Suddenly just gazing at her body excited her. His body and hers; that at least was simple, thrillingly so. Their sensuality amidst such neatness, their nakedness in this over-clothed room; especially her *parents*' room! She lingered there, just gazing in the mirror at her bare shoulders and breasts, while he lay waiting for her in the big bed.

But when, a few moments later, he lifted her parents' sheets and she slipped between them, she closed her eyes as she reached out her arms.

The next day, Easter Sunday, catastrophe struck. Later Laura found herself blaming it, with a puritan logic she thought she no longer possessed, on their sacrilegious night in that bed, their fornication in a setting so totally tabooed that nobody had even put it into words.

It started gaily enough. Laura suggested they take Badger out to Harrow Common; they got into the Morris; she had just reached the end of the road and was turning right when Mac said: 'Give us a go. Be a devil, my sonner.'

'But you can't drive.'

'Yes I can. At least, I know how.'

'You haven't got a licence.' That sounded prim, so she added: 'Anyway, you don't know the pedals or anything.'

''Course. That one starts it and that one stops it.'

'And this one?'

'That's the clutch. I know all about that too.'

'Honest?'

'Honest. Go on. I'm an ace driver, my sonner. You'll be amazed.'

The sun shone, the trees waved their branches, Badger's yellow eyes in the driving-mirror danced with eagerness. Why not? she thought.

Into the passenger seat slid Laura; into the driver's seat slid Mac. 'OK bud, over to you,' she growled. 'Show us her paces.'

With a jerk the car sprang forward. 'Hey, watch out!' she cried.

In a shuddering series of jerks, jerks like huge hiccups, the car juddered across the road.

'MAC!' she screamed. 'BRAKE!'

In sickening jumps it jolted across the white centre line,

across the other side of the road and in a final spasm crunched into a parked car.

A loud, horribly loud crunch.

They straightened themselves and sat still for a moment, staring through the windscreen. Badger wagged his tail and barked at this jolly game.

Laura didn't look at Mac. Slowly she got out of the car and walked round to the front. Wordlessly she stared at the crumpled bonnet, at the shattered lights, at the buckled bumper of the beloved Morris. Then she stared at the parked car, at its caved-in door and the handle that hung on a wire, pointing downwards like a finger of doom.

She heard Mac getting out and standing beside her. 'Monkey's bollocks, I'm sorry, my sonner. Honest. What did I do wrong?'

'I suspect you didn't find the brake.' She stared at the car, not at him.

'Hmm. Just like the dodgems.' Probably he was trying to smile but she didn't look. 'Come on,' she said. 'I'll back it out.'

She got into the driver's seat. A jerk, then an ugly grinding noise and she eased the car from its nuzzled union. She parked it on the other side of the road. Badger's tail was still wagging; it made her feel even more irritable.

'Well,' she said, 'what shall we do?' He'd bashed it up, so he should have the ideas.

'I dunno.'

By now faces had appeared over garden fences. Someone, no doubt the owner of the car, came out into the road.

'One thing's for sure,' said Laura. 'It's got to be me that's done it.'

'Why?'

'Because otherwise I'll be prosecuted for letting you drive, stupid. If I say I drove it I'll only get a fine.'

'I'll pay.'

'You can't,' she replied witheringly. 'You haven't got any money.'

This was so true they both lapsed into silence.

The shadow of the man fell across the car. Laura got out. Mac stayed inside.

And as she explained in detail how her foot had slipped off the pedal, and as she saw the superior look on the man's face, perversely she wished that Mac would burst out of the car and cry 'I did it! It wasn't her fault!' It would be foolish of him but at least it would be, well, positive. Chivalrous. But chivalry, as her father so frequently said (just then she felt a pang; *he* would have taken care of everything), chivalry seemed to have died out nowadays. And of course it would only get them into worse trouble if he did. Much more sensible to stay in the car as he was doing, ruffling Badger's hair and avoiding everybody's eyes.

Addresses were exchanged, apologies given and finally Laura drove back to the house. Inside the drawing-room, for the first time that weekend, she opened the curtains to let in the light. She needed to think clearly. Mac sat next to her, humbly, but her mind was on her car, and Claire, and her parents. By comparison Mac seemed flimsy.

'Forgiven me yet?' he asked with a hangdog look.

'I suppose so.' She gave him a watery smile and turned back to the window from which she could see the car, its blunt nose crumpled. It was real, that car, its caved-in metal and shattered headlamps were real, just as the pound notes and the no-claims bonus that would pay for it were real. More real, suddenly, than her sunny Bristol room where she could play at home-making, and its non-husband coming home in his silly uniform.

But most of the time, of course, she felt just the opposite. It was she and Mac who were the real ones; only they knew how to live. All the other lives, those lived behind trim hedges, lives like those of her parents, weighed down, hemmed in, busy with trivia, those were mere existences. Weren't they?

Later that day Mac left for Bristol. Laura cleared up the house, made the bed and turned the pictures the right way round. She opened the windows. She put the cushions back on the chairs. By the time her parents returned the house was looking as welcoming and as boring as it usually did.

Her father took the bags upstairs to the bedroom. Laura thought of its satin counterpane, smooth now. Holly hugged the dog. Her mother bustled about. Then they gathered round the pretend logs in the drawing-room and her father made them Martinis.

'So what happened to your car, then?' he asked, quite cheerfully because he'd enjoyed his Easter.

Laura said: 'I bashed it up.'

They waited for more. None came, so her mother asked: 'How?'

'Well, my foot just sort of slipped off the brake.'

'How extraordinary, darling. You're usually such a good driver.'

'It just did.' How uncomfortable she felt lying, and even worse seeing her father's cardigan shoulders. Feeling tense, too, whenever they looked around the room in case they saw some relic of Mac.

Her mother left the room to prepare the supper. Laura could hear the kitchen sounds she'd heard a thousand times before . . . fridge being opened, mother murmuring to Badger, bowl clattering as he ate his supper . . . more fridge noises, water running, then a clanking of saucepans. Sounds whose normality was heightened, tinnily, by her guilt.

And the worst of it was that her father would pay. The sounds grew tinnier; her guilt increased. He always did. I just play games, thought Laura, and if anything goes wrong I can scuttle home to safety. Complain I might, sneer at Harrow I might, but home I scuttle. And Daddy's always there, safe and reliable, to pick up the bill.

twenty-two

Marriage, the thought of it, changed things completely. Claire forgot what it had been like before Geoff had turned off the engine and, addressing the steering wheel with fervour, had spoken those words. Though she knew she loved him she hadn't yet given him an answer. Instead she dithered and drifted in a warm May limbo; it was like lying on her back in water, to one side lay one shore, to the other side the other, and just for the moment she was unwilling to turn either way and force herself to swim.

And as she drifted she watched. She didn't like herself for it, but she couldn't help it. Nothing was too small to be noticed: in restaurants, how much he tipped (enough; a sigh of relief here), in the car, what programme he chose on the radio (sometimes pop, occasionally classical and often, for he was very masculine, the Test Match). Love is not blind, she thought, it is analytical, exhaustingly so. Is he sometimes *too* masculine? Buttoned-up? Sometimes a bit pompous? Could some people, Laura for instance, call him dull? Once, when he was trying on suits in Austin Reed and one looked funny, she laughed and he was irritated. Was this significant? A pointer to the years ahead? For everything, like plants towards a window, now leaned towards the future.

In Austin Reed she thought she wouldn't marry him. Geoff's bothered expression, something twitchy about his shoulders, repeated itself, as in a hall of mirrors, far into the years ahead. But after she visited his mother she thought she might.

His father had died and his mother, who lived alone in leafy Finchley, was treated by Geoff in a courtly, ceremonious way. Affection had been translated into small deeds. He only half-filled her coffee cup, Claire noticed, and guessed that otherwise her trembly hands (she seemed remarkably old) would spill it. In such details Claire could glimpse, as pressing a button illuminates a street plan, a whole network of tender routines, taken for granted by their practitioners but a source of considerable pleasure to herself, their witness. His tact, unconscious and dignified, touched her; so did the way he folded his mother's newspaper at the right page before they left. How unlike most of her friends with their parents! He was kind; Claire loved him; she did say yes.

For a few days they enjoyed together their first large secret. They even house-hunted. Geoff prodded walls and she stood in gardens imagining the rows of hollyhocks. They were suburban gardens, for they wanted children and couldn't afford to live in the middle of London. But Claire didn't mind. She would do whatever he suggested, so oblivious was she; oblivious and warm and relieved to have made her decision.

And of course she longed for Laura. She must tell her the news, but not by phone. There was so much to tell; she had to see her face, her expression. 'Let's go to Bristol,' she said.

'By all means,' he replied. He often said things like 'by all means'. 'Actually I have some business down there in a couple of weeks. Why don't you come with me and visit Laura while I work?'

Until she'd spoken to Laura she didn't want to tell anyone. So they kept their secret for two more weeks. They went to Harrow for a drink one night and everything was bland and polite. Claire felt big with her secret; impatient, almost fretful with it, and longed again for Laura. Laura would shake them up!

Laura would have no time for How nice it must be to have an open car in this weather. She'd take one look and know what had happened. None of this polite chat and then a tinkle of ice as everyone, with a pause, inspected his glass before the next topic. How English they all were, herself included, speaking in code, oblique, skirting round things. Pleasant, but how could they ever get to know each other? Would Geoff and her father always nod, with a little smile, after the other one had spoken? Would they never disagree? It was at moments like these that she could understand Laura's hot frustration. Difficult to imagine Laura and Mac sitting here, keeping things so very safe.

And yet she did nothing, for she felt herself strangely in a limbo, suspended above normal life in this period after the decision and before the flurry of telling everyone. At school she drifted through the day . . . Roy, Lance, Clive, their faces floated in front of her, she could see their jaws moving as they chewed their gum, they might even be making belching noises; she must be talking to them, but she could never remember what she said. It was like a dream.

'Penny for 'em.' It was the biology master, gallant as always. 'If I may venture to say so, Miss Jenkins, you look a thousand miles away.'

She settled into an armchair and smiled vaguely at him, amazed how all men, even one so bald, had become mysteriously infused with Geoff-ness. She hadn't expected this, how all Geoff's sex was enhanced, made in some way more welcoming, by her passion for one of its number.

twenty-three

It always gave Laura a shock when Mac mentioned his parents. Part of his fascination lay in his self-sufficiency. Amongst his few possessions it pleased her to find knife, fork and spoon wrapped in a spotted hanky. So neat and self-contained he seemed, compared with those students whose identities, struggling like hers out of some parental mould, were all blurred edges. They dragged their upbringings around with them; Mac, his belongings in a hanky, seemed complete.

So the fact that he had parents there in Bristol, that his father had just retired from thirty years at Rolls-Royce, that his one sister had married and gone to live in New Zealand (all of which she'd collected, sieve-like, from conversations she'd otherwise forgotten) – all these facts, though in themselves hardly earth-shattering, were for her unexpected, and of course all the more tantalizing for that. She wanted to know more.

'I was on the 97 today,' Mac informed her when he came back one afternoon. Summer term had just started. 'It goes right past me folks' place.' He sat down in an armchair, threw his busman's cap on to the mantelpiece and stretched out his legs in their busman's trousers that her efforts to taper had only made odder. 'Shitting bricks, I was, that someone I knew would get on board.'

'Why?'

'It'd get to the old man, wouldn't it.'

'What, that you're a bus conductor? Would he be terribly upset?'

'He was pleased as hell I got into Design School. If he knew, like, I'd quit . . .'

'Why did you?' She felt like prodding again this shy subject.

'I told you. It was a real rat race. All closed in.'

Oh well, she supposed he must be right. It just seemed a bit sad.

'It froze up me painting, you see,' he said.

'Yes, but when's it going to unfreeze?' She kept her voice

pleasant but she felt impatience creeping in round the edges. For some reason she'd been feeling it creeping in quite often since the episode with the Morris. Or perhaps it had existed before and the car thing had just put a name to it. 'I've known you three months and all you've done is one drawing of me in the bath and two Airfix model bi-planes.' She added: 'You never finished the drawing, either.'

'That's what I was thinking,' he said, unrattled. He never got rattled. So mild, he was; sometimes it disarmed her, sometimes it didn't. 'I thought we might saunter down that way this afternoon and fetch the rest of my stuff. Some canvases and suchlike. I've got a couple of stretched canvases in my room.'

His old bedroom! She perked up. 'And I can come?'

'Why not? My mum'll like you because you're so classy.' He stood up, reached for his jeans and started undoing his busman's trousers. 'But I'm still at Design School, remember.'

They took the bus because the Morris was still in London being repaired. The conductor, who knew Mac, sat down beside them, produced a battered copy of the *Sun* and started reading out the jokes. Laura, laughing, saw the grey university buildings slide past the window. Much better to be here in the bus, she thought. Amongst real people, not suspended up there above it all, sealed into rooms full of billions of words, windows closed on the street outside, doors closed on life itself. She gazed out at the shop fronts. Ron Balls, Turf Accountant said one, *Tyres 40% Off!* said another, *Retreads Our Speciality*. Life itself! *This* was life, wasn't it? This rumbling bus, these busy streets, this marvellously free feeling – well, not quite free because that clock said 3.30 and she ought to be at a lecture now. Still, the guilt was just part of her bones nowadays; something to be lived with, rather than the hot sediment in the stomach that she'd felt in those early weeks of seminar-dodging. She could ignore it if she tried.

It was quite a suburban street actually, Mac's. Not as romantically working-class as she'd expected it to be. A good deal of crazy-paving about and flowerbeds edged with alternate clumps of white and blue flowers. Gnome country. Mac's house was particularly neat, its windows veiled by net curtains of a dazzling white.

After a pause the door was opened.

'Why, John,' said his father. Although she knew it existed, she had a jolt hearing Mac's real and more boring name. 'This is a surprise.'

'Just, like, thought we'd drop by. Get some stuff.'

'Come in, come in the two of you.' He looked as if he'd just woken up. As she passed him she smelt, stale on his breath, a lifetime of smoking. 'Just having my little nap,' he said. 'I'll call Mother.'

They sat in the front room while he stood in the hall. 'It's John, Mother, and a young lady come to see us.' In a moment he returned. 'Just making the tea, she says. Make yourselves at home.'

He looked at Laura expectantly and for once Mac remembered to introduce her. He shook her hand. 'And what's your line of business, Laura?'

'I'm at the university.'

'Ah, a college girl. Like our John here. We're very proud of him, his mother and I. And what is it, may I ask, that you study?'

'Psychology.' There was a pause and she felt awkward, knowing that he must be longing to talk to his son.

The silence was broken by Mrs MacDonald entering with the trolley. Odd to see Mac's features sunk into a softer, altogether more ample face. 'Nice to see you, Johnny,' she said. 'And your friend.'

'This is Laura.' Mr MacDonald patted her knee as if he'd just discovered her.

'Pleased to meet you, dear.' She leant across the trolley. 'You know, we haven't seen our John for such a long time. Four months is it, or five, Johnny? He's so busy at his Art College he never has any time for his old parents any more. Do you, dear?' Mac muttered something. 'They do the funniest things,' she went on, 'though you probably think it's quite normal, Laura, but I mean to say, when Johnny was living here, the things he used to put up in his room! Once it was sort of cobwebby things, wasn't it, Johnny, all made out of string. Yours truly had quite a surprise, I can tell you.'

That must have been Mac's first, enthusiastic term, before he went . . . well, *limp*. The word shook her.

'These students,' said his father, gazing fondly at Mac.

Oh, but he's not one any more, thought Laura, feeling embarrassed and avoiding everyone's eyes.

'Please help yourself,' said Mrs MacDonald. 'There's Maries here and Digestives. If I'd known you were coming we would have had a better spread.' She passed the plate to Mac. 'Go on, Johnny, I know you love the Digestives.' She leant over to Laura. 'Shall I tell you something, dear? When John here was little there was no stopping him once he'd got hold of a packet of Digestives. He loved them, didn't he, Father! Diggies, he called them, and he'd crumble them up and then mash them with his tea and – '

'Hey!' Mac was roused to protest.

' – a greedy little scamp, he was.'

A greedy little scamp! How different from now. Laura tried to picture a smaller greedier Mac stuffing himself with soggy biscuits. Things had altered since then; less consuming of Diggies, more consuming of booze. She looked at him. What else had altered?

Mr MacDonald settled back with his cup and asked: 'How's it going at College then, John?'

Laura stiffened.

'Fine, fine,' answered Mac.

'Getting on all right then?'

'Uh-huh.'

Laura shifted in her seat. It was dreadful, this pretending. This non-communication too, for when she looked at Mac's face she saw it was closed; shut off from his parents.

Mr MacDonald put his cup carefully back on its saucer and felt in his pocket for his cigarettes. 'You know, John, your mother and I are very proud of you. We're not the ones to make a song and dance about it, but I think you know our feelings.' Laura felt a stab. She looked out of the window at the neat, painfully neat garden. 'I know we don't see too much of you nowadays, it's only natural, of course. I can appreciate that you've got your diploma in a few months, all sorts of possibilities coming up . . . I know that Mother will back me up when I say we don't expect a lot from you, but . . .' Obviously not one for long speeches, he paused, gazing at his smouldering cigarette. 'It's just that, well, with Jeannie gone off to New Zealand I know your mother would appreciate it, she misses her a lot, you see, I know she'd appreciate it if you saw your way to paying us a visit a little more often.'

'OK. OK.'

'After all, it's not as if we're very far away. It doesn't take long –'

'OK. I said OK.'

The conversation trailed off into silence. Laura felt awkward, urging Mac to say something, anything rather than just sit there like – yes, like a moody adolescent. Glum but prickly with it, definitely adolescent. She'd never seen him look like this before; but then of course she'd never seen him in his home.

Goodness, she thought, he's just like *I* am at home. How very surprising. She looked at him; he was frowning at the carpet in an irked, inward, put-upon way. How young he looked now he was here! Home seemed to change how people looked; he'd never seemed adolescent before, he'd always seemed so free, what with all his weird and careless friends, his general irreverence and his belongings tied up in a hanky. Rootless.

Ah, but he had roots and here they were, his parents, sitting staring into the fire grate in a silent, subsided sort of way. Her own parents flashed through her mind. She turned to Mr MacDonald. 'Will you show me your garden after tea?' She at least could say something.

'I'd be delighted,' he said.

But Mac, she could see, was already standing up looking restless. Past the age for Diggies, he was rolling a cigarette with those supple hands, bending over as he stood with that concentration that had once so moved her. Once? All she could think today was: He smokes too much.

She ate three Digestives to make up for him. Parents, she thought. Poor parents, all of them.

'C'mon, Laura,' he said. 'Let's get the stuff.'

'But I must see the garden.'

'OK, I'll get it while you see the garden.'

Laura hesitated, torn. She ought to see the garden. Yet how she longed to see Mac's room and, above all, his paintings! She paused. 'Oh,' she looked at Mac. 'I'll come with you, then.'

As they left the room she looked back at his parents as they sat, one to the right and one to the left of the tea trolley. 'Do we have to go now?' she hissed, following Mac up the stairs.

'Yeah, we'll get the stuff and go. This place gets on my nerves.'

'But your parents are so nice,' she said tentatively. They were.

'They depress me. Their dismal lives. Their nagging.'

'But they didn't nag. They only wanted to see you more often.'

'Huh.'

'But it seems quite reasonable really.'

'Hey, don't *you* start.'

She watched him going up ahead of her, up the narrow stairs flanked with wallpaper of a bamboo pattern. Hunched and moody he looked, even from the back. She felt disappointed. Somehow she'd expected him to be better than her about this. But he'd just sat there, with that look. And yet he felt so much for other people, children he met in the street, old dears in the pubs with their halves of stout, for dogs even . . . why then couldn't he feel for the two humans who above all others were closest to him? It must be *because* they were closest to him. Funny, that.

'Here we are then.' Mac's voice. 'Me masterpieces.'

Thoughts of parents vanished. Laura sat down on the bed, cast a swift look around the room (bare really, no sign of Mac's past, she was sorry to see), and concentrated. This was it then. Mac's inner essence was about to be revealed.

Mac started pulling canvases out of a cupboard. He leant them against the wall. She clasped her arms round her knees and looked.

She looked at one and then at the next. She looked at the next. She looked all the way along the row. She felt just the faintest sinking feeling. She could ignore it if she tried.

Mac finished propping them up and stood to one side. She could feel him watching her. She kept her eyes on the paintings. She looked at them, one after the other, again.

Heavens, they must be good! They *were* good, weren't they? They must be!

Round and round went the words in her brain. For some reason she'd always presumed they'd be good. She looked at them again. She hadn't realized how important it was that they *were*.

And yet the first thing about them that struck her – oh, but quickly she stifled it. They weren't bad. Well, not exactly. They were very *neat*, and painstaking. Not wildly original, no, but inoffensive. Abstracts, they were; tidy, planned-looking abstracts of big bright shapes, some straight, some curly, all edged with thick black lines. They reminded her of something. What was it? Yes: those Swedish tablecloths one finds at places like Heal's.

Mac was watching. 'Well?' he asked at last. She could tell by his humble look that he thought they were good.

She paused. 'Hmm. Yes, well, they're rather nice.' She clenched her fingernails into her knees. 'You know, I can never think of what to say about paintings. It always sounds stupid.'

'Sound stupid. It won't bother me, my sonner.'

The trouble was, she could only think of negatives. They weren't offensive, or vulgar . . . nothing positive sprang to mind at all. Somehow there wasn't enough in them to be positive.

'Er, they're very, you know, neat.' She cleared her throat, aeons away from her beloved Mac.

'Right. I was trying to purify things. Like bring them down to basics. No fuss.'

'Yes, I can see that.' She spoke slowly and considerately, for this was worrying. She'd always presumed that he'd be good or, if not strictly good, at least innovative and unexpected. Not boring and predictable.

There! Now she'd admitted it. His pictures were boring and predictable. As boring and predictable as Daddy's — actually, even more so, if she was absolutely fair. Daddy at least could draw.

'Glad you liked them.' Mac started stacking them back in the cupboard. Then he selected unused canvases for them to take back with them. She watched him, watching a certain substance and mystery drain from him. He seemed so ordinary all of a sudden, here in the ordinary room with its bamboo wallpaper.

But then, she thought, perhaps I've been unfair to him all this time, making him what I want him to be. Filling him with my own longings and glossing over the bits that don't fit. Claire wouldn't do that; she'd love somebody for themselves, she's clear and honest. But I can think anybody into anything. If I think them into being fascinating I bet I can find it interesting even when they're saying things like 'two sugars please'.

Laura got up, dismayed that from now on she would have to keep a secret from him. Beastly pictures; she wished she'd never seen them. She went over to the window. Below her the gardens stretched out side by side, narrow, neat, the furthest portion studded with vegetables. She really should have gone to look at his father's flowers with him; it would have given such pleasure and she would have avoided all this. But that was an escapist notion and, anyway, wasn't she being a bit histrionic? As if it mattered whether someone was a genius or not!

But it did matter a bit because it had exempted him from certain things. She realized that now. Parts of Mac that had disappointed her, like his not getting things done and being a bit feeble some-times and not even doing his bus conducting very well — these she'd seen not as failings but as the sort of thing one put up with when one lived with talent. The price of his Art. She'd presumed that he'd been sapped by his genius.

But then, couldn't one be just as preoccupied with bad pictures as with good? She was getting into awful tangles here. Perhaps, when she'd finished her psychology course, she'd be better at this sort of thing.

As they walked home a clock struck her eye. 5.30. One double-period lecture sunk without trace. Panic. She could rush over to the department and ask somebody for their notes. But would she ever be able to catch up? Just for a moment work seemed more important than it had done for weeks.

But they didn't take the way home past the university. They went another way and her worries, like the buildings themselves, started to recede. She could feel them draining away the further she walked. She had always been able to close her eyes to things she didn't want to think about. Soon, when she turned her head she could see that the department roof had become blotted out.

In front of them loomed the docks. They decided to go home that way. Past warehouses, echoing and empty, they found themselves walking; along narrow streets at times shadowed by walls and at times open to the glinting water. Cranes reared up above them, motionless; to one side rose a building desolate with its broken windows.

Suddenly she shivered, thrilled by the huge shapes and empty spaces; all at once they were changed into outlaws, for around stood notices saying KEEP OUT. Her petty muddles dwindled away, dwarfed by such vastness. Silly to be worried by things like that.

At that moment Mac took her hand and put it with his into his pocket. That felt nice and warm. No, she wouldn't go back to the department. He looked down at her and smiled, hitching his canvases under his other arm. Against this background, so romantic and forbidden, so reminiscent of a film set, he looked different from the way he'd looked back in that house. His wild hair, his smile, those KEEP OUT notices behind him, the way he was now clasping her hand in his pocket and starting to run . . . they were jumping now over some planks that lay strewn over the cobblestones. She kept close to him; he tightened his grip. She was flooded with love. Her laughter echoed back at them from the high buildings.

They were alone, but through gaps in the warehouses she could see cars and people streaming home after their hard day's work. She laughed again.

twenty-four

One day in June Great-Aunt Josie died. Mac gave Laura the telegram in the garden; she was sitting beside the lettuces. She looked at the dancing letters and tried to concentrate.

She'd been weeding. At least, she'd been sort of weeding but it was rather a struggle because she was stoned. Zonked. Really and quite definitely zonked. Definitely and definitively zonked. It was funny how long it took to get the weeds out. They kept on moving about before she could catch them. It made her laugh when they did that. Sometimes she did get hold of them, and then how funny it was when the whole plant came out with a nice rustling noise. All its tentacle roots came out with it, too.

Whoops! Looked like a lettuce. That was even funnier. Never mind. You could hold it up to the sun and shake it so the roots rustled again and all those little showers of earth came down. If you shook it over your hand, it tickled it. It speckled it with black. Such nice speckles.

She giggled. Do Mummy a power of good, it would, to have a drag or two of Afghani Black before she ventured into the old flowerbeds. It'd get things going with her dahlias all right. They'd all, well, sort of *welcome* her. My weeds welcome me, giving them their little shake.

'Hey, what d'you know?' she called over to Mac. He was lying on his back in a patch of grass; nice big thistles all round him. 'My Great-Aunty's died. Passed away.' She giggled. 'Popped off.'

'Wow.'

'Isn't that just something? Poof! Just like that. One moment she's there and the next . . .' She couldn't stop giggling. She looked down at the paper, crumpled yellowish paper with the writing all dancing. The letters just wouldn't stay still. 'I think she needs a proper burial, don't you? A little ceremony is called for at this juncture, right?'

From the thistles came: 'Mmm.'

Carefully, very slowly, she smoothed out the paper on her knee. It slipped but she could keep it there if she tried very hard. Then, her fingers like rubber, no bones in them somehow, she started to tear the telegram into strips. She was so careful and slow. It took a long time because it was interesting seeing just how narrow she could make them. Sometimes they broke and that made her giggle. Sometimes they didn't and that made her giggle too.

Slowly, with her fingers she scraped out a hole in the soil. 'Down she goes! Farewell, Aunty Josie.' In the hole she laid the pieces of paper side by side, very, very neatly. 'Jolly Josie, rosy Josie . . .' She scattered the earth over them and heaped it up so that it was a nice neat little dome.

'Farewell,' from the thistles.

She started putting little flowers on the dome but somehow she felt she hadn't quite grasped something. Aunty Josie, she was sure, wasn't rosy, but for the life of her she couldn't remember what she *was* like. It was so difficult to get hold of . . . but soon she'd feel better and then she would remember.

'I'm so sorry, Aunty Josie,' she said, smiling at the dome, trying so very hard to concentrate. 'I'm so very, very sorry that I can't quite remember exactly who you are. I *do* apologize for my pitiful state – ' she felt quite moist-eyed here ' – and I'm sure I'll be able to remember *very* soon. Extremely soon. Definitely extremely soon.'

She smiled at the little dome. It looked so pretty with all its dancing flowers; they seemed to be jumping all over the place. Aunty was in there somewhere.

The second telegram arrived that night. DUE FUNERAL COINCIDING HALF TERM HOLLY ARRIVING BRISTOL 11.15 TRAIN 18 JUNE. RETURN NEXT DAY.

Laura started. Holly coming to stay! Her head was almost clear now, and with a rustle and a thud all this afternoon's events settled down in her brain. Great-Aunt Josie was dead.

Dear Aunty Josie! She hadn't thought of her for years. Fresh out of storage, pictures and smells appeared. For a start, that musty pepperminty scent – somehow it was both – of her cottage at Windermere. Aunt Josie lived alone, and when they were younger

Laura and Claire would take the train up to visit her. At Josie's, things they couldn't do at home seemed fascinatingly allowed. There was the glass of thick sweet sherry to be wickedly drunk by them when they were only thirteen; there were the olives which were swallowed in handfuls because in some mysterious way they were adult; best of all, there were the shelves and shelves of books whose covers showed chisel-faced doctors and nurses with long eyelashes, that sort of thing. Aunty Josie had lots of books like that; they read them all but they never borrowed them to take home. Instinctively they knew that their father wouldn't actually forbid them; it was worse than that. He'd just look pained.

Aunty Josie sometimes came south and took them out to lunch, just Laura and Claire. Once she'd mentioned, casually, that it was one mile from their house to the restaurant. That fact stuck, as some facts do. Walking to lunch was therefore one mile exactly, and all distances after this became multiples of that one stretch of road – high hedges, low hedges, a shop with bread in the window (nowadays called Safeways), a shop with vests and clothes-pegs in the window (nowadays called Young Mods Boutique). Even now, though she was nearly twenty, this strip of Harrow had wedged itself in her brain and re-emerged usefully when her calculations needed it.

Illness, too; Aunt Josie was connected with that. She was a most satisfactory reader-aloud. Satisfactory meant she went on and on; to quench their shrill demands she even read the same book all over again, because sometimes if one was feeling really awful it was reassuring to listen to a story one knew backwards. Preferably Noddy. Long after feebler souls would have given up and said they had to cook dinner or something, her voice would be droning on. A good performer, Aunty Josie. The memory of her was still connected with being comfortably tucked up in bed at the wrong time of day.

Still is, actually, thought Laura, lying on the sheets, queasy from cannabis and longing for that stout figure. Not to read to her or even talk, but simply to be there and not to be dead. She could see her in the armchair, her sturdy legs slightly apart and, when Laura was older, embarrassing her when her friends were there because then she'd notice that Aunty's stocking-tops were showing. It didn't matter when they were alone, of course.

'What's it say, then?'

Laura jumped. Mac had come in. 'Oh, that my younger

sister's coming to stay tomorrow. My parents have to go up to Windermere for a funeral, and it's her half term, so she's coming here instead.' It was no good starting to tell him all about Aunty Josie; he'd never known her and now he never would. Of Laura's small rooms, one closed its door to him. Just for a moment she longed for Claire; there was simply so much they had in common. Again Mac seemed flimsy.

She gazed at the stack of books she should be reading. How would her psychologists classify Aunt Josie? Unfulfilled? Frustrated? Someone unable to cope with men except between the covers of Mills and Boon romances, someone even with latent lesbian tendencies? It made Aunt Josie quite different to think of her like that. Psychology did spoil things sometimes.

Speculatively she looked at Mac. 'Where shall I put you, then? You can't sleep here with Holly around.'

'Why not?'

'Honestly!' she answered primly. 'It wouldn't be right. Anyway, she'd tell my parents.'

Mac thought for a moment. He rubbed his hair thoughtfully, for he'd just had a bath. 'You could put me on the roof,' he said at last. 'I like it up there. I can bring your binoculars and see what the neighbours are watching on telly.'

He looked so helpful, and his wet hair stuck up around his face so funnily, and his body looked so lovely and clean that her heart quite turned over. She sat up, childhood forgotten, and held out her arms. 'Come here,' she said.

Laura always felt unreal when she kissed Mac goodbye before she went off for a lecture or before he went off for a day's work. The little doorstep ceremony, so nearly conjugal, deepened her suspicion that they were only playing. It was all so easy; a game of Mothers and Fathers financed (she hated to admit it, but it didn't seem to lose Mac much sleep) by her father. The fact was, Mac hardly made enough to keep him in beer, the amount of days he missed work, and so she paid the rest. Or to be accurate, her father did. Since she'd seen his paintings this had started to disturb her. Somehow it seemed more valid to keep a good artist than to keep, well, not *quite* such a good one.

It was the next morning. 'Are you sure you'll recognize her?' she asked Mac. She hardly ever asked him to do anything; it was seldom, in fact, that they had any outside complications.

But today Holly was coming.

"Course, my sonner. She gave me sausage rolls at that party; in fact, I got her to fill up me pockets with 'em.'

'And it's the eleven-fifteen train. I'll be back soon after twelve.'

'Trust old Mac. Bye-bye, my love.' He kissed her. She walked down the street, past the houses of all those neighbours she'd never met, busy family houses with Hoover noises coming from them. She arrived at the psychology department.

She had got to the stage where, as somebody who has once visited a far country likes to hear news bulletins about it, she had to have confirmation once in a while that such a thing as psychology still existed. And today of all days she had to go because there was a special lecture she couldn't, she mustn't, miss. Holly would just have to be met by Mac, that was all. It seemed inappropriate for him to do something practical and familified like this, but she had the desire to involve him.

Outside the lecture hall she bumped into Mike. 'Hello stranger,' he said. 'What have you been doing lately?'

Lying tranced in the rumpled sheets, she wanted to say.

'Oh, this and that,' was what actually came out.

'Come down to Hall tonight. I'm auditioning for my play.'

'What play?'

'Something I've written. I want you to be in it. I'll audition you with marvellous bias.'

'But I can't, I'm afraid. My little sister's coming down to stay the night. With us,' she added.

There was a pause. 'You're getting very domesticated,' he said, looking at her, making her feel shy. 'How is he, by the way?'

'Fine. He's a bus conductor now.'

Another pause. 'Anyway,' said Mike. 'It would have been nice. Lots of people have been asking about you. But nobody ever sees you nowadays. Shame, really.'

The words hung in the air. She looked at his bony, clever face; then he left and she watched him as he crossed the street. A faint sense of loss, but she ignored it.

The hall was crowded. She sat alone at the back, looking at the rows of listening heads in front of her, thinking of all that information going into them and all that information already there. Her own head felt quite empty, a clear pool round which swam, lazily, train times and bits of shopping lists. Panic rose; she tried to concentrate.

And as they all shuffled out she noticed, for the first time, how all the others seemed to know each other, and greet each other, and disappear into the Berkeley Café or the library with each other. And yet all she could do – or all she wanted to do – was to bundle her books under her arm and hurry away up the street, back to that charmed room.

Back to Holly, too. Squeezing past the pram in the hall she strained her ears for sounds from upstairs. Perhaps Mac had taken her out for a walk; perhaps they were sitting on the floor and Holly was helping him with his Airfix plane. In tender detail Laura could picture it. Mac was so easy with children; so childlike himself. In advance she smiled, loving them both.

Up the stairs she clattered two at a time and flung open the door.

Mac sat in the armchair reading *Beano*.

'Well, where is she?' She looked round the room.

Mac shuffled his comic. 'Couldn't find her.'

A silence.

'*What?*'

'She wasn't there, my sonner. At the station.'

'She wasn't *there?*'

'No. I looked.'

'What d'you mean, you looked?'

'I looked. She didn't come out of the train.' He looked down and fiddled with the *Beano* – the *Beano* she'd bought specially. Could she trust him with nothing? Did they have no claims on each other at all?

'Oh God!' she cried. 'You fool! I told you she was waiting in the train. With the guard. You had to go in and *fetch* her!' She flung down her books and rushed to the door. 'The train must have left ages ago!'

She slammed the door. She heard him calling out after her: 'Shall I come?'

'Don't *bother!*' Out of the front door she ran, down the road, round the corner and down the steep lane that led on to the main road.

Fifteen minutes later she was at the station. Her heart beat fast. The platform was empty. She looked wildly around, visions racing through her head – Holly raped, Holly murdered, Holly abandoned with the left luggage in some mid-Wales shunting yard.

'Hello.'

A door marked RAILWAY STAFF ONLY was open and there she stood.

'Oh, thank goodness!' Laura rushed over and flung her arms round the small stolid form.

'What's the matter?' Holly gazed up, unmoved. 'I say, steady on.'

'I thought you were lost. Ra – I mean, murdered. All sorts of things.'

'Of course I wasn't. What a silly thing to think.'

Inside the staff room a man put a teapot back on a stove; then he came out to Laura. 'Glad to see you, miss.' He patted Holly's head. 'I told the little lady you wouldn't be long. She was –' he gave Laura a significant and sage look over Holly's head ' – a touch, you know, anxious at the beginning.'

'I wasn't!'

'All right, Duchess. You wasn't.'

'I wasn't really, Laura. He gave me a cup of tea. And – ' here she looked polite ' – he showed me an engine. It was very interesting; he told me what everything did.'

Laura turned to the man. 'Thank you so much. I'm terribly sorry. My friend got, well, a bit confused.'

'Not at all, miss. We had a nice little chat.'

They went home, the bus rumbling up the hill and Holly gripping the seat in front and glueing her nose to the window. Despite the bravado she had been frightened, Laura could tell. That stolidness had been a bit too stolid.

She looked out at the passing shops that now and then, joltingly, froze. She would never marry Mac, she suddenly realized. Even if he wanted to, which she doubted; she couldn't quite picture that scene. She loved him but no, not marriage. Not for life. She couldn't spend her days rescuing Hollies; so to speak.

After lunch they crossed over the Suspension Bridge and went to explore the woods on the other side, with their giant trees and surprising wildness. Up a bridle path the three of them straggled and into a darker part. Holly dawdled behind, pulling off grass heads and practising her whistles. Mac strode ahead, hunched but jaunty, his curly hair rising and falling, rising and falling with each step.

All of a sudden the whistling stopped and Holly piped up:

'Celery raw develops the jaw but celery stewed is more quietly chewed.'

Laura laughed. 'Gosh, did you make that up?'

'No, it's Ogden Nash. I know lots more. We learn them after lights-out in the dorm.'

'In the dorm, eh?' Mac's voice floated back. He'd put on a silly grand accent. 'In the dorm?'

'Yes. Why?'

'With your lakky sticks and your Angela Brazils?'

'What's that?'

'And your Mummies and Daddies coming down in their Rovers and eyeing each others' hats – '

'Oh shut up!' Laura said this with surprising venom. It left Mac, she could see, unrattled. She looked over her shoulder at Holly who, despite the renewed whistles, looked rather solitary amongst the tall grasses. Why did Mac sometimes feel he had to say things like that? Funny. Funny, too, how sisters pulled one's loyalties; more than men did. Blood was thickest.

The path darkened; the trees closed overhead; the ground grew muddier and midges hung dancing in the air. They picked their way around the puddles. Tranquillity restored, Laura became conscious of squelching behind.

'Holly, what on earth are you doing?'

'Breaking in my shoes. They're new, you see.' Holly stood still to explain, ankle-deep in the blackest of mud. 'You must get them Experienced. First they need mud, especially smelly mud like this.' She squelched around a bit. 'Then you've got to stick 'em in water. Get them properly soggy.' She waded out of the mud and into a tractor rut brimming with oil-filmed water. She stood still, reverently. Lines shot through the oil and it separated into silken squares. 'Shake 'em around a bit.' She did this, thoroughly. She stepped out. 'Then they really should have some cow's mess, but they seem all right already.'

Laura inspected them. 'They certainly look full of experience now. So do your socks.'

She glanced at Mac. Perhaps he thought that only a spoilt private-school girl, used to an unending supply of new shoes, could indulge herself like this.

Ah, but she could never predict. His teeth showed white in a grin, and with a grunt he jumped into the middle of the water. Holly stared, then she giggled.

'Ha!' he shouted over the splashes he was making. He was stamping up and down. 'Now your mum can get at both of us for our dirty shoes!'

With a suck and a plop he pulled his feet out of the muddy water and started to run in great striding leaps, hair rising and falling, up the path and into the distance. Soon he turned off into the trees and Laura, who had taken Holly's hand and was running, laughing, after him, saw his wild figure flickering between the tree trunks.

They caught up with him eventually. He had thrown himself down on the dead leaves and lay, arms outstretched and the hair round his face dark with sweat, beside an inky pool.

'Lo! A Narcissus!' cried Laura, not expecting a reply to *that*, and with a crackle of leaves flung herself down beside him. Holly stood next to the pool and prodded it with a stick; Laura just leant on her elbow and contemplated that outflung arm with its faint miraculous veins. After she'd gazed at that for a while she undid, very gently, two buttons of his shirt to reveal a triangle of chest. She contemplated that.

He was such a mystery to her. Sometimes, that is. Despite misgivings and disappointments, despite the times he irritated her, he could still startle her with his strangeness. As an animal would startle her. She gazed down at his muddy plimsolls. Or like a child.

Holly's presence made it altogether an odd sort of day. Laura had seen so little of her lately that she couldn't predict at what stage of maturity Holly had arrived. At home Holly never seemed to change or get older, but that was probably to do with the backcloth. Hard to appear different in the same old nursery. It would take the sullen heavings of adolescence to shake up *that* fabric, and Holly hadn't reached adolescence yet.

But what stage *had* she reached? Laura tried to picture her suspended in limbo, a young female, and wondered what sort of day she should provide. A jolly day exploring and mucking about, or was she too dignified for that now? A gentler day, cutting things out of felt? A more adult day, gardening and chatting, perhaps even exchanging confidences about clothes? And should she, Laura, tidy up the room for her as she would for an adult, or leave it messy and explorable as she would for a child who would muck it up in ten minutes anyway?

Finally, being lazy, she'd left the room as it was, the only concession to her virginal visitor being the removal of Mac's more obvious possessions and the concealing of them in the cupboard. And she changed the sheets in honour of the chaste couple who would be occupying them that night.

And anyway, once Holly had arrived it was at once obvious that no effort had been needed at all. It didn't matter what they did. Everything was delightful to Holly because every rule could be broken. How fascinatingly lawless to lie on the carpet at one o'clock on a *sunny day* and read *Beano*! 'Holly, really!' her mother would have said. 'Just look at that sun outside.' But all Laura had said was 'There's a *Beezer* in my bag when you've finished that,' and gone on stirring something in a saucepan, something that smelt funny and foreign. Everything was so different here, even the meals.

And then she'd seen some ants walking across the floor, a little line of them carrying crumbs towards a crack in the wall. 'Oh look, Laura!' she'd said, and Laura had stopped stirring and knelt down beside her. 'Mac!' she'd called, and Mac had woken up (a funny time of day to be sleeping!) and got off the bed and they'd all knelt down together and watched the ants for ages. They both seemed really interested. Back home Mummy would have swept up all the ants with tut-tutting noises. But then, back home, there wouldn't have been any crumbs on the floor anyway.

After lunch they'd gone off into the woods, which was fun, and she'd broken in her shoes which she'd been meaning to do for ages when she was at a safe distance from Mummy and Daddy.

Then they'd come back and seen some chairs piled up behind a fence. Mac had climbed over the fence and taken some. 'Aren't you stealing?' she'd asked. 'I expect so,' he'd said, calm as anything. How naughty! It had made her feel quite peculiar. Nicely peculiar, she'd decided after a bit. And back in Laura's room they'd broken them up and had a real fire. At home it was just a dreary pretend one. This one was lovely.

And now they were all sitting round the fire and she was teaching them how to do cat's cradles. At home nobody would have sat with her long enough. Certainly not Mummy and Daddy at the same time. Mummy and Daddy were always looking at their watches. Mac didn't; he practised them again and again and got jolly good at them. Nobody told her to wash or anything boring like that; in fact, nobody got boring at all, except once or twice

Mac got funny about school. Questions like Did the girls have any power in the running of the school? And she'd said No fear.

Later they had another meal, sort of soupy stuff with bits in it. 'What's this funny branch?' she asked. She lifted it out on her spoon.

'Time,' said Laura, or something like that. 'It's a Herb.'

She sucked it. All new tastes today. After supper Mac went out and she thought he'd gone back to his home. Laura kept saying what a nice home he had. But he came back a bit later with a bottle. The fire had gone out because they'd run out of chair and it had got rather chilly. There was only one light, too, so she had to crouch on the floor to finish her *Beezer* while they poured out whatever it was into glasses. She had a sniff; it smelt horrid, like Badger's big jobs in the sandpit, and sick, and stuff the doctor had given her when she had tonsilitis – no, actually, it didn't smell like them, she was just thinking of all the worst things she could.

They took ages drinking it, as if it was *nice* or something and she, Holly, was feeling jolly cold by now because she'd not brought another jersey with her; but she couldn't get into bed because Mac was still there and she certainly couldn't get undressed with him there, no fear, because her bosoms were starting to show. So she found a book and looked at it beside the lamp. It had peculiar pictures in it of bare men climbing all over each other, and monsters.

'That's bosh,' Laura said, or something like that. 'He's good, isn't he?'

It was funny, they were doing such odd and rude things, she spent ages looking at all the rude bits. She never knew people did things like that. But she didn't like it much, it made her feel queasy. And anyway, to tell the truth she was rather sleepy. It was eleven o'clock and Mummy always made her go to bed at half past nine, which was soft of course, but –

'By the way, Holly, if Mummy and Daddy ask if anyone was here, just say Mac came to tea.'

'But he didn't.'

'I know, but say that. Please. Be a sport. Anyway, he'll be going, er, home in a minute. So it's nearly true.'

'OK,' she said, but she felt confused. Why must she say that? What was wrong with Mac being there?

She hid a yawn behind the violent pages of her book. How

sissy to look tired! Specially after the fuss she always made about going to bed at half past nine!

'By the way,' said Laura. 'Claire's coming tomorrow. She wrote and said Geoff has some business here so she's coming for the day. And they'll take you back to London in the evening.'

'Claire?' Surprisingly, Holly suddenly felt better. Somehow, Claire and Geoff meant things being done properly. And just for a humiliating, homesick moment that was just what she wanted. Silly, but she did. It was something to do with it being night and nobody minding what time it was, and that book and things.

She yawned again, and when she woke she was lying with Laura's legs all tangled up with hers and it was morning.

twenty-five

'Claire!'

They hugged each other, then stood back, each sister with so much to say.

'Excuse the stink, excuse the mess.' Laura led Claire into the passage. They squeezed past the pram and the potty cupboard. 'There's a family with about thirty children upstairs. They have a social worker visiting and everything.'

Claire picked her way over the curling lino. 'I feel I know this place, every inch, from your letters. Where's Mac?'

'Out for a walk with Holly.' It pleased Laura to link their names together, so that Mac was a part of them all. 'Let's go straight into the garden and wait for them there.'

They edged their way down the passage and out of the back door. 'And Geoff?' Laura asked over her shoulder.

'Seeing some client. He said he'll come here after lunch.'

Something in Claire's voice made Laura stop in her tracks. This Geoff business couldn't be more serious than she thought, could it? He seemed so much part of Claire's day, accepted into it.

Geoff. Mac. The names hovered round their speech, but for a moment they just let them hover. 'Here's my garden, then,' said Laura. 'Our garden.'

They stepped across some rusted iron spokes, the bowels of something long past recognition, and sat down in Laura's small square of cut grass.

Claire gazed round, smiling at the sun on Laura's lettuces which struggled through the weeds. Then she gazed at a clump of cornflowers; such intense blue – if she closed her eyes until everything went blurry, the blue still pierced through, 'It's idyllic,' she said. 'Your own room, your own garden, your own Mac. Do you feel all fulfilled and happy?'

Laura lay back on the grass and closed her eyes. 'I suppose so. Yes, I'm sure I do. It's just that sometimes I feel it's all a bit *too* idyllic, if you see what I mean.' She lay still. If for once I organize my thoughts, actually speak my doubts, won't that make them concrete? And then won't I have to do something about them? Better just to lie back and feel the sun warm on my arms and listen to the hum of the traffic.

But then she thought: Geoff must be amongst that hum somewhere. And she felt uneasy again, especially as she could hear Claire pulling up bits of grass. Claire, usually so straightforward, wasn't the sort to fidget.

Laura took a breath, kept her eyes closed and asked: 'What gives with Geoff, then?'

A pause, a long one.

'Well,' came Claire's slow voice. 'That's really why I came down here. I wanted to tell you first.'

Oh no, thought Laura. Oh *no*.

'You see. Well.' More grass-pulling sounds. 'Well, I was thinking . . .' She paused. A silence, but for the tearing sounds. 'What I mean is, Geoff and I were thinking of . . .' Another silence. The tearing sounds stopped. 'Amazingly enough, we were thinking of getting married.'

Laura let out her breath. Christ. She sat up and stared at Claire. Claire's eyes looked bright and enquiring; anxious too? She stared at Claire's hand, stilled on a clump of grass.

'Well?' asked Claire.

'Well, how about that! Claire! When did you know?' It hardly mattered what she said.

'Just a week or so ago. I wanted to tell you in person.'

'Hmm.' Honestly, she couldn't think what to say. So she said: 'Congratulations!' as if Claire were a total stranger.

The grass-pulling started again. Claire was watching her. 'Go on, Laura. Tell me what you think.'

'Honestly, I think it's all jolly exciting. Jolly exciting, I must say. What a thing to happen, eh? You and Geoff. Goodness.' She burbled away at random. 'He's very handsome.' She nearly added: 'And he's got such a lovely car,' which showed how hard up she was.

Avoiding Claire's eyes, she stared at the backbone of iron that stuck up through the grass. The sun went behind a cloud and she shivered.

'I can see his faults,' said Claire brightly. 'I'm very level-headed. Anyway, I've got faults too.' Oh no! Laura shouted silently, not like his! 'It's just that, although he may not bowl one over with excitement at first glance, one discovers more and more as time goes on. He's very very nice. Decent. He's so sensible. I like that.' She was still searching Laura's face; Laura, avoiding her gaze, could yet feel it burning her cheeks. Claire went on: 'It's all right for me, you see. I don't mind about intriguing lifestyles and all. He doesn't have to set the world alight.'

'Do you love him?'

'Of course I do,' she replied simply. 'And I do hope you will. Give him a bit of a chance. He's very English, you know. Sometimes you have to break through a sort of code.' She was still pulling at the grass. 'I know you'll love him too.'

'Goodness,' protested Laura, 'I'm sure I like him already. I think he's very nice, honestly.' How terrible to have to be polite to one's sister!

After a while Claire got up to wander about the garden. Laura felt suddenly lonely. All at once she and Claire were miles apart; it was the same desolate feeling as when Mac had shown her his awful paintings. From now onwards Geoff stood between them; from now onwards she would have to pretend about him. She could never say what she thought.

For Geoff surely was *boring*. Now Claire was down the garden she could sort him out better in her mind. Wasn't his the dullness she so despised, the well-nurtured dullness of Harrow? The most comfortable emptiness? She tried to picture their married evenings, Claire looking out of the window and Geoff totting up his Barclaycard counterfoils. Dead! Dead!

She threw herself back on the grass. Perhaps she was unjust; perhaps he was the type to blossom as a husband. After all, he was perfectly pleasant, not unintelligent, he'd care for Claire.

He'd had no brothers or sisters to loosen him up. Perhaps he'd improve; she must give him a chance.

She sat up and watched Claire walking towards her, brown hair billowing round her face. Oh, but nobody was good enough for Claire, with her unshowy, independent life! Claire, who never lost touch with her fellow humans whatever they were like, and who was so special just because she believed herself to be so ordinary.

Just then Claire started waving to someone behind Laura's back. Laura turned round. Mac had appeared at the back door with Holly. She got up. Claire approached, brushing the bits of grass off her skirt. Grass lay everywhere, green scatterings of her huge news.

Mac and Holly looked companionable standing there together; this warmed Laura. She also needed him at this moment. Bereft of Claire, he suddenly seemed more important to her. She ran towards him.

But as she approached, her warmth drained away.

'Hello folks.' Mac looked sheepish; he scratched his head. She could see at a glance that he had been drinking. There was something about his smile lingering forgotten on his face; anyway, she could smell the booze now she was this near. And she'd wanted him so much. He gave Claire a kiss; it would be, unmistakably, a beery one.

'Where did you go?' she demanded, feeling shrewish as she said it, the nagging wife.

He replied, unabashed: 'To the Downs.'

'Then where?' Her patient voice. 'Which pub?'

'Oh, just the Oak. On the way home, that is.'

'Where did Holly go? She's not allowed in pubs.'

'I sat outside in the garden,' said Holly. 'It was lovely.'

'What, all alone?'

'But I could see him inside. And anyway I played with a dog. It really was fun.'

But sinkingly Laura could see that Holly protested too much. She wouldn't have told her it was such fun if she hadn't thought it was odd. And from this she gathered that he must have spent ages in the pub; longer, for sure, than a quick one.

Oh Mac! Even the fact that his jumper was inside-out failed to melt her. As he stood there, scratching and blinking, she thought:

Is this what my father feels? This disappointment and feeling of sheer waste? 'Come on,' she said. 'Let's go in.'

They started towards the door. Just then they heard some thuds amongst the thistles, followed by a pattering noise. They looked up at the house; in an upstairs window they saw a figure sinking back into the darkness of the top room. Closer inspection of the thistles revealed eggshells and two tins saying Batchelor Peas.

'It's too much,' said Laura. 'They can't go on just chucking out their rubbish.' She turned to Mac. 'Will you go upstairs and tell them to shut up?'

Mac paused and considered this.

'Go on!' she urged.

He scratched his head again. He looked uncomfortable. 'Can't you go?' he said at last. 'I'm scared of that big bloke. He always gives me dirty looks when I meet him on the stairs.' He put on a persuasive face. 'Honestly, my sonner, he likes you. You do it.'

Laura blushed, ashamed of his feebleness – or of his gentleness – he became coloured differently according to her mood. She knew Claire must be thinking of Geoff and how he would have leapt up the stairs wordlessly, no hesitation. 'You're hopeless,' she said with a laugh. But it was important, for her. Claire was always calling Laura's life bohemian, but in truth it was bohemian only in its trivial things, like odd hours and harmonium playing. Its essentials, such as her feelings about Mac, were of the most ordinary kind. Nothing exotic about her disappointment, or her impatience, or her love. At the bottom she was exactly the same as everybody else. Whether that was a comfort or not she couldn't, for the hundredth time, decide.

Lunch had gone on so long that at three sharp, when Geoff arrived, they were just thinking about coffee. On the doorstep Laura didn't know how to greet him. Should she give him a kiss? He was now definitely in the kissing category. But she didn't dare, he was so tall and straight. Not unpleasant, though, at close view. She would next time. After all, he didn't know that she knew yet.

She led him past the junk, apologizing for it this time with a touch more smugness than she had with Claire. His leading such a very conventional life made her prouder of hers. Upstairs he shook hands all round, even with Holly. Holly looked pleased;

hardly anyone ever shook *her* hand. Laura poured out the coffee.

And as they took their cups, Geoff was informed that they knew. Congratulations were given, even Mac wished them good luck for the great unknown, and suddenly, sitting round the table, they were united. It was quite unexpected. They gazed into the brown liquid; as they stirred the sugar they were hushed, each gazing into his cup and into the mysterious years ahead. They sipped and drank as if drinking a sacrament. Claire and Geoff sat side by side, impressive; even Holly for an instant looked older. The weight of marriage had taken them all by surprise.

But the moment passed. Conversation broke out, Claire got up to clear the plates and the general feeling changed to: What now?

And the consensus was: The Zoo. An agreeable enough way for this little assortment, this motley fivesome, to spend the afternoon.

'My favourite place,' said Mac. 'Some truly amazing creatures.'

'I haven't been to a zoo for years,' said Geoff.

'There's an otter,' said Mac, 'who I have deep conversations with.'

'Really?' asked Geoff.

'And a very motherly giraffe.' Mac started foraging under the sink for some carrots, another farewell haul from the gardens. Getting them past the foreman, he'd told Laura, had been very cinematic. 'Let's bring these. They must get pissed off with all those buns.'

'But I don't think one's allowed to feed animals in zoos,' said Geoff. 'People give them the wrong things, you see. Their diet's carefully worked out, I've been told.'

A pause. Laura looked at him sourly. He was right, of course. Holly asked Mac: 'Can we see the white tigers?'

'Uh-huh. They're amazing, but snooty.'

'And can we stay a long time, not be hurried?'

Mac nodded.

'Good.' She did like Mac. He made things special, somehow.

Geoff was shuffling through his briefcase. 'Lucky I brought my camera along, wasn't it. Is there a shop on the way where I can get some more film? I only have six exposures left and I'd like to get the Zoo down on record.'

Laura looked at him severely. He was the sort of person, she decided, who only enjoyed something if he could take a photo of it. Document it. In fact he seemed to surround himself with apparatus. Now he was rummaging around for his umbrella, looking out of the window at the sky as he did so. She watched him, thinking of the series of boulders that must constitute his day, each one to be heaved aside or negotiated somehow. The equipment he used to weigh himself down! No doubt he was right about the possibility of rain. People like that usually were, whereas people like her got drenched.

She pushed back her hair and wondered why she couldn't be reasonable. He was only acting like any normal person, really. It was just that, because he was marrying Claire, she couldn't feel sensible about him at all. She mustn't exaggerate everything he did. She must try to make an effort, for Claire's sake.

'You'll like the Zoo,' she said, smiling at him. 'And on the way we have a lovely view right down into the Avon, with cliffs and the Suspension Bridge.'

'I shall look forward to that,' he replied, and smiled down at her from his tall and manly height. She could admire him, perhaps, if she tried. She must.

They left the house and walked up the road. At Geoff's car they stopped and gave the usual exclamations at its beauty. Yes, thought Laura, and at least Geoff can drive a car. She gazed with sudden sourness at Mac. She'd just discovered from Claire that the garage was still sorting out the damage done to the Morris. It would probably take weeks.

'Yes, she's not bad,' said Geoff, patting the bonnet, 'but there's an odd rattle in the ignition, and when something small goes wrong I always think it might be the symptom of some larger problem.'

Laura was pleased; he'd actually confided in them – even if it was just about a car. Claire was looking at the Lotus, her head on one side. She said: 'Like a dirty face suggesting that a person's knickers are grimy too.'

The others burst out laughing. All except Geoff, that is. He straightened up and stared at Claire.

'Sorry,' she laughed, linking her arm with his. 'It just slipped out.'

The problem is, thought Laura, he needs loosening up. He might be better then.

As they walked up the road Geoff, after a moment's hesitation said: 'I always think that with cars there are only two noises.'

He paused. 'Cheap noises and expensive ones.'

Never was a feeblish joke more heartily laughed at. And the longest laughs came from the two sisters, one who loved him and one who was intermittently trying to. They felt so relieved.

The famous film was bought and then they wandered along a gracious crescent that curved, columned and creepered, around the lip of the hill. Deep below lay gardens, tall trees and, still further below glimmered the next crescent. The houses might be mouldering but the harmony of stone and branches was lovely; an orchestration of man and nature.

'Claire, remember the last time we walked through these streets?' Laura asked.

'Of course, when we visited those pot people. It was raining and it was still beautiful.' How long ago it seemed when these crescents, then veiled in mist, had veiled the future too; before, in their different ways, each sister had claimed and been claimed.

'Found anywhere to live yet?' Laura asked.

'No, but we've started looking.'

Laura gestured at the view. 'Try and find somewhere as gorgeous as this. You must live somewhere beautiful.'

'Actually we're thinking of the suburbs.'

'Claire! No.'

'It's the only sort of place within our price range, isn't it, Geoff?'

Laura's eyes swept the landscape. Don't! she called out silently. This beauty is what you deserve. Don't let Geoff drag you down into the humdrum; pull him out of it instead. I can't have my sister living in a semi with a ding-dong doorbell.

'You see,' said Claire. 'We both want children very soon.'

Both. Several decisions already taken that she, Laura, knew nothing about. A lifetime of such decisions to come. Laura felt that lonely feeling again. Married conversations, unintelligible to her, from which girlish giggles would be absent. Conversations which, as the years passed, would grow denser with shared jokes and mutual happenings until they would be all but incomprehensible to herself, an outsider.

She was jealous; she had to admit it. She stole a glance at them; Geoff was bending his head towards Claire and pointing out something to her, something in one of the gardens. When we get our house we'll get one of those – the tilt of his head said that.

Claire nodded and murmured something. She, Laura, was with a couple now.

Geoff paid for them all to get into the Zoo and became, by this generous act, their leader. They hovered around on the tarmac waiting for him to speak. Not that they didn't feel he was the leader anyway; there was something unmistakable about his masculinity, coupled with Claire's desire and Laura's more spasmodic decision to bend whichever way he wanted and thus to please him. Already, wherever he turned they would have followed.

'White tigers?' he suggested mildly, unaware.

'Bet you 10p,' said Holly, 'they're not really white.'

'Done,' Geoff answered jovially. Laura felt that after lunch, with a click, he had put himself into a different gear, a Saturday-afternoon one, known as Recreation and Fun. His Saturday-morning gear must have been Commerce and Duty.

They saw the white tigers. Geoff took a photo, no doubt identical to a score already taken that afternoon, and gave Holly 10p because she was right about the whiteness. Obviously a man of honour.

'What now?' asked Geoff, rubbing his hands. 'Any preferences?'

'Chimps,' said Holly.

'Chimps it is.' He adjusted his camera strap over his shoulder and strode alert and purposeful in the direction of the chimps. How wispy Mac looked in comparison, meandering, his jumper still inside-out, and coming to rest in front of cages that the others were passing without a glance. Vaguely scratching his hair, he was oblivious to all humans and, waiting for him, Laura warmed to him anew. His absorption in the animals humbled her; they four were hurrying but he had time for everything. He was even talking to the sparrows. She waited, half impatient and half endeared. Often she felt like this.

There was a crowd round the chimps' cage, for one of its inmates was practising some particularly ambitious and elaborate faces. Sneers, pursed lips, screwed-up eyes, wriggling eyebrows, it was working through its entire repertoire in front of its admiring audience. Holly gripped Claire's hand, entranced; Laura called Mac over to have a look; Geoff raised his camera to his eye. The crowd pressed closer, staring with fascination at the rubbery contortions. Nobody seemed aware of the pair of cold and beady eyes buried in the folds of the face. Calculating eyes.

Without warning cheeks swelled, lips drew back, eyes gleamed and everyone standing near was sprayed with a spatter of evil-smelling saliva. With shrieks and giggles the crowd scattered; with a smirk, the chimp retired.

Laura, weak with laughter, turned away and suddenly noticed Holly. 'What on earth's the matter? What's wrong?'

Holly was crying. Her head was bent over and covered with her fists. Claire and Geoff clustered round. Claire sank to her knees beside her. 'Tell us, Holls. What is it?'

A pause, then muffled words. 'Some got in my eye and it stings.'

They stared at each other. Mac collapsed in chuckles on the grass. Laura and Claire looked at each other, on the verge of chuckling too. 'His *spit* went in your *eye*?'

Holly, still crumpled over her hands, nodded.

'Here, let me look.' Claire eased Holly's fingers apart.

'Ow!'

'Come along, Holly.' It was Geoff's voice, calm and no-nonsense. 'Stay still.' He took out his handkerchief – of course it was large and white – and twisted it to a point. 'Here we go.' He knelt down, looking big beside her, and they watched as he damped his handkerchief on his tongue and gently put it into the eye. Holly relaxed. 'You must lift the lid, you see,' he explained. 'There, now that doesn't hurt a bit, does it?'

Silence from Holly, who was actually starting to feel uncomfortable. It was dawning on her that she'd made rather too much fuss and, now she thought of it, it hadn't really hurt at all. Just surprised her. But she couldn't say so now. And she'd been trying so hard to impress everybody with how grown-up she was! If she was babyish they'd have to act special with her and then she'd feel out of it, a tagger-along.

Mac was still chuckling. 'I'd feel *honoured*,' he told her, 'you're unique. It's not everyone that has a bleeding monkey spitting in his eye, you know.'

Laura looked at him. Geoff at least got things done. She remembered once when she'd cut herself, how Mac had just gazed admiringly at the red blood on the yellow of her sleeve. He'd been genuinely surprised that the colours hadn't entranced her too. But then, at least he appreciated, he saw the colours, just as he appreciated and saw the sparrows. He was an artist after a fashion, wasn't he? That was the difference between him and Geoff. Geoff did; Mac looked. She giggled; and it *was* rather funny about the monkey.

They were walking back home now. Spread across the pavement, they were chatting. Would Geoff, Laura wondered, be the jealous type? It was part of the *Woman's Realm* appeal. It went with the open car and the straight nose.

She looked at Mac. Tranquil, harmless, he was springing along the pavement, rattling his baccy tin along the railings, on, off, in time with his own private thought-rhythms. No, nobody could call him jealous. Once she'd told him about her past amours. He'd listened with interest but with none of that studied non-reaction, that careful light laugh when one had finished, those tense little questions popping up unguarded at odd moments during the following days – none of those signals of the truly disturbed. She glanced from Geoff's tanned profile to Mac's hunched shape. Was Mac just not masculine enough to be jealous? Or was jealousy an emotion to be despised, anyway? She did remember feeling put out, though, at the time.

She put an end to these comparisons. They were taking up precious time when she could be gossiping with Claire who, she realized sinkingly, would soon be called Claire Hare and living in a semi.

Back in the room, the two sisters left the men sitting about in armchairs and began to prepare supper. 'It's all so quick, Claire. Tell me how it all started. What stage had you got to by that cocktail party?'

They started chopping vegetables. They worked well together; Laura didn't have to explain where things were kept. With some sisterly sixth sense, Claire knew. It pleased Laura to see on the soap dish their companionable rings, her assorted ones of twisted copper next to Claire's single diamond. From time to time one of them with automatic hand would reach out and stir the garlic and onions that glistened in the saucepan, or take a swig of wine from the smudged and shared tumbler.

'. . . and that was that.'

'A romantic story.'

They laughed, they chatted. Laura felt happy having Claire at last to herself. They were making risotto. The gay mound of vegetables grew under their busy fingers. Just for a while those two complicating males were distanced, despite their presence three yards away, leafing through newspapers. Despite the fact, too, that they were the subject of the conversation.

The risotto was cooked. The dishes were put on the table.

'FHB,' murmured Laura, looking at the food she was spooning out. 'Right, Claire and Holly?'

'What on earth,' Geoff asked, 'is FHB?'

'Family Hold Back. There's not enough risotto.'

'I'll FHB,' said Holly, 'if I can STP afterwards.'

'It's a deal,' said Claire.

'What's STP?' Geoff asked.

'Scrape the Plate, dope.'

'Holly!' cried Claire. 'How should he know?'

Sitting there, the two men suddenly felt united in being outsiders; this sisterly repast seemed to be governed by its own secret code. Infantile that code might be – FHB, STP, honestly! But its very silliness distanced them further, proving that it sprang from somewhere far deeper than mere taste, sprang indeed from the sisters' long and linked roots which no one, husband or lover, would ever quite reach. They'd done a million things together; they'd known this Aunty Josie who'd just died; how many other aunties, for a start?

For once Mac and Geoff were thinking the same thing. They might make new roots of their own but they'd never be tangled up in those deep, deep childhood ones.

On the journey back to London, Claire felt uncomfortable. This had nothing to do with Holly, curled asleep on her lap with *Beezer* still clutched in her hand; nor with Geoff, so capable in the driving seat. No, she was worried about Laura. As they passed the same verges her parents had passed eight months before, discussing the very same girl, Claire asked: 'Geoff, did she seem all right to you?'

'What do you mean?'

'Happy. It's just that she struck me as, well, too anxious about looking happy. A bit confused. She kept striking different attitudes.'

'She certainly made me feel as if I was doing everything wrong.' Now! With his foot down he was managing it. 7,500 revs! No doubt about it. The dial said so. Not bad, that. Into the red sector.

'Poor Geoff! I hoped you wouldn't notice. And then sometimes she was so nice. She's like that at home, you know. She's so changeable.'

'They both seemed happy enough to me. Quite idyllic really, if they can stand the mess.' He double de-clutched.

'I think that's part of the trouble,' Claire went on. 'Laura herself said it was almost *too* idyllic. Unreal, I think she meant. Despite the rubbish and the family upstairs. They just make her *feel* it's real life, the gritty stuff, but it isn't.' She was warming to her theme. She liked talking to Geoff about Laura; it cemented them round a problem and made him part of the family. 'She used to be a big fish in Harrow. Then she suddenly found herself at Bristol, amongst thousands of girls exactly like her, the same denim skirts. So she felt submerged and got out so she'd feel individual again.'

'You might be right there.' Really, compared to humans cars were so pleasantly simple. Things went wrong; all, in exchange for a certain number of pound notes, could be put right. People, especially great involved families like the Jenkinses, all discussed their problems as if nothing else existed. Heavens, they should lift up their heads and look around them. See some real problems.

Not, of course, that he wasn't interested in Laura. She had many of Claire's qualities, she was his future sister-in-law, he enjoyed her company and he was not insensitive to her beauty. It was just that she simply got too much attention for her own good. He said: 'Laura and Mac know that in Britain they can never starve. That's what I think.'

'You mean, they're basically secure so they can make rude faces at all the things that are in fact letting them live their lovely free lives.'

'Something like that.'

His voice held an air of finality; Claire had some sense. She stopped talking about Laura. But the trouble was, there was nobody she *could* talk to; everyone took sides. Geoff, her parents, none seemed to understand the delicate balance of good and bad in Laura's present life. People liked to put things into slots; they'd take one look and either dismiss it as irresponsible etcetera or extol it as liberated etcetera. Both were too simplistic, for Laura's life seemed a mixture of many things; even Geoff, adequate though he was proving himself in such conversations (much better than when she'd first known him), even Geoff disapproved too much to be very helpful.

'I've been thinking,' he said. 'Shall we go to Scotland for our honeymoon?'

'Yes! Yes!'

They talked about Scotland then. Geoff had it all worked out; a small hotel near Inverness (run by a friend of his aunt, so they'd get very favourable rates and of course the best treatment), and then a motor trip round the lochs, staying at the kind of inns Britain was supposed to have: whitewashed walls and wooden beams. They did exist, didn't they? The whole holiday a mixture of the practical and the romantic, for wasn't he both of these things, though he might keep the second hidden? It would be good to sweep Claire away from all those burdens that she took on herself – burdens of her sisters, and flatmates, and horrible schoolchildren. She even worried in case the people she saw in the launderette were lonely! She was so complete and strong herself she attracted people who clung, that's what he'd worked out. He thought about this sort of thing more often than people guessed, actually.

'Can we fish in a loch?' she asked.

'Of course.'

'And climb the purple hills?'

'Yes, except I don't believe they'll be purple yet.'

'And go out with a picnic in a small leaky boat?'

'I expect that can be arranged.' He wanted to call her *darling* but as yet he hadn't quite managed to slip the word easily into the conversation.

Claire clasped her hands together. A real holiday, and they could go exactly where they wanted. Alone and free, just the two of them. Alone and free, come to think of it, just like Laura and Mac. But Laura and Mac were different, for wasn't their whole existence a sort of holiday; yet, because they had nothing to holiday *from*, not a real one at all? In fact as unreal as Laura, lying amongst her half-hearted but sunny lettuces, had hinted?

twenty-six

One week later. It was Saturday night and already twenty past seven.

Hurry up, Rosemary! Dan twisted the car keys round his finger; he shifted his weight from one foot to the other; he waited, but impatiently. From the faint sounds upstairs he tried to guess how nearly Rosemary was ready. A tinkling clatter – she must be at her dressing-table now, fiddling around with those glass jars and pots of cream. Hundreds, she had. That meant the last stage of the ritual had been reached. A soft swish as she shut her jewellery drawer; the creak of floorboards as she stood up. Such familiar sounds, each accompanying an act he no longer had to witness to see. After twenty-five years of marriage they were as much a part of him as his breathing, and as much a part of the fabric of the house as the grumbling of the pipes and the sigh and scrape as Badger adjusted his position on the middle stair. At this sort of moment he always lay on the middle stair; he liked an eye on each of them.

Tonight, though, even Badger's sounds made him irritable. Steps overhead as she went back to the cupboard. She'd be looking for her shoes now. A long pause. Twenty-two minutes past seven. She couldn't decide which ones to wear. So clearly he could picture her, kneeling down and plucking at the heap with fastidious fingers (she'd just painted her nails and they'd still be wet), with furrowed brow drawing out shoes one by one as if she were drawing them out of a Christmas stocking. What did she buy all those shoes for, anyway? He never saw her wear half of them. Typical.

He missed Holly. She was always quick at getting ready; in fact, she despised any sort of preparation at all. In the hall she'd fidget with him; they'd commiserate together on the hopelessness of women and their boring preoccupation with how they looked. But today Holly, especially imported from school for the occasion, had gone ahead in Geoff's car, so he waited alone.

'For God's sake, Rosemary, hurry up can't you!' How peevish

he sounded! 'The table's booked for eight and the others left hours ago.'

'Bags of time, darling.' The voice floated down. Even when she was late like this she managed to sound brisk and superior. 'We needn't leave for five minutes.' How did she do it?

Laura and Mac (odd name that; still, Laura always did specialize in odd friends), Laura and Mac were joining them at the restaurant; they had come up from Bristol specially. And naturally enough, Claire had gone with Geoff. So there was just the two of them left to go together. The two old fogies.

'Get a move on, will you!'

'*Almost* ready.' That maddening sing-song floated down.

'Heaven knows why you're taking so long!' Tonight he not only felt irritable; he also felt assertive. He hardly ever did; it was something to do with going to a restaurant and footing the bill, also something to do with being the prospective father-in-law for the first time. He must do the thing properly. For Claire and Geoff. Claire Hare, funny how it rhymed. The fact that it rhymed made him even more irritable. He twisted the key-ring round and round his finger.

In the cramped darkness of Geoff's car Holly slid her feet backwards and forwards, backwards and forwards, in and out of her shoes. It was a fascinating feeling. Slip-on shoes! Proper grown-up shoes! Her very first pair. No babyish laces, no soppy straps. This was the proper thing. Mummy had bought them for her that afternoon; they'd gone specially to Harrods and she truly felt a different person now. At least three years older, like the girls at school said they felt when they'd got their first bra. She'd be getting one of them soon, too.

And staying up late, *and* going to the Post Office Tower Restaurant which was terribly high up, she could see it from the flats' roofs down the road. Someone said it went round and round too. How fast?

And all because of Claire being soft on Geoff. Sitting there all soppy in the front with her arm round him! Honestly, she couldn't see why she liked him so much. He was all right but he was like a lot of grown-ups. Interested in all the wrong things. Not like Mac.

Still he did drive nice and fast. He was talking about it now. '... round we go ... that's the job.' They shot ahead and round a corner. Holly was too wedged to sway.

'Just think,' Claire's voice, 'this is the first time we've all been properly together. The whole family and everybody knowing and celebrating like this.'

'Should be eatable, too. Should be, I mean, knowing the prices they sting you for in that place – whoops, watch it there!' Lights flashed by. 'Beats me how they passed their test!'

'In a way,' said Claire, 'I feel quite nervous. I wish we weren't going to such a grand place. It's always so difficult to relax, I mean, it would have been easier if Mummy just cooked something special at home. But I suppose my father wants to make the big gesture, do the thing properly. He likes to do that. Just hope we won't be too stiff.'

'These occasions are always on the stiff side, aren't they. Bound to be. Prospective son-in-law and all that. I'll enjoy it because of you. Darling.'

'Really?'

'You see, you always bring out the best in people. Darling.'

'Sweetheart!' She leant across and kissed his ear. Dangerous, thought Holly severely. And silly.

She got bored with listening to them and started picking at the car seat. But then she remembered it was Geoff's car seat and she oughtn't to pull out all the loose bits. Apart from its nice loud engine, Geoff's car was actually rather dull. It was too tidy and there was nothing to fiddle with. It smelt of cigarettes and some soppy man's scent he always wore. She preferred her parents' car; it smelt of dog.

She turned her attention back to her feet. Such lovely shoes! In, out, in, out slipped her feet, so easily; so grown-uply.

The sisters did look lovely in the candlelight, one had to admit that. Their beauty seemed increased by being repeated, with variations, in the three faces. Up in the restaurant they were sitting on the edge of an abyss, suspended above a void, for behind their seats and far, far below glittered the lights of London. So fragile, the girls looked, against that space which stretched out around and below them, the three of them poised at this historic moment.

Rosemary was looking at them. Especially she was looking at Claire, the orange glow of the city behind her. It was Claire's evening. A warm flush – of joy? Not exactly; more of significance –

a warm flush spread over her face, she could feel it. Hope my powder won't run, she thought. She also thought: hope, *hope* Claire will be happy.

Daddy, Claire realized with a sinking heart, was finding it all rather a strain. No wonder – meeting Geoff formally like this, Mac turning up and adding to the burden, coping with an elaborate menu – no wonder he had on his selfconscious look. He often got like this in restaurants; pubs, too. He was inspecting the menu; Claire watched him. Even in the dim light she could tell by the tilt of his head and his too furrowed brow that he was about to say something pompous. He was. He looked up, paused and stated: 'I always find duck acceptable, don't you? The *canard à l'orange*.'

'Right,' said Geoff. 'I'll take your word for it. Duck for me, sir.'

Claire stiffened. *Sir?*

'I can't understand these words,' Holly said in a clear voice. 'I don't know French. I just want some fish and chips.'

'Hush, darling!' said her mother. Mac looked admiringly at Holly.

'Don't be silly, Holly,' said her father. 'If you want some fish then I would suggest the *truite aux amandes*. That's trout, you know. A delicious fish.'

'Yeah, but I don't want it messed up with anything.'

Laura looked nervously at Mac. Was he suddenly going to say he wanted baked beans? She wouldn't put it past him. He was looking from face to face with an inner grin and she didn't trust him an inch. Not that she wouldn't giggle a bit if he *did*. How odd, too, he looked in his suit – at least, Mike's suit. He looked so uncomfortable in it, as if someone had sewn him into it then left all the pins behind. It had been an effort to get him to wear one at all, but she'd wanted him to so he wouldn't stand out too much. But how he hated suits, with a personal intensity, as if putting on some pieces of cloth made him into a different person, someone to be despised.

'Daddy,' said Holly, 'if I have some peas, will they be little ones like I have at home or big ones with potato in like I have at school?'

'They'll be perfectly delicious, Holly, whatever they're like. Now will you please choose? We're waiting.'

Mac said nothing. Laura thought: Am I disappointed? Then she thought: God, for a moment I'd forgotten. How could I?

Geoff leant towards Claire. 'Your parents are doing us very well, I must say,' he whispered. He pointed to the menu. 'See what I mean by the prices?'

Claire nodded, looking across at Laura and Mac. She could tell by Laura's fixed, smug look that they were holding hands under the table. Just for a moment she wished that Geoff would hold her hand. But she knew he wouldn't, for somebody might see and he'd mind that.

The wine list arrived and Claire, hating herself for noticing, still couldn't stop her eyes being drawn to her father's face as if to a magnet. It was a solemn face; she watched it with dread. He spent a lot of time over the list, turning the large shiny pages like a scholar. 'Any preferences?' he asked the young men at last.

'I leave it up to you, sir,' said Geoff. 'I'm sure you're the expert.'

Claire didn't look at Geoff. She turned her attention to the salt and pepper pots. She placed them in the mathematical centre of the table, concentrating on getting it exactly right. It must be that he was nervous. Mustn't it? Nervous like Daddy, in his different way.

'As long as it's wet,' said Mac, 'and made from grapes.'

Everyone froze. Laura looked down and fiddled with her napkin. There was hesitation all round, then thank goodness Rosemary laughed lightly: 'Yes, darling, none of us are connoisseurs. Just choose something you think'll be nice.'

Dan retired back into his wine list.

There was a general pause. Now that the ordering was over, everyone was feeling rather stiff and waiting for Dan to start asking the questions for this sort of evening, for really they had never talked much. Shouldn't he ask about job promotion, the future, the proper son-in-law questions? Though there was nothing about Geoff that she particularly admired, Laura felt a wave of sympathy for him at this moment, and another for her father.

Most of all, though, she felt sympathy for herself. What am I going to *do*? she thought.

Mac let go of her hand and scratched round his collar. In mid-scratch he caught the eye of a waiter, a sleek specimen who was standing about fancying himself. She saw Mac rolling up his eyes and making his imbecile's face. The waiter stared back unblinkingly. Mac grinned.

Laura didn't grin, though. She hardly noticed, for again she was thinking.

Dan looked at the bottle of wine. It was being held out in front of him in a caressing, expectant way, the waiter pausing for the affirmative he, Dan, should be giving. He looked at the label; Chateau Chasse-Spleen, it said. The words failed to cheer him. 1961, it said. Still he felt desolate. Does every father, he wondered, feel like this? The sense of loss? The unreasonable irritation with the young man? The excessive politeness with which one covers this up?

'Well, Geoff,' he began. He nodded at the waiter. 'I hope you realize how lucky you are.' He stopped and gazed into his glass. Some liquid, just a small dark pool, lay at the bottom of it now, and beside him he felt the waiter hovering. He gazed at the little pool; it made him feel rather sad. Really he ought to be enjoying all this.

'Accountancy's not my line,' he said. He drained his glass. It was delicious of course; he nodded to the waiter. 'Does it offer a young man like yourself plenty of scope?'

'Yes indeed. There's a lot of space to play around with in accountancy. Once you know your objectives you can branch out . . .'

Geoff knew his objectives; it showed. All of them could recognize that. The two men started talking and Claire relaxed. Not that she needed to be tense in the first place, really. Geoff was obviously impressed by the meal and hiding any nerves he might be feeling. What did it matter that she longed for one of Laura's messy, free-for-all sort of meals, even a quarrelsome one? In this place her father and Geoff, despite the talk passing between them, were just two unopened packages sitting there opposite each other.

Still, Geoff handled things very well, despite the *sirs*. She hoped Laura hadn't heard them. But he was so capable and most extraordinarily handsome. How she longed to hold his hand!

Just then her eye was caught by something Laura was doing. She stared harder. The waiter was standing beside Laura and – could she be seeing right? – Laura was actually putting her hand over her glass.

'What, no wine, Laura?' her father asked.

'Er, no thanks.'

'You don't approve of my choice?'

'Don't be silly, Daddy. I, er, just don't feel like it, that's all.' She laughed lightly. 'I've gone off it.'

At that moment she caught Claire's eye and Claire saw, with a shock, that she quickly turned and looked out of the window. That was what did it. That furtive look. Claire went cold.

Just then the starters arrived. A bevy of waiters appeared bearing artistic little arrangements elaborated with parsley and curled, impaled bits of this and that. Claire pushed the thought out of her mind.

Dan looked down at his prawns. Fat, rosy and complacent, they seemed to mock him. The luxurious restaurant, sumptuous food, velvety wine – all seemed inadequate substitutes for the loss of his daughter. Somehow their very deliciousness made this inadequacy the greater. Twenty-one years of her and suddenly she was gone. She might have lived away from home for a while but that was a question of geography not of ownership. He looked across the table. Ownership by a well-dressed, bland, alien male. A sensible-looking chap, no doubt, but still . . . No more laughing at his, Dan's, jokes; from now on she'd be laughing at Geoff's. If he ever made any, that is.

Dan glanced over at Mac. Now here was a different proposition. *Not* the sort of person to keep Laura in the style to which she'd been accustomed, one could tell that a mile off. Still, under all that hair he looked as if he might have something to say. If he, Dan, knew the code, that is. So many young people nowadays seemed to be operated by some secret key possessed only by each other. They sprang alive then, they actually talked and laughed.

Claire finished her avocado and left the skin, limp and oily, on her plate. She looked down at it, thinking of her sudden startling worry. Perhaps she'd been mistaken. A hand whisked away her plate. She looked at the blank linen mat. Yes, perhaps there was nothing there at all.

A theatrical pause. Then, at some secret signal waiters appeared; with a flourish the main course was brought in. There was much whisking about of napkins, solicitous stoopings, little flurries, and finally the production of sizzling plates some of which were flaming.

If only she could speak to Laura alone! Perhaps later they would go to the cloakroom and there, females together, she could ask Laura the urgent question: Why don't you want to drink? Do you feel sick? How long have you been feeling sick for? Is it, oh is it what I think it might be?

The pattern of the evening, quite satisfactory up to now, at least not disastrous, had suddenly been jolted apart. The fact was, she could imagine it happening; Laura was so very careless. Still, if it wasn't the cloakroom it could always be Greenbanks tonight, for they would be sleeping together in their old bedroom. That would be the time for confidences. Perhaps the last time, as in two weeks from today she would be married.

Laura's eyes, avoiding Claire's, came to rest on Holly. Holly was tearing her paper napkin into tiny balls, each one exactly the same size, and arranging them in a circle round her glass. Such calm self-absorption seemed rather refreshing. Restful too; Holly wasn't exactly the type to look up and start prodding one with questions. Good old Holls.

Just then she stiffened; her mother was turning to Mac. 'Mac's an odd name,' she said pleasantly. 'What's your real one?'

'John.'

'And where does the Mac come from?'

'MacDonald.'

An expectant pause, but no more information was forthcoming.

'Er, is that your surname?'

'Yeah.'

'You're from Scotland, then?'

'No, Bristol.'

Mac was eating Lobster Thermidor. At least, thought Laura, he could answer in words of more than one syllable if he was shovelling down four quids' worth of shellfish. Obscurely it disappointed her that he hadn't made a more humble choice and thereby shown his indifference to this sort of set-up.

Her mother was battling on. 'You're a student, I expect?'

'Nope.'

'Ah. What do you do then?'

'Bus conductor.'

A hush. Forks poised, mid-air. Laura looked down at her lap.

The napkin in it was completely shredded by now. In fact she'd torn it further than shreds; it was at the wisp stage. Silly to get so nervous! She looked round the table, her nervousness mixed with defiance. Nervousness won. 'Actually, he's really an artist,' she said.

'Ah.' Her parents subsided, just a little. 'So it's only temporary, I expect,' said her father.

'That's right. I got the sack today.'

'What?' gasped Laura. 'No! Mac, is that true?'

'Uh-huh. Non-attendance.'

A ripple ran round the table. For a moment everything was swept from Laura's mind.

Dan was cheered. All of a sudden he was actually thankful that Claire was marrying Geoff. After all, she could have ended up with someone like Mac. There might be reservations about Geoff but at least he wasn't a *failed bus conductor*.

Mac, probably to escape the attention, dropped his napkin and ducked under the table. Laura could imagine him down there; a moment of pure peace. Very nice. Down there he could breathe; he could also inspect the shadowy underworld of legs amongst which he found himself. She forgot her nerves; she forgot her other dreadful worry; she couldn't help smiling. Intriguing things, legs. She could imagine them, some trousered, some skirted, some crossed, some planted firmly apart, some shoeless and dangling (Holly's), and all innocent of their owners. Down there, such a serene world of guiltless appendages; up here all this stilted chit-chat and fiddling with napkins.

Her legs stirred, suddenly selfconscious after this long perusal of them. She saw her mother shifting in her seat. Mac, with a last regretful look, straightened up.

Geoff was enjoying the meal. Mr Jenkins was certainly doing them very well. When could he dare to start calling him Dan?

'Geoff.' Claire was leaning towards him, whispering. 'Don't you think Holly's going to be beautiful? Doesn't she look lovely tonight, like a princess who doesn't yet know she is one.'

'Yes, she'll be very pretty, but you're looking fairly stunning yourself. I like that dress. Darling.'

In fact, he felt proud to be part of such a family and above all, of course, proud of Claire. He liked being part of this massed and candle-lit spectacle of Jenkinses. And he'd captured her now; unbelievably, she wanted him. Him, Geoff.

He gazed down at her engagement ring; £220's worth of diamonds there. Still, diamonds didn't depreciate and a girl like Claire deserved them. The best for her. He'd always liked to do things properly.

On impulse he covered her hand with his; who cared who saw? Right there, in front of everyone. Quite bold he felt, all of a sudden.

Claire turned to him and smiled. She was his beautiful girl. He tightened his grip. 'Really excellent claret,' he called across the table. 'Dan.'

By the end of the main course things, aided perhaps by the really excellent claret, were relaxing a little. Laura, to everyone's surprise, had remained practically silent all evening; but Dan and Mac were actually conversing.

'To tell the truth, Mac,' he was saying, 'I'm rather glad to meet someone who's not a student. They've had such a bad press recently – you know, sit-ins for higher grants and so forth. Politically very confused, I think.'

'Are they?'

'Seem to be. Disrupting every institution yet making a fearful fuss if those same institutions don't get them their money on time. That sort of thing. I'm glad you're not political.'

'How do you know?' challenged Laura. 'Actually, Mac's a Marxist.' I think, she added to herself.

'Tell me about Marxism,' her father said. 'I'd like to know.'

'Well,' mumbled Mac. 'Bit complicated.'

'In the thirties, you know, it was rather different. Chap in my office lost a leg in the Spanish war. Compare that to your – '

'Ah, the trolley!' Rosemary's gay voice interrupted them. Dan was getting on to one of his hobby horses and she liked to keep things harmonious. 'Do let's choose a pudding!'

'Yes, but Dad – ' began Laura. She wanted to carry on, to have a proper discussion. Real talk at last. She had a feeling, too, that her silence was arousing attention. Besides she was proud that, whatever had happened since, her father had actually once been a Communist; she wanted Mac to know that. She didn't know much about politics but what she did know was that she should admire the Left.

But her weak urge faltered at the sight of the sweets trolley, a truly kitsch wonderworld of snowy peaks, drenched valleys and layers of ooze. Drab politics were forgotten. For a moment, everything was. 'Bags the last rum baba!' she said.

Holly cast a swift professional eye over it. 'You can keep it. Not enough juice. I want some of that pie, please, and an eclair. Can I have both?'

'I'll swop half your baba, Laura,' said Claire, 'for half this cheesecake. Done?'

'Done.'

'Girls!' cried their mother. 'You're behaving like babies.'

'Heavens, I've just spotted the trifle,' sighed Laura. How she craved sweet things, just lately!

'Have it as well,' said Holly. 'Go on, ask the waiter. If you're sissy I will, but only if you give me a mouthful of your rum thingummy.'

'Think about your guests,' said their mother.

But Geoff and Mac liked it. All at once they felt more comfortable. What a relief, nobody being polite any more! It pleased them, this wearing away of the formality; this glimpse of the family underneath, as the veneer on a table might be worn away to reveal the no-nonsense pine. They liked a bit of bad manners.

Dinner was over. Brandies were poured. Even Holly was given a tiny glass of something green. Dan took a packet from his pocket and leant over to Laura. He always offered her a special Black Sobranie after a grand meal.

'Er, no thanks awfully,' she said.

'Given up? Goodness, Laura, you used to smoke like a chimney.'

'Er, yes, well I've stopped.'

'Don't be ashamed of it girl! Congratulations!'

Claire's eye was on Laura; Laura looked out of the window. Dan passed the cigarettes round to the men.

They settled back. Wreathed together in aromatic smoke, the three of them became drawn into the ageless and masculine spell of after-dinner contentment and fine brandy. Black cigarettes were tapped over ashtrays, amber liquid was tilted in its balloon glass and inspected as if it held all the secrets; upon them a timeless air descended.

And simultaneously the four women drew together, silently marvelling how some lost clannish spell, or perhaps just booze, was accomplishing before their eyes the very state of affairs they'd been striving to achieve all evening. And, cosy and clannish themselves, they talked about the wedding, its little details, all the dull and practical things which they would be selfconscious about mentioning in the company of men but which, just because it was Claire's wedding, were surprisingly absorbing. Bridesmaids? Canapés? How many invitations had been answered? Even Laura, who believed she frowned at such things, found herself caught up and leant forward, quickened into discussion about the number of glasses and should they have one usher or two? It helped to keep her mind off what she had disclosed as yet to nobody. No time could be more inappropriate than the present, and anyway she was still unsure. Nothing was definite.

Just then Holly stifled a yawn and Rosemary, with her alert mother's eye, stopped. 'Dan darling,' she said, 'isn't it time to make a move? It's long past Holly's bedtime.'

'It's not!' protested Holly.

With twenty years of whiny bedtimes behind her, Rosemary didn't bother to reply but just stood up. They all four stood up and looked at the men.

Mac had taken off his jacket and looked definitely cheerful. He was showing the other two some complicated – too complicated – trick with matches and they, fingers busy trying it out, were carrying on with their conversation. Murmurs could be heard. 'Sound year,' was one; 'investment,' was another. 'How about clubbing together on a crate of the '69?' Claire heard. She smiled.

Standing by the coat rail, all three men were very gallant at helping the ladies into their coats – all except Holly, that is, who struggled into her anorak alone and would have tautened, affronted, if anyone had tried to come to her aid. Geoff held out Claire's enduring Harris Tweed affair; with a blush and a smile she slipped into it as if slipping into his arms. Dan helped his wife, with rather too much of a flourish, into her powder blue number that exactly matched her dress. Even Mac, *Mac*, felt prompted to lift Laura's ratty fur and hoist it round her shoulders. It was no good pushing her arms into it because the lining was all holey, so she could only wear it draped around her shoulders, the parody of a mink.

After this Geoff and Mac disappeared in their different directions and the Jenkinses squashed into the Rover. Holly, who a year ago would have sunk herself, sleepy and fragrant, into the nearest arms, now sat up, stiffish but slightly swaying. She was too old for such soppiness.

Or so she thought; but slowly she was toppling. By the time
they had passed Regent's Park she was truly asleep and breathing
into the comforting Harris Tweed of Claire. Dreams later the
car stopped. Holly woke with a jolt. Doors were being opened,
skirts gathered together. Tumbling out, she found herself standing
on the pavement outside her house in her bright red tights. No
shoes. She had to wait until everybody else got out and then
scrabble amongst the collapsed Kleenex boxes, battered maps and
moulted Badger fur for them. At last she found her stylish slip-
ons; slightly less convenient, perhaps, than her babyish ones which
at least stayed on. Still, a small price to pay for growing up.

Laura lay in her bed and waited. Claire was still in the bathroom;
she could hear the mumbling of the hot water pipes deep in the
walls. 'As if the house had indigestion,' her father used to say.
She heard the rush and thump of the lavatory. With Claire here
her memories were stirred; stirred too by the sinking knowledge
that this must be the last time they would sleep together. They had
always shared this room, right up until Claire's move to Clapham,
even though there were two other rooms next door to it. But
they preferred to sleep together because it was more fun. Their
midnight murmurs were fun, so were their muffled giggles, only
temporarily stilled by the sound of a footstep on the stairs.

With a click the bathroom light was turned off. Laura lay
gazing at that familiar mark on the ceiling which, when she was
horsey, had seemed like a thoroughbred's head and when she was
older just seemed abstract again. She turned and gazed at the
Sellotape marks where her Beatles photos had been, most of them
of George, whose gentle shagginess she'd loved the best. She looked
at the fan-shaped brown smear above the gas fire where in spiritual
adolescent moments she'd lit joss sticks. And she looked out of
the window and remembered countless evenings when, gazing
out at the Harrow swallows swooping, elastic, against the ribbed
sunset, she'd dreamt of future lovers and a happiness impossible
to put into a shape. Had it any shape yet? Ominous clouds, that
was all.

Another click; the landing went dark. Claire crept into the
bedroom and closed the door behind her. The end of an era,
Laura thought. In August this room is to be redecorated and
everything – the ceiling mark, the Sellotape ones, the joss stick

smear – they'll all be painted over. In August Claire will be lying alongside her own husband, and I? What about me?

Claire switched off the bedside light; the bed creaked, sheets rustled; she was in.

'Wow,' Laura sighed loudly. 'I'm glad that's over.'

'Why?'

'So painful. What an ordeal.'

'Oh, it wasn't that bad.' For some reason Claire felt prickly. 'It was a lovely meal, anyway.' Perhaps it was that to criticize the evening was to criticize Geoff, who was at its centre.

'But such a vulgar place! The whole business would have been much better at home.'

'Daddy wanted to make a thing of it.'

'Yes, but Daddy's things always embarrass me.'

Claire pulled the cool sheet up to her chin. 'Anyway, Geoff enjoyed it.' It was her and Geoff from now on. She gazed at the darkness into which she was placing her words. Much easier to send them into the black than to speak them to another face. For even with a sister one could be shy; especially when the subject was Geoff, as surely it would be. She dreaded this but it couldn't be avoided. How often were they alone like this? They must talk.

'You're lucky,' came Laura's voice. 'They seem to like Geoff. I wish they'd like Mac.'

Ah, we shall talk about Mac, thought Claire with relief. That was easier; the whole thing was definable with Mac. 'Mac's so different,' she said. 'They just don't understand him. Anyway, they just think he's another of your boyfriends. If they knew you were *living* with him . . .'

Words failed both of them. 'But Geoff,' said Laura, 'they can understand what he's about.'

Was there wistfulness there, or condescension? Difficult to tell. 'I just hope,' said Claire, 'there are other things they like about him too.' She was edging nearer and nearer to what she really wanted to ask; even in this room steeped in past confidences she couldn't quite ask it outright. *Are you pleased about Geoff?*

'They seemed to be getting along fine, anyway,' said Laura. 'All that talk about what stereo to buy and what wine to lay down.'

'Oh dear, it sounds awfully boring.'

'Count your blessings, my girl. It's good that they talked at all. Nobody except you and Holly can ever think of anything to say to Mac. Not that he helps much.'

Laura relapsed into silence. A silence thinking of Mac or one thinking of Geoff? Or a silence comparing them both? Claire waited, then gave up and started explaining into the blackness: 'The thing about Geoff is that he's adult. Capable, you know, not like most of the people I've met. You know, narrow-shouldered youths you have to mother – ' She stopped. Narrow-shouldered youths sounded just like Mac. 'Er, you know, hopeless ones like that flapping overcoat one in Bristol. Not nice ones like Mac.', She thought for a moment. Shame having to choose one's words with a *sister*, of all people. 'Or else unhappy existential ones you have to be careful with, ones who keep you awake all night while they chain smoke and talk about their complexes, and analyse just what you said to them all day and did you really mean it – you know, sensitive ones who're not really sensitive, just touchy.' She stirred her toes clockwise round the cool tucked corners of the sheets, searching for words. 'Or else sad middle-aged school-masters who live in bedsits and somehow missed out on a wife. You see, Laura, I'm not beautiful like you, or even amazingly intelligent – '

'Don't be stupid! Honestly, don't feel you have to explain Geoff or apologize for him. I think he's very nice. He's the sort of person who gets things done. I saw that at the Zoo.'

Oh dear. Claire stared into the dark. It was as she dreaded; Laura was choosing her words. Mac and Geoff had entered this room now and altered everything. There they lay, two sisters in their parallel beds, miles apart.

A long silence. Staring into their separate darknesses they lay there. Behind them stretched the past, the shared midnight murmurings, the electric crackle and cling of the winceyette nighties as they squirmed with muffled laughter, the secret words whose meaning was known only to themselves, the wickedly late chime from the clock downstairs, the mystery of their parents' closed bedroom door and what went on behind it – all that was over. It had become the Past and now they lay in limbo, for what was to replace it? A far horizon faced Claire, a misty landscape of marriage whose actual stones and grass her feet had not yet felt. Soon they would be stepping there.

And Laura? Claire tried a question. 'By the way, how come you had no wine? Or cigarettes? Do tell me, please.' She slid her toes about, blushing into the blackness. 'Are you by any chance pregnant?'

A quick laugh. 'Oh heavens no! 'Course not! I'm just being healthy, aren't I, cutting down the booze, saving money on fags . . .'

'Thank goodness! I thought, just for a moment, at dinner . . .'

'No no.'

'That's all right then.'

Laura relaxed. That was over. No, she would tell her fears to nobody, not even her darling sister who just lately seemed so far away.

Downstairs there was a familiar whirr and ting as the clock struck one; outside the door there was a scrape and a sigh as Badger, who had moved upstairs to guard his girls, shifted himself in his sleep.

'Night-night, Laura.'

'Night-night.'

Laura stayed awake the longest.

twenty-seven

The doctor took off his spectacles and by the way he did it, rather carefully, Laura knew it was all over.

'Do sit down, Miss Jenkins.'

The large expanse of leather-topped desk and the framed diplomas on the wall reinforced his authority and gave the words she knew he was going to say, when he said them, a weightier significance – as if they needed any more of it.

'Yes, your test was positive, I'm afraid.'

Funnily enough this didn't flood her with realization and emotion. Perhaps it was that the whole room spoke of this little scene endlessly repeated; a past procession of girls like herself creeping here to be confronted by the same calm words, the same routine with the spectacles. He was polishing them now. The hygienic surroundings emphasized that she was a statistic, though a regrettable one.

'Goodness,' she said, and closed her mouth again. That was all she could think of saying. It did sound polite and extra-ordinarily feeble, but still. The rubber domes on the tray looked smug. Bad luck, they said. Too late, weren't you? Should have used us from the beginning, shouldn't you?

The doctor, being kind, put on his spectacles, shuffled some papers and gave her no lecture. Probably he was tired of giving lectures. He did ask what she intended doing and he gave her an address in London, but as she had never been absolutely sure, she had thought out nothing. He did mention that by her calculations she must be nearly three months pregnant and therefore any, ah, *decisions*, should be made swiftly. No mention was made of the young man, for which she was thankful. Mac's face in the midst of it all could only confuse her.

She went out. Faced with a streetful of shoppers, she felt suddenly transparent, as if not only the embryo inside her but all her emotions just beginning to cluster round it were visible. She paused a moment outside a shop and tried to arrange her face. Behind the glass rose tier upon tier of shoes, single shoes, shiny and virginal. She gazed at them, each one new, each one as yet un-mated, and so hopefully displayed. Through them, spectral, her reflection faced her.

She turned off the main road and started climbing the hill towards Clifton. The summer holidays had begun; there were few students about and the streets were empty. Tall and noble houses stared down at her. What, *what* shall I do? How on earth am I going to tell my parents? How am I going to tell *him*? Will I want to marry him? Christ.

She turned the corner into Jacob's Crescent, her thoughts reeling. What should she do? At the word abortion, black wings flapped in her head.

Just then the sun came out and swept down the street, stunning her with its brilliance and lighting up the pitted old brickwork. The long slender windows of the houses winked down at her, suddenly confidential. In an instant all was radiance.

She stopped and leant against a lamp post, for now she thought of it this way she felt heavily ripe, a pregnant woman in need of rest. It was the fact that her body actually worked. It had changed. It felt different. No longer was it that well-inspected shape she saw in the mirror, nor that warm bearer of pleasure, nor that web of veins she felt at the blood clinic or the prickling, aching skin she felt in illness. None of these. Now, suddenly, she felt its central reason.

Ah, that was very fine, but across the road stood number 18 and what was she doing to do? Mac was in there. Didn't she know in her heart what should be done? Despite leaning like this against the lamp post, glamorous with fertility. Wasn't the decision made? All she had to do was to tell him; hadn't she?

'Stop! Stop! No entry.'

Mac flexed himself in the doorway; he was gripping the lintel, the lighted room behind him. She hesitated and peered through the angle of his limbs barring her; she could see nothing but the unmade bed.

'What on earth is it?' God, everything was unreal today. Wasn't he going to ask where she'd been all afternoon?

'Close your eyes,' he said. 'Go on. No cheating, my sonner.'

She closed her eyes.

'Now I'll lead you in. Promise not to look. You must see him from the right angle.'

Cringing behind him, she let him lead her into the room.

'It's a surprise, you see,' he explained. She felt his hands on her shoulders as he stopped her, then a dramatic pause. 'You can open them now, my sonner.'

He had actually lit the fire. The flames cast a flickering light on to the place where the hearthrug would have been if they'd ever bothered to get one. Also on to a large cardboard box that stood there.

'Go on. Don't be shy.'

She hesitated. To add yet another shock to the day suddenly seemed too much of an effort. By now, had she any reactions left?

'Go on. Open it.' Mac was watching her expectantly, so she knelt down and pulled open the flaps of the box. Her heart turned over.

Crouched down in the box, it stared up at her with bulging eyes. Horror (what were they going to do with it?) fought with a surge of love. Her very own rabbit! And a black and white one, too. She hadn't had one since she was a child.

She picked it out of the box; it was deliciously heavy. Her heart melted as she felt the softness of its belly and the fragile elbows of its front legs. It didn't struggle but allowed itself to be held in her arms, simply.

She lowered it on to the ground where it sat for a moment, quite calm, sniffing the floor and then lifting its head with its beautiful enquiring ears; the firelight glowed through them and she could see their tracery of veins, the miracle of them. Round its face sparkled its busy whiskers.

'How about him, Laura?' Mac was watching her nervously. 'Like him?'

'I think he's the most beautiful rabbit I've ever seen,' she said truthfully. 'When did you buy him?'

'After – sort of lunchtime today. I had a drink with – you know – some of the lads, and when we came out we were going past this, like, petshop, and I started talking about you liking animals and all, you know. Especially rabbits, I said. So they said let's just look at them inside, and we saw him and they said why not buy him; for you. As a nice surprise, like.'

Mac, mellow, a few pints inside him, blinking in the sunlight as he shambled out of the pub. A bit maudlin, boasting about her to his mates as they wandered down the street trying to focus on the shop windows that kept dancing before their eyes. Straining with vague good intentions towards her; also a bit soppy about a nice rabbit sitting all lonely in its cage. She could just imagine it. Booze, or dope, or even neither of them; he need be under no influence but his own. How infuriating, how endearing, how *typical*!

'So I thought, why not?' he said. 'We can take him for walks. I can fix up a cage. Just like a baby, he is, without the hassles.'

She froze. Just for a moment she'd forgotten about that. How could she possibly tell him now, while he was watching the rabbit as a fond parent would, a pretend parent, as it lolloped round the floor exploring the place with bright eyes and busy whiskers? Damn and blast, why did he always have to do such nice things at the wrong time. Such very nice things; and yet such hopeless ones.

She sat down weakly. Claire. Yes, Claire was the one. Claire could help her; she would go there, for how she needed her!

A few minutes later Mac went out. He was going to Hal and Min's old house to get some wood for a cage. As soon as the door closed behind him, Laura darted to the chest of drawers and filled a case with clothes. She rummaged in her bag; £3. Hardly enough even to get to London, but somehow she felt hesitant, even repelled, by the thought of using her cheque book, for wasn't it her father's money that she would be drawing? Today for once she felt compelled to act independently. She would hitch.

The rabbit had been put back and she heard rustling noises in the cardboard box. The softest of noses, black and whiskery, poked out between the cardboard flaps. Amongst the fur she saw its nostrils breathing. She didn't like to look at that soft face, nor those nostrils, for she was leaving and she would be having an abortion.

Yes, she was sure of it. Despite the ache for Mac that, now she knew she was going, tore her insides, pulled at them as if a strong hand was inside twisting and tugging. She went into the bathroom to fetch her things. She looked at the bath which she and Mac had often shared, natural as children; oddly sexless they'd been, scrubbing each other with scarcely a linger. She gathered up her things and picked up her copy of 'Sons and Lovers' that Mac had pinched to read on the lavatory. He'd got to page 23. She closed it; she felt a pang that he couldn't finish it; silly, but she did.

Back in the room the fire had died down. She snapped her case shut. The rabbit was restless, she could hear it moving about in its box, bulkily turning in the small space; she didn't look, though, in case she saw that nose. Nor did she look at the room. Nor did she even write a note, for how could she explain it in a note? She just picked up her stuff and left.

The university clock chimed five as she hurried down the hill. It must have been nearer six before she had walked through the centre and had seen, between the buildings, the big blue signs for the motorway. It was a long walk, and past her, blowing fumes and dust into her face, swept the cars of the rush hour commuters. Her suitcase weighed her down and as she walked she kept her eyes on the piece of ground the next step ahead. Sometimes it was pavement, sometimes sooty grass, damaged grass littered with rubbish.

As she drew nearer the motorway it reduced in width, edging her further and further into the road. This was not a place where people walked; the rubbish was the sort that is thrown from passing cars. The edge narrowed down until finally it was just a rim of concrete lining the motorway approach road. A stretch of non-space between town and motorway, a no-man's-land where no human foot is presumed to tread. A windy frightening place. Ahead, separated from her by a flyover and glinting traffic, she could see the blue sign for EASTBOUND: M4 LONDON. But how could she get to it?

She trudged along the verge, her case – oh so heavy! – bumping against the steel barrier at every step. The cars were crowding her; the verge was too narrow. It was difficult to keep her balance.

'*Coo-ee!*' She jumped. A belch of exhaust fumes. '*Fancy a bung-up, then?*'

A car swept by, blowing her skirt up. She choked in its dust. The words drowned in the roar of the traffic. Waving arms, staring eyes; she could see the people turning round and laughing at her; then the car was swallowed up into the mass of others.

She felt trapped on her concrete strip. Sliding streams of cars . . . how could she possibly get on the right bit of road for London? Some of the cars slowed down and she could feel people staring at her, but she kept her eyes on the ground. She felt sick, as she felt every evening now that she was pregnant, and the exhaust fumes nauseated her. Those slowing-down cars – she felt humiliated by them and knew they were inspecting her laddered tights and her thighs that kept being revealed as her dress blew about in the wind. Especially they were inspecting her thighs. She couldn't hold her dress down; the wind from the cars kept blowing it up again. She could conceal nothing. Oh her little room, her rabbit, her Mac!

'*Cunt!*'

A horn blared. Exhaust belched at her. She regained her bit of verge.

It seemed to take an hour to walk from one gigantic sign, towering above her, to the roundabout that it indicated. Miles of no-man's-land stretched in between, miles of her narrow rim with its odd blackened and buffeted plant clinging to it. They made her feel sad, those plants. She got to the roundabout. She edged her way to what seemed the right exit, walked down it and found herself at last on the wider edge of the proper approach road. She put her case down and stood there, thumb out.

Minutes passed. Hours, it seemed, passed. The sun had gone down and it was getting chilly. She shivered. Hundreds of cars passed; many of them slowed down to look at her but none of them stopped. On the ground beside her lay the contents of an ashtray, like spilled sick. She looked down at the stubs. Who had smoked them and where was he now – Wolverhampton? Crewe? She couldn't keep her eyes off the stubs spilled by this passing male – she was sure it was a male – forgotten by him as he speeded off, but lying scattered here on the grass to nauseate her.

Yes, her pregnancy was like that, wasn't it? No miracle, nothing to do with Mac or with passion. Just spilled seed. That's how she would think of it. Hardly connected with him at all, for didn't aching miles of concrete separate them now?

She looked up. A car had stopped and a man was leaning across the passenger seat towards her. Before she could gather her thoughts he had stretched out his arm and swung open the back door for her suitcase. Then he swung open the passenger door and she got inside.

'Thank goodness!' she said with a little laugh. Her voice startled her; she'd said nothing for hours. She glanced at him. An unmemorable sort of face; an anonymous man, another spiller of seed.

'Going far?' he asked.

'Just to London.'

A silence. 'But this is the road to Birmingham,' he said.

Laura swung round and stared out of the window where the EASTBOUND: M4 LONDON sign was passing underneath. Their car was taking them up over another flyover.

'You've got on to the wrong road,' he said. 'This is the M5. Would you like to be put down?'

'No, no.' The clear road stretched ahead. What did it matter? 'No, I don't mind, I'll go to Birmingham.'

The man's face, she felt it, turned round and looked at her. She turned away; she looked out of the window and gave her little laugh. 'Er, it's just as easy to get home from there, you see.'

'Ah. Where do you live then?'

'Somewhere between the two.' She might as well be a dweller in no-man's-land, an inhabitant of nowhere, for wasn't she on her own now? Truly alone. She might feel like running home, back to sympathy and a place defined on the map, but fate and the motorway had declared otherwise. She would have to forget those little nests.

'Er, you're a student then, I take it.'

'Sort of.' She was a nothing person, in limbo.

'Ah. Part-time, perhaps.'

'In a way.'

'And it's home for the holidays, I expect.'

'Uh-huh.'

'Yes. Well.'

The air was tense. He was thinking of something to say. She

wished he would shut up and leave her alone. She wanted to
think. She had a lot to think about.

'Yes. I expect funds get a little low at this time of year.'

'Uh-huh.'

'I have the same trouble myself sometimes.' He laughed.
'Funds, I mean. Don't we all? You know, inflation and all that.'

She gave her little laugh and stared out at the landscape,
willing him to stop asking these silly questions. It was almost dark
by now. Headlights were being switched on, blacking out the
surrounding countryside.

'Yes. Well.' He cleared his throat. 'And you have some brothers
and sisters?'

Honestly! 'Two.'

'Brothers or sisters, or perhaps one of each?'

'Sisters.'

'Yes. Well, that must be very nice.'

A pause. 'Er, younger or older?'

'Both.'

'Ah, I see. So you're the middle one. Best of both worlds,
perhaps!' His enquiring little laugh.

She didn't reply. Good God, they had miles to go. Was he
going to keep this up all the way? This was the last thing she needed,
this awful invasion of her privacy just when she had so much
thinking to do. How could she get him to shut up?

'Yes, well it must be very pleasant to come from a large family.
Three of you, all sisters together, it must be really very nice.'

'Uh-huh.'

'Very nice. And do they all have such beautiful legs?'

She froze.

'Yes,' he said with an apologetic little cough. 'I'm afraid I can't
keep my eyes off them.'

She didn't move. Frozen, she stared into the blackness. There
was a long, long silence in the car, broken only by the rhythmic
moan of the windscreen-wipers, for it had begun to rain.

He cleared his throat. 'It's all right, dear. I won't touch you.
Not unless you want me to, that is.'

A pause.

'Er, but there's no need to sit right over there like that, you
know.'

She couldn't turn and look at him. She couldn't move. Was she
going to be sick?

'Really, dear, it's quite all right. I won't do anything you don't want me to.'

She couldn't speak, her mouth was too dry. And her hands – she kept pulling her skirt down over her knees – her hands were trembling. Her jumble sale dress was so thin, of such silky stuff, the shape of her thighs was obvious but she had nothing to cover herself with.

'Come along, dear.' He patted the empty space between them. 'Do sit a little nearer.'

'Er. No thank you,' she managed to say at last.

'All right. I won't force you, you know. Of course I won't.'

Another pause.

'Perhaps you'd like to hold my hand?'

She wasn't looking at him. She kept her eyes fixed on the blackness outside the window. The cold metal of the door handle was pressed against her thigh and she could press herself no further.

'It would be nice,' he said.

She felt fingers touching hers. 'Stop it please!' she whispered. 'Could you stop it.' Silly words, refined.

'I would like it so much.'

His fingers were lightly touching hers; his, too, were trembling, just slightly.

'It's just a little thing,' he said. 'It won't do you any harm.'

His fingers curled round hers, holding them tightly, squeezing them. His hand was hot and moist; trembling too.

'I must get out!' she whispered, but no sound came out. His fingers started rhythmically squeezing hers. Harder and harder he squeezed. It started to hurt.

'Let me out please! I must get out please!' she whispered, just audibly. She couldn't stop being polite. But oh God *he* was so polite!

'Really, don't be frightened. Wouldn't you like us to hold hands, dear, just like this? It is so nice. I do so enjoy it.'

'I'm going to be sick. Let me out please! *Now!*' Her voice broke. '*Now!*' she shouted.

His hand stopped; he let go. The car was slowing up.

'I'm not well, you see,' she said, suddenly apologetic now he'd stopped. She stumbled out on to the verge and bent over. The rain trickled icily down her neck; she could hear the soft moan of the windscreen-wipers and the murmur of the engine ticking over. Lights flashed by, spraying her legs with water.

He had not got out of the car. It was too dark to see him, but he must be sitting in there waiting for her to finish. She couldn't vomit. She wanted to, it was surging up, but she couldn't. It rose and then sank. She could only stand there, bending and humiliated. Was this being independent, this utter and terrifying vulnerability? He could do what he liked with her. Beside this flashing, roaring motorway nobody would see. They were both but another pair of headlights in the night, stationary headlights perhaps, but who was to notice? Anything could happen and nobody, absolutely nobody, would know. She was somewhere in the nameless Midlands and not a living soul knew where she was. Except him, of course.

'You all right, dear?' From his voice he must be leaning out of the car looking at her.

'I'm just not well.' The tears came, chokingly.

'Get in, dear. Don't be worried. Come along.' She could hear him patting the seat.

And slowly she climbed back in. What else could she do? Start running?

He let out the clutch. 'I think you need a nice cup of coffee, don't you? You're soaked.' He patted her thigh. 'Yes, really soaked.'

His hand remained there a moment while she sobbed. She fumbled for a handkerchief.

'Here,' he said, and took his hand away. He opened the cubbyhole, took out a box of tissues and gave them to her. His hand returned not to her thigh but to the wheel. He indicated and drew out into the traffic.

She blew her nose; he cleared his throat. 'Feeling better, are we?' His voice was bright. 'I hope so. We'll pull in at the next service station. That should do the trick.'

She said nothing.

'Really dreadful weather, isn't it,' he went on. 'So chilly. When I saw you beside the road I thought – she really must be freezing in those clothes. Just a slip of a girl, I thought.'

She blew her nose.

'Looks so lost, I thought.'

The hand remained on the wheel, she could see it out of the corner of her eye. But she stayed pressed up against the door.

'I do hope you're not too wet.' His voice was staying bright and enquiring. 'We don't want you catching a chill.'

Could he possibly be pretending that nothing had happened?
'No, I'm all right, thank you.'
'That wouldn't do at all, would it.' So polite, he was!
'No, I feel much better, thank you.' So she was.

Soon lights loomed up through the rainwashed windscreen. He indicated to the left and slowed down into the service station.

If it had been a film, she reflected later, he would of course have ravaged her in the back seat and then strangled her with her own laddered tights. Then she would have been dumped behind a clump of landscaped motorway conifers. But it wasn't a film; it was too humdrum and too real for that. She was just an ordinary girl like a million others who, that night, were participating in some tepid pick-up; some lonely, sad, unlikely little scene not too different from this one.

They stopped in the car park. She hesitated before getting out. Should she get her suitcase? If she did, she could leave the man here, but then what? She'd only have to chance it with another one, another pair of headlights in the darkness.

'Looking for something?' he asked politely, waiting for her.

There was a pause. 'I was just thinking,' she said.

'Well, I shouldn't bother. Thinking, I mean. It'll be all right, you see.' He smiled a bright smile in her direction, not meeting her eyes. In the neon light she could see his face clearly, an un-memorable face trying to keep its dignity. It wouldn't happen again. Whatever it was, whatever he had been feeling, was over.

'I'd like some coffee,' she said.

The café was blindingly bright. Her relief was soon replaced by a helpless feeling of exposure. Behind the counter stood a pimply youth. He was staring at her chest; she could see him working out, with his eyes, exactly where her nipples were. She looked down at the rows of plastic packets of food. She couldn't move.

'Do you take milk?' the man asked. He was waiting at the urn.

Yes, she'd like milk. On her tray she placed a roll, some butter and some honey, for she should be hungry. With an effort she could remember her day and recall that she hadn't eaten.

The man, still nameless, paid for it and they went over to a table. 'You'll get back all right, will you, once we get to Birmingham?' he asked.

'Oh, I expect so.'

'When we arrive you can tell me where to drop you. What station and so on.'

'That would be very kind.' How odd for them to sit here so politely when her face must still be blotchy with tears!

'On my calculation, averaging about sixty we should make it in half an hour. No one will be expecting you?'

'No, no one.' She fumbled with the honey, trying to open it. Being such a sealed little sachet it was difficult. 100% *Pure*, she read. *Grade 1 Honey. Granada Catering Ltd.* But it was sealed, laminated, hygienically and hermetically soldered. Precious honey, labour of bees. Patient bees, their secret toil had been sucked up into the *Catering Ltd* division of *Granada*. Priceless honey entombed in plastic.

Her eyes blurred with tears and she put the little packet back on the table. Tears of pity ran down her cheeks, tears for the bees, for the embryo inside her, for things she couldn't put a name to. With her sleeve she wiped her eyes.

The man must be noticing but he pretended he wasn't. Instead he unwrapped his sandwich, unwrapped the sugar for his coffee and began to eat. Mindlessly Musak played; beyond the windows the motorway traffic hummed; at the next table someone pushed aside his refuse of packets. Laura tried to sip her coffee but her mouth was bleary with tears and it tasted glutinous. She put down her cup, more desolate than she imagined possible. She was helplessly alone. But then so were those countless millions being swept along the motorways just as she was, swept through the windy corridors of high-rise cities and round wastelands of flyovers. Everyone was alone; silly to pretend all these years that they weren't. Alone but just occasionally one of them would reach out and touch a human thigh.

'Er, have you finished?'

The man was looking not at her but at her uneaten roll. He never looked at her. 'It's just that we ought to be pushing along, I think. Don't want to hurry you, of course.'

'I don't want anything to eat, actually. Sorry.'

'Don't mention it. Perhaps you don't feel well.'

The pimply youth watched her as she crossed the café. She wanted to put her hands over her stomach, hiding her womb. Nothing was safe.

They were outside now. He opened the door for her, polite to the last. They drove across to some petrol pumps where they were served by a muffled shape to whom they were but an empty tank and a proferred note. The shape was in a Texaco uniform; *Marlboro*, declared two patches, one on each side, dead over the lung. Laura shivered.

Even the man, by this time, was silenced by her behaviour, and they drove the last stretch to Birmingham in a quietness that was lulled, rhythmically, by the windscreen-wipers. In the car all was darkness but for the winking lights and wavering dials of the dashboard.

Just once the man leant over. Laura froze. But he was only switching on the radio.

Hush now, don't explain,
You're my joy and pain . . .

It was Billie Holliday singing. Not those words, not that voice. 'Could you possibly turn it off please?'

The man leant forward; with an apologetic little cough he turned it off.

When they got to Birmingham he took her to the railway station. He passed out her suitcase, polite to the end, then he hesitated. Was he going to ask her something? Two lost souls, they were. Between them there was a bond of some sort; one of them, or perhaps both, had passed through so much. But he said nothing, and she must have thanked him for now he was leaving.

When the tail lights had disappeared, swallowed up amongst the others, Laura set down her suitcase. What, exactly, was she going to do now?

The station clock said 10.30. A few people wandered about. She'd never been to Birmingham before; New Street Station was glassy and modern. She took her case and sat down on a bench facing the Departure Board. A train for Euston, it told her, would leave in seven minutes and she had easily enough money for the ticket.

She sat there, suitcase in lap, hands on suitcase. She could see the ticket office over to her right. The hands jerked. Six minutes.

In six minutes she could be settling back in her seat, speeding out of the station towards London, towards her sister. Claire! Claire wouldn't mind how late it was; she'd hug her and tuck her up on the sofa and listen, and help, and laugh, for by then she, Laura, might feel like laughing. With Claire there, she might.

But she was too late, for Claire was married now. Of ceremonies none could have been more normal. For Laura, though, none could have been stranger; in front of her people had moved, smiled, raised glasses, but silently, as if on a television screen with the sound off. All of them, even her darling sister, moving like tiny robots, distanced and dwindled by her worry. Now ten days had passed and Claire would be lying beside her husband in her new house. What right had she, Laura, to disturb them? Something was stopping her; perhaps the need to go through a certain amount of this alone. Perhaps the fact that Geoff would be there. Strange to sit here, caught in a spell of desolation, unable to break it. She felt more lonely than she'd believed possible, but oddly enough strong too. She'd go to Claire tomorrow; Geoff would be at work then. She'd get through tonight on her own; in this spell-like state she actually wanted to.

And then, of course, there were her parents. And never had she needed them more, them and that warm, known house, them and that soothing suburban normality. They'd welcome her, too. Seeing her in such a state they wouldn't fuss or ask the wrong questions – not tonight, anyway. They'd be at their very best. They would make her some Horlicks like they used to.

She looked up. The clock had jerked four times. Three minutes to go; she could still just make it. She thought of them in their shared and legal bed where with clear minds they'd be slumbering. No, she couldn't upset them. She'd upset them so many times.

The loudspeaker boomed and a few last figures hurried towards the platform. She could see the train. In Bristol, of course, Mac waited. She could imagine him, bemused, wondering if he'd missed something she might have said about going out; totally unsuspecting. Their bed, his and hers, waited. The most welcoming place in her universe; the centre of it. Mac, who made the most barren of places come alive! How clearly she could remember that first day in the supermarket, the way he'd dawdled and larked about. He'd understand so well what she'd felt in the M5 café and why she'd cried over the honey. He wouldn't think that was silly.

Darling Mac, darling sweetest Mac – she could call him these things now, after all those months of longing to whisper them but not daring to because she'd been too selfconscious and he'd never talked like that – darling dearest Mac, who made faces at the faceless. Such a rattler of the old baccy tin against the railings of the vast and the impersonal. Attached to nothing, committed to nothing, least of all to responsibility; better at Airfix kits than driving a car three yards across the road. Her sweetest, maddening Mac, bringing home a rabbit when he'd actually produced a child.

She shivered. She couldn't, wouldn't go back. A whistle blew and she could see the train backing out. It was the last one for London. She got up and walked to the Ladies' where she changed into her warm jeans. She put on two pullovers. She'd long ago stopped caring what she looked like – blotchy face, streaked mascara most likely, and now lumpy jumpers one on top of the other. Who minded?

She bought her ticket for the next day, then for a long while she sat in the station café, 'Sons and Lovers' propped up against her empty cup of coffee. Some of the time she thought, and some of the time she read her book, which told her of firelit parlours. She shivered again. She was chilly even in two jumpers and no doubt would get even chillier. Such a long night it was going to be. Minutes passed so slowly; each time she looked up the clock hands had hardly moved.

When centuries later the hands told her it was 12.30, she returned to the Ladies' and washed her face in the cold water. The basin lacked soap; nevertheless the water soothed. The roller towel hung down dampish and grey, but pressing her face into it comforted her. My body, she thought, rubbing her face; what will happen to it? What's it done?

The Waiting Room was down by the London platform. It was a bare, glassed-in box, its seats polished by the bottom sides of thousands of waiting bodies. No one was there. She closed the door and settled down on one of the seats. Some clothes she spread under herself; some, once she'd lain down, she spread on top. Her slippery silky dress she rolled up and used as a pillow. In her hasty exit from the room she'd forgotten her fur coat; something else to read, too, for she'd long ago finished 'Sons and Lovers'. It hadn't been a practical getaway, but then nothing had been very practical about the last few months.

It was uncomfortable and it was tedious. Though the platform outside was deserted, she felt exposed in her glass box. Being unable to sleep or read, all that remained was to lie on her back and gaze at the ceiling. Or she could turn on her side, padding her hip bone with another handful of clothes, and gaze at the row of seats, imagining those countless people who for ten minutes or one hour had stared at this same convector heater, shared this same space. On the wooden seat someone had tentatively scratched his initials, rather wavery ones, as if he'd felt impelled to fix his personality somewhere, just once. An Inter-City network map hung, framed, on the wall; on the dusty glass someone had drawn with a finger a stick man with a blank circle for a head; no features. The whole room in fact was curiously anonymous. Those thousands with bodies like her own who had sheltered here today, yesterday, a year ago, and who would no doubt be sheltering here tomorrow and next year – this unseen multitude had left little trace. Just as she, Laura, as unremarkable as any of them, would leave little trace. Not even a fag end, for she'd stopped smoking.

She gazed around the room in which she lay, for once unembellished with all those accessories with which she'd once had to fix her personality. She no longer felt she needed them. Bare room, bare facts, simple facts that she was only just recognizing. That she was neither more nor less unique than anyone else, for a start. Under their clothes they had bodies like hers; inside their heads dreams. How dismissive she'd been! Snobbish and stupid. There was nothing to distinguish her from the others who had sat here, blown their noses and followed with their eyes for the hundredth time the Inter-City lines between Birmingham and Crewe, Leicester and London, London and Bristol.

She lay back, oddly humbled. Things settled into place. Funny to feel suddenly comfortable inside one's skin when outside it one's more uncomfortable than one has ever been in one's life. The buttons of her pillow-dress were nudging her cranium; she readjusted it, and before she fell asleep she remembered Mac in his shelter in the Rec. Daffodils and someone else's Burgundy; the most playful of exiles, that had been. What a contrast to this one! Which, she wondered as she closed her eyes, which is the most real?

The rungs of the seat digging into her spine told her that it might be this one. Was it this one?

twenty-eight

The night passed; two days passed. Now it was morning and Claire was putting out the milk bottles. She straightened up. Nobody could call their street remarkable, she thought, looking at it. They had taken Laura's advice and moved in as far as they could afford, but one had to admit that they were still on the wrong side of Kilburn. Queen's Park, to be precise. Who cared? She loved it, the way it started as red-brick villas and ended as semis, the way it dazzled after all that rain yesterday, the way that number 12 was theirs. When Laura saw it, what would she say? She'd be bound to visit soon; wouldn't she be bound to sneer?

Claire walked back down the hall. She felt a particular fondness for the hall because Geoff kissed her here every morning, a swift, fresh, aftershave-and-toothpaste kiss, not at all like the deep dark kisses of upstairs. Until the evening and his arrival home, his presence lingered around the area of the coconut mat. She liked that.

Claire went back into the sitting-room. They had only moved in last week and already the room looked settled, Geoff's stereo speakers like monuments on each side of the fireplace, his pipes on their rack looking as if they'd been there since the Romans. They reassured her, those pipes, of his solidarity. She liked his things settled in with hers, his records slipped in amongst her records, his toothbrush sharing her glass; small unions throughout the house. Upstairs their clothes still lay in trunks, and it pleased her to rummage amongst his shirts for her jumper; as the days went by the clothes got more and more untidy, his entwined with hers, an embrace of weaves. At this moment she was wearing one of his shirts; it satisfied her, and though it had startled him at first, no longer did he grunt with surprise when he found her wearing such things. He was learning; they were both learning.

He was back at work now, but ahead of her stretched summer weeks. No more Roys and Lances until September. Her holidays already seemed to have lasted ages. A few days ago they'd been in Scotland; before that the hectic days of the wedding. Holly had been bridesmaid and it had been necessary to insert darts into the bodice of her dress for she was now thirteen years old and no longer flat-chested. One era ending; another beginning. Claire had surprised herself by feeling damp-eyed at her own nuptials; she'd had to scrabble for her mother's handkerchief – damp already, of course.

With a thump the letters arrived; Claire went into the hall. She liked seeing Geoff's mail. Addressed at times to G. Hair, J. Here and G. Hore, it was usually something boring from the Diners' Club or a brown paper copy of *Drive, The AA Magazine*. Still, even to *Drive* a frail mystique clung, the mystique of the past, Geoff's previous twenty-five unknown and Claire-less years. *Drive* had to be turned over in her hand and inspected. She was very much in love with Geoff; anything unknown about him tantalized.

She was picking up the letters when the doorbell rang. Ding dong; yes, it was one of those. What would Laura say when she heard it? Claire opened the door. It was Laura.

'Good grief,' she said.

'Hello, Claire.' Laura smiled, but why did she look so pale? 'I say, what's the Morris doing out there?'

'We got it from the garage yesterday.'

'It looks lovely. All different.' Laura looked different, too. Not at all as she normally did; she looked almost dowdy in those thick jumpers.

'It purrs along now,' said Claire. 'All overhauled and refurbished.'

'Like me.'

'What?'

'I say, Claire, its roof looks new too.'

'I thought it ought to have a treat while the rest was being done. Like a hair-do when one's undergoing surgery.'

Laura burst out laughing. She looked better then. She gazed about. 'So this is your street. I've been longing to see it.'

'Pretty suburban, eh?' Claire answered brightly. 'It's not exactly scintillating; all lollipop men and mums pushing prams and learner drivers creeping round the corners at one mile an hour.'

'I think it looks cheerful. Cherished.'

'Goodness, Laura! I didn't think you'd approve. I mean, it's what you always thought was worse than death, this sort of place.'

'I don't think I do now.'

Claire looked at her curiously. What had happened to her? She wasn't being polite; she could tell by something relaxed in Laura's voice that she was telling the truth. Why was she so gentle all of a sudden?

'Come in, come in,' said Claire. She inspected her. 'It's marvellous to see you but why are you here? Anything happened? Come into the kitchen. I'm just starting a pie. We'll have it for lunch.'

'I'm starving. I haven't eaten for days.'

'Laura, what *has* happened?'

'Can I sit down first?'

Claire drew a chair up to the kitchen table. She started rolling out pastry. There was a silence; she kept quiet, waiting for Laura to speak, but this meek, washed-out girl seemed to be keeping it all inside. She, Claire, must wait; whatever it was, it was too big for the usual proddings.

'You're so deft,' said Laura. 'I can't make pastry.'

'I love it. Kneading and rolling, big wholesome pies. All floury and bosomy it makes me, such a fertile feeling.' She looked up. 'You know, I think I'm pregnant already.'

A silence.

'*What*?' asked Laura.

'I can sense it, somehow.'

Laura was staring at her. Why was she staring like that?

'Heavens,' Laura said.

'Quick work, eh?' Wasn't Laura going to smile?

Laura stared at Claire, standing there so serenely and acceptably pregnant. The pie was finished and Claire was picking the dough off her fingers and putting it into her mouth. Laura watched her picking round her wedding ring, peeling the dough off it. How could she tell her such botched and untidy news! Now, of all times. She might long to unburden herself, but what about Claire? How distressing, how hopelessly inappropriate her news had suddenly become. She watched Claire sucking the gold ring, then putting her fingers under the tap. The gold glinted as she dried her hands. Her married sister.

Then she rallied. Of course she'd tell her! Impossible to keep it buttoned up any longer. Who cared if it was inappropriate? Claire of all people wouldn't mind.

'I say, Claire,' she began. And she told her. Speaking the words, she relived it; the whole strange, flustering then peaceful sequence. The stiff awakening, the train journey, the arrival at Euston. The telephoning of the number her doctor had given her, the number of a Doctor Stein. Things happening quickly then. By mid-morning she was sitting in the most elegant of rooms somewhere in St John's Wood. A dark red room, its blinds down. As she talked to the doctor she kept her eyes away from his hands which were soft and white. Fingers. Fingers reaching out the night before. Why were this man's hands so white? Fingers sliding between legs. Oh it was a cruel business, all of it. Until lately she hadn't realized that.

'What did he say?' asked Claire.

'Was I absolutely convinced I wanted the termination? A lot more questions like that. Probing ones. He wrote the answers down on a form.' At one point he had lifted the telephone and spoken to her doctor in Bristol; they obviously knew each other well. While he talked he carried on writing on her form. She had the sensation of things being taken out of her hands, of the smooth machinery starting to work. He'd nodded several times and she'd started to relax. Then he'd sent her into another room to get the form counter-signed by an equally suave doctor sitting at an equally elegant desk.

'Then he said that the red tape usually took a day or two, but that they had an unexpected vacancy in their clinic. By sheer chance they could fit me in the next afternoon. Sheer greed, more like. Obviously business hasn't been too good lately.'

Claire was sitting watching her. 'How cynical you sound! It frightens me.'

'I didn't like them, either of them. I didn't like their hands.'

'And money?'

'Remember Josie's money? The Building Society? I'd forgotten she'd left us those little deposits.' She smiled. 'Funny Aunty Josie, with her shelves of romances. What would she say, I wonder, if she knew how her money had been used?' She paused, thinking. 'Actually, remember that sherry and those olives? In her way she always was a liberator.' She paused again. 'Anyway, I rushed off and cashed it, didn't I.'

'And then?'

'Then I was hustled away. Most efficient, the whole business.' Laura looked at the floor, looked at her hands, looked at her legs in their jeans. She did it all slowly, in a quiet way that was new to Claire. Claire didn't move, so transfixed was she.

'And later?'

Consciousness glimmering brighter and brighter until Laura was awake. Sleepy still, but awake. For a while she couldn't believe it had happened for she felt nothing but a comfortable drowsiness. The room was white and anonymous; timeless too, for blinds were down and she had no watch. All was silence. Minutes passed, perhaps hours, as she lay back in the soft pillows. Cleansed, she felt. The past lay behind, the future ahead and in the middle lay her own self, drowsy between the sheets. Lying there she was the blank space between two chapters; between two halves of a film she was the white notice saying INTERVAL. Not an unpleasant sensation.

'Puritanically,' she said, 'I felt it should have hurt.'

Time passed; a nurse entered with some tea. More time passed; the doctor came in and told her she could leave in the morning. More time passed; the blind grew grey and the nurse entered and switched on the light. It must be late. She lay in her vacuum, not thinking, just existing, in the room that was no longer white but lit yellow and with shadows in the corners. The confusions of the past seemed to be slipping away.

'And this morning you came out?'

This morning she had come out. Behind the clinic stood sooty privet bushes and dustbins; she'd seen them because she went out of the wrong door. They were large dustbins. Inside her body something cold knotted itself. She might be released but she would never forget.

'And I peered through the bushes and looked at the forecourt. The side marked DOCTORS was sleek with Jaguars.'

That was that, then. Claire sat back and gazed limply at Laura. Many questions swum around her head and one surfaced. 'Why on earth didn't you tell me, you idiot? I could have been there with you.'

'It happened so quickly. This vacancy and all. Anyway, I wanted to see if I could do the whole thing myself for once. Be really adult.'

'You chose a drastic time to start.'

'It was rather drastic.' Laura lapsed into silence, thinking it all over again. It took the greatest effort, a heaving apart of heavy curtains, rows and rows of them, to get back to the beginning and remember that the day before yesterday she'd woken up on a waiting-room bench.

'And what now?' Claire asked. She looked pale, drained, her hands clenched together. She was gazing at Laura, her eyes searching Laura's face. There was a long pause.

What now? 'Money to be earned,' Laura said. Josie – the memory of her – to be paid back. Things to be sorted out in her head and in her body. Things to be done in a different way. She looked up at Claire. 'I feel rather changed but I don't feel all goody-goody. I'm not some reformed paragon of purity. It's just that I feel my attitude's changed.'

'Wearing the same dress but with a different expression on your face.'

What shall I do? thought Laura. Tomorrow, next week, next month?

'Enough about me,' she said briskly. 'What's it like being married, then?'

'Nice,' said Claire, and stopped. Where could she start? There was a silence. The very size of events, the headline nature of them – Sister Has Abortion, Sister Marries – overwhelmed them. They gazed at each other.

'Let's look at the house,' suggested Claire.

They did look at it, its ordinary bay-fronted downstairs, its ordinary bay-fronted upstairs. Things already had their place; Laura felt safe. Downstairs on Geoff's desk those long buff envelopes with windows that she, Laura, never bothered to investigate, were open and stacked on his IN tray. Not her sort of life, but she could see the use of it. And here upstairs the bed was made. Married people always made their beds. She and Mac never did. Looking round this bedroom she could tell that mornings here would be brisk bathroom noises and the murmur of the BBC News. Very different from mornings in Jacob's Crescent; she and Mac never switched on the News, for who would wish strikes at Leyland to break a trance as sunlit as theirs? Instead, if they had the energy one of them would get up and put on a Bach Violin Concerto; or else they'd just lie there listening to the birdsong outside, and those unfortunate people who had to go to work trying to start their cars. Oh the freedom, and oh the sneaking guilt!

Claire gestured towards the window. 'No huge sky or epic

landscape,' she said apologetically. 'Not quite the Jacob's Crescent panorama.'

Tiny gardens and the back views of semis. In fact, a row of equivalent back views. 'I like it,' said Laura. 'Cared-for gardens. Ours never was, not really.'

Laura gazed at the neat bed, at the order. Was this freedom? The view might be restricted but did that matter if one's mind was not? And Geoff and Claire *would* listen to the BBC News, she knew it. They *would* care about what happened outside their own hallowed patch. Now she could look back on it – just a little, foreshortened as it was – she could see how shuttered her life with Mac had been. Despite that huge view, despite what she had considered that limitless freedom.

Her life wouldn't go the same way as Claire's, she knew that. But she could understand now.

Claire stood gazing at the back view of the opposite house. 'I like it, I must say.' For a moment she forgot Laura and smiled. Every night a light shone in the upstairs window equivalent to theirs; a bond lay between the two lit rectangles. A secret bond, for the occupants of the two houses would never recognize each other in the street. But they shared their nights, nights when Claire would lie, her husband's body against hers, his arms around her, and gaze into the dark. Her night-time view, dear beyond words.

Downstairs they had the pie for lunch and then they started sorting through packing-cases in the sitting-room. The two of them sorted piles of junk – things with lids missing, things not quite broken enough to throw away, things that some day just might be useful – into piles. Suddenly Claire realized she wasn't humming. With Geoff there, she would be. During the silence of any shared occupation she felt compelled to inform him, by a hum or a whistle, that she was cheerful. She was conscious of him beside her, that was why. With Laura, she realized, she never felt the need to hum, for Laura was completely accepted into her life and always would be. How long, she wondered, would it take her to get so utterly used to her husband? To his mind being in the same room as hers? Longer, for sure, than it took to get used to his marvellous body.

Laura looked out at the street. The semis stared back at her, yet curiously enough she didn't feel closed in by them as she should.

She felt larger and calmer, actually, than she'd imagined possible. Whatever her surroundings she felt free – freer, she realized with surprise, than she'd felt in that independent room in Bristol which at the time had seemed the threshold to such fascinating liberty. Then she'd been blank and unused, and how very much younger, dabbling about with her little efforts at individuality.

Outside a mother and two children were getting into a car. An unremarkable suburban family like her own had been. So why did she feel overwhelmed with fondness? A child pulled open the door; a large dog got into the back seat and sat in there, aunt-like, big and complacent, blotting out the rear window. The woman lifted the children in and closed the door. She won't go down in history, thought Laura. Nor will I.

Her image of people thickened – of Geoff, of her parents. Barriers were falling, vistas opening. The figures in her life were becoming more human by the minute. How could she have been so rigid about people, so intolerant?

She sat back on her heels, looking at her suitcase. Soon – later today or tomorrow morning – she would go. Perhaps back to Bristol, but it would be a different Bristol now.

For the first time in her life she would work, really work. That was the answer. She had a debt to pay. She looked out of the window; yes, perhaps she'd even work on the buses. Why not? There would be something right and proper about that. She'd sort out her stuff and find somewhere cheap and she'd make the money because she would work differently from the way Mac had done. She would tell nobody, not even Claire, until it was finished.

It would be a strange few weeks, she knew that. A time cut adrift from Harrow, and textbooks, and Jacob's Crescent with its little square of vegetables gone to seed. She looked up; adrift, too, from this Queen's Park sitting-room with its returning husband and its little square of earth so carefully nurtured. What do I want? she thought.

At the moment, just to pay back the money. It would satisfy her, that.

twenty-nine

September, with autumn scents on the air. In the herbaceous border many flowers had seeded and podded; spears of them, brown, now rose up behind the mauve blur of the michaelmas daisies. Dampness underfoot, under leaves.

And hanging over the garden the blue smoke from a bonfire. From her bedroom upstairs Holly could see her father standing there throwing armfuls of leaves on to it. The flames leapt into the air; she could even hear them crackling. Her father bent down and gathered some more.

She was supposed to be packing her trunk. Actually, she'd got very cross with Mummy about it because Mummy had kept on nagging and nagging about why didn't she, Mummy, help, because she was so quick at it and then she, Holly, wouldn't get into a fluster at the last minute.

Yes, she'd really got quite cross with Mummy. She was getting to be such a nuisance, always telling her, Holly, to do things. The fact was, she wanted to do this particular thing in private; she wanted to do it in private because of the book.

Whenever she went over to her chest of drawers to fetch something like her navy blue games knickers or her white shirts she had to pass her pillow. Under her pillow lay the book. If she just lifted the pillow she could see its orange cover. And if she opened it . . .

She was sitting on her bed now, bundle of knickers in her hand. She opened it at the list of contents. She knew the list by heart, of course, but she wanted to see it again.

Chapter 1: Sexual Development. Chapter 2: The Sex Act. Chapter 3: Some Difficulties Experienced by Couples. Chapter 4: Morals and Society. Chapter 5: Birth Control. Some bits were boring. She hadn't bothered at all with Chapter 4. It was Chapters 2 and 3 that were the ones.

She hadn't believed any of it, of course. Not when she'd read it first. She thought there must have been some mistake, or she must have been reading it all wrong, or else it was some long and complicated joke. People couldn't *possibly* do *that*, could they? Could they? Ordinary people like Ann's mother and father, or the Hacketts next door, people who she'd regarded as quite sensible grown-ups in every other way. People – and whenever she thought about this she went icy inside – people like Mummy and Daddy.

But they must. In the midst of all this awful muddle one thing was becoming clear. They must, or else she, Holly, wouldn't be sitting here on her bed. Unless, of course, they'd found her in a phone box and adopted her when she was a tiny baby. She would like to think that was the answer but there was still the problem, she had to admit it, of how much she looked like Laura and Claire. 'You must be sisters,' people were always saying, and how much she looked like her mother, too. 'Doesn't she have Rosemary's lovely eyes!' people said, bending down and inspecting her. Anyway, for her parents to have the book downstairs was surely proof enough of their treachery: 'Young Marrieds', obvious as anything, right there in the shelf between 'Roses for Everyone' and 'Rambles Through the Cotswolds'. Looking at her parents now made her blush.

The burning question at the moment was: should she or should she not bring it to school? There were many, many things she wanted to get clear; many, many bits she must read again, and Chapter 5, which on first glance looked the most peculiar of all, she hadn't even read yet. Anyway, she could show it to Ann and perhaps Ann could explain the funniest bits – if she knew anything about it, that was. And if she didn't – well, what a marvellous feeling of power to be able to tell her! She could read it out loud, and probably with her it wouldn't seem so odd when she thought about her parents; she might even be able to laugh about it or wave it aside in a grown-up, knowing sort of way.

It would be simpler if Laura were here. She could ask her. She might tell her, Holly, a bit more about it. Funnily enough, though of course Laura had never done It, it was easier to imagine her doing It than her parents doing It. Claire, now she thought of it, must have done It else she wouldn't be having a baby. Still, that didn't seem too awful. It was just that her mind went blank and buzzing when she tried to picture her parents doing It. And now Laura was back in Bristol, and her room was painted white and looked so empty. Oh, but just now she needed a sister!

A creak on the landing. Holly froze. There was someone outside the door. A grunt and the door moved a fraction.

Seized with panic, she bundled the book under the pillow and wedged herself against it, knickers clenched in her hand. She stared at the door.

Another creak and it pushed open to reveal – Badger. He padded in, tail waving, courteous and kindly. He had come to pay her a visit; he liked to keep in touch with what everyone was doing.

Holly let out a deep breath and realized she was hot all over and damp under her arms. Her hands clutching the knickers were damp too. It was quite a new feeling, this. Never had she felt she'd had to hide something before. Of course, she'd had special secret treasures she'd kept in special secret places, like those holly trees beside the sand pit. But they'd been nice things. She hadn't felt, well, guilty about them like she was feeling now. Come to think of it, she'd never felt guilty like this before at all. And now Badger was here, so trusting and such a friend, who'd done everything with her and who she'd shown all her secret places in the garden and in the Rec. Now Badge was here she felt worse because, with his wagging tail and bright eyes, he looked so straightforward, and for the first time she had something she would be ashamed of telling even him.

Holly went to the window. She could see them in the garden, her father beside the bonfire, her mother squatting in the middle of a flowerbed, tying those mauvey flowers to sticks so they didn't wave about in the wind. She heard laughter. She'd always thought adults led complicated lives, but just at the moment she had never seen grown-ups look so carefree, and it was herself, Holly, who was weighed down. She gazed at the apple tree she'd climbed a thousand times. It had ferns, she noticed, sprouting out under a branch. Ugh! Like hairs in an armpit.

She avoided Badger's eye and got up, took the book from its hiding-place and crept downstairs. The coast was clear and she slipped it back into the shelf. No doubt she'd go on reading it next holidays, but just at the moment it seemed too much of a burden to bring to school. Anyway, someone might notice it was gone.

She started to walk towards the garden, but as she was passing the mirror she caught sight of herself in it. She was fascinated by mirrors, not because of vanity – she never actually looked at her face at all – but because of Inguedoc. Inguedoc was the place, almost like home but not quite, that she could see in the mirror, and it was full of people who were just out of sight. When she passed a mirror, then, she had to give these people a wave because they were her subjects and they expected it of her. She knew, as certainly as she knew anything, that they were craning round the very edges of the mirror frame, pushing and shoving to get a glimpse of her, and so she must please them by a wave. Apart from mirrors, the only other place she got near to them was when she was in her bath and she knew without looking that they were all around the sides of the bath on the floor. When she was sure they were ready she'd flick out little sparkling drops of water, which was money of course in Inguedoc, over the edge of the bath and keep her eyes averted so she didn't see them scuttling away across the floor, undigniedly, with their treasures.

But today as she passed the mirror, for once she didn't raise her hand. Instead she stopped, looked into the glass and, instead of studying that reassuring Inguedoc, she studied her face. It wasn't half so reassuring. Her nose, her mouth, her eyes which, now she inspected them properly looked surely far too piggy – was this what she looked like to everybody else? That fat nose! This was the face, she knew it with a sinking heart, that was *her*, Holly, and she'd be stuck with it for the rest of her life. She'd never ever thought of her face like that before. Could anyone ever find it pretty? Or even not absolutely disgustingly ugly? Would anyone ever want to do It with someone with such a fat nose and piggy eyes and – she was sure she could see one – an actual beastly red spot in the middle of her chin?

More laughter outside. They'd been much more laughy this holiday. Holly turned and went towards the french windows, feeling older.